Among the Lilies

Among the Lilies

Daniel Mills

UNDERTOW
PUBLICATIONS

Contents

Below the Falls

Gentlemen, I am tired of ghost stories.
They are always the same. A respectable narrator visits a country house where he experiences a series of unsettling incidents before the final appearance of the ghost bursts on his mind like a thunderclap. His faith is shattered or his sanity. He is changed forever.

But if the defining quality of a ghost is its mystery, its *otherness*, I propose to you we are surrounded by such spirits whether we acknowledge it or not. In pain the mind hides even from itself, becoming a darkened star around which light bends but does not pass through.

I hope you might permit me to read from an old diary. The story it tells is a kind of ghost story, though the dead do not walk in its pages, except in the usual way by which the words of the deceased survive on paper after their graves are filled.

The diary came into my possession some years ago when I was practicing medicine in Lynn, Massachusetts. A nurse at the State Hospital in Danvers had learned of my interest in psychoanalysis and sent it to me after the death of its author.

Her name was Isabella Carr and she was born in Walpole, New Hampshire. Her father died when she was seventeen. Her mother married again and Isabella lived with her mother and stepfather for a time until age eighteen when she married Horace Carr of Beacon Hill. The diary begins shortly after Isabella's wedding to Mr. Carr and depicts the weeks prior to her committal.

❧

Apr 2

Alfie was here again last night.

I heard him at the door, his faint scratching. He was just outside the room, waiting for that late hour when the whole of the house lay sleeping and there was only me to hear him.

I opened the door. He scuttled inside, dragging his belly on the floor. He was terribly thin, his hair all in patches. It came away in tufts beneath my fingertips, baring the pitted skin beneath, the sallow flesh speckled with rot: they had buried him alive.

I dropped to my knees and wrapped my arms around him. He did not resist but merely lay with his head against my chest as I whispered into his ear.

I'm sorry, I said. I thought you were dead.

His breathing was strained and rapid but still he did not stir. He listened as the words poured out of me, an undammed torrent. I spoke for hours, or what seemed like hours, and later, I awoke to find him gone with the bars of sunlight on my face.

Bridget woke me. She entered the room while I slept and now applies herself to the tasks of stripping the bed, taking down the curtains. She whistles as she works—an Irish song, I suppose, for I do not recognize the tune.

Downstairs, the clocks all sound the half-hour, and I know that I have overslept. Mr Carr awaits me in the breakfast room. He will be dressed for his clients, his club, checking his watch as the minutes tick past and still I do not come—

❧

Apr 7

A letter from Uncle Edmund—

This morning I woke early, before dawn, and padded downstairs in my nightgown. In the hall I found the mail where it had been dropped through the slot. In amongst my husband's correspondence was a letter addressed to me in my uncle's hand.

I recognized it at once. Edmund is my father's brother, his senior by ten years or more. He is a big man, like Father was, and likewise well-spoken, if occasionally given to maundering, and his avowed agnosticism once made him a figure of some controversy in our household.

When Father died, Edmund took to writing me long letters, and these I cherished like jewels, for I heard my father's voice in his words and seemed to catch his scent upon the page. The letters ceased with Mother's marriage to Mr Orne, who is a Methodist of the meanest sort, though it was months before I realized they had hidden them from me.

Uncle Edmund had obtained my husband's address from a gentleman friend in Walpole of some slight acquaintance with Mr Carr. He rarely speaks of it, but Mr Carr was born in Walpole and is, in fact, my mother's cousin, though he relocated to Boston as a young man and was subsequently estranged from his family for years.

Now Edmund writes to say that Father's house has been sold and is soon to be demolished. My mother has moved with Mr Orne to Vermont, to be nearer his church, while our neighbors the Bosworths have bought the property. They have plans to erect a gristmill, damming the creek where it plunges to the falls.

Soon it will all be gone: the gardens, the paths down which we walked on summer evenings, Father and I, when the damp lay thickly on the air and the rosebushes rustled all round. I remember. We crossed the creek at the footbridge, where the petals lay like a blood-trail, and sat together in a place above the falls while the current frothed and broke among the rocks below.

ᔐ

Apr 8-9

Midnight—
I hear the church bells tolling, the passing of the mail coach. An old man sings his way home, and a young girl weeps in the alley. In the silence of this hour, each sound recalls to me my shame and the solitude that

followed. Days and nights in that bedroom with the curtains drawn while Mr Orne kept watch outside and Mother walked the halls, screaming.

From the bed I watched the curtains change in color from gray to yellow to crimson. On cloudless nights the moon shone through the fabric, flesh-white and glistening with grease, making stains on the bedclothes and running like an oil in the blood—

For months I listened for the swollen creek, fat with autumn rain, white water roaring as it fell. Sometimes I thought I was dying. Other nights I was certain of it. In the evenings, I heard the winds blowing outside, and Mother weeping, and Mr Orne ascending the stairs—

Then one night he unlocked the door and entered the room with his bible under his arm and the usual prayers upon his lips. He knelt beside me and took hold of my wrist. He said some words. There was a sharp pain, then, and a light washed over me, cool as spring rain or the touch of God's breath on my forehead, and finally, I slept.

৺

Apr 11

Sunday, no church—

I will not go. Mr. Carr is away on business, and for all of her coaxing, Bridget could not rouse me from the bed. She is a Catholic girl, of course, and quite devout. From the window I watched her hurry off to Mass, wearing her Sunday hat with the brim pulled down to her ears.

Then I dressed myself in the blue silk he had loved and sat by the window with my diary in my lap. As I write, I watch the birds circle the rooftops opposite. I admire their ease, their lightness. They drift like bracken on the churning current, carried this way and that with the wind through the chimney-pots, dropping like stones when they sight the river.

The ice is out of the Charles. Every morning reveals a surface more degraded, riven with forks of liquid water. Last week Mr Carr walked home with me after church. He was meeting a client after lunch, a young man of my own age, and was in rare good spirits. The day was fair and warm and we took the bridge over the Charles.

Halfway across, I paused and gazed down at the river with its plains of blue-gray ice and glimpsed the creek behind them like the words in a palimpsest. I could hear the falls, too, over the clatter of wheels and footsteps, and recalled the garden at night. The rush of water spilling over rocks, foaming far below. The answering hum of the blood running through me.

Mr Carr joined me at the railing. I asked him of what the ice reminded him. He thought for a moment and said that it resembled a map.

Yes, he said, more confident of himself. It is much like a map of the city. Do you see? he asked, pointing. There is my street, my house.

April 11th and the ice is gone and Mr Carr's map with it. Beacon Hill has dwindled away into the black water, and soon my father's house will follow. There will be only the river, only the creek, two channels feeding the same sea. I must go back—

Apr 15

This morning at breakfast I raised the matter of the house in Walpole and asked Mr Carr for leave to travel there. At first I thought he had not heard me, for he did not answer, and did not wrest his gaze from the newspaper.

I must see it, I said. While it remains standing.

He turned the paper over. He continued to read.

Hmm? he murmured.

Father's house, I said. Our neighbors, the Bosworths—

Mr Carr slapped down the paper. His cheeks were flushed. They had darkened to purple and the pores stood out below his eyes. We have been married three months, but I have never before seen him angry.

And how is it you have heard of this? he demanded.

Uncle Edmund wrote to me.

Is that so? How interesting.

He reached for his coffee cup. He sipped from it, seemingly lost in thought as a carriage passed in the street outside, rattling the buds on the trees.

He shook his head slowly. When he spoke, his voice was low and level.

He said: It is entirely out of the question.

I will be discreet, I said. I will say nothing of your—

He slammed down his cup. The saucer cracked beneath it, upturning the cup and sending the hot liquid spilling across the table. He leapt up and called for Bridget. The girl appeared in the doorway with her eyes downcast, looking terrified.

Clean this up, he said. He indicated the mess before him.

Yes, sir.

He glared at me. Leave us, he said.

And I left—but I listened outside the door.

Mr Carr was furious with Bridget. He hissed and spat at her and threatened her dismissal. It would seem he believes that she sneaked a letter to my uncle on my behalf. The good Catholic girl, Bridget did not deny the accusation, but bowed her head and accepted this punishment as her due, speaking up only to voice her agreement, and later, her apology.

See that it does not happen again, he said. Good day.

Bridget swept out in her apron and skirts. She scurried past me with her face in her hands, reaching the staircase at a run. For his part Mr Carr pushed back his chair and vanished through the opposite doorway. I heard the front door shut behind him, his footsteps on the stoop.

He will visit his club when the working day is done. He will not return for hours.

Bridget

☙

[The next page appears to have been removed.—*ed.*]

☙

I still think of it, that first sight of the Atlantic. When I was sixteen, we visited the coast south of Portland and stayed with Uncle Edmund in a cottage on the sea.

Evening fell, and we followed the reach of the shore beyond the lighthouse. By then the tide had gone out, leaving the dead fish piled all round and the great ropes of seaweed like sheaves in a summer field, waiting to be taken up and carried in.

The stench was overwhelming, sour and sweet and sharp with the tang of the sea. Father fell ill. He broke from me without warning and stumbled to the water's edge where he emptied his guts into the ocean. Afterward, he lay feverish on the cobble and muttered to himself of the battlefields of his youth: Fredericksburg, Chancellorsville.

I held his hand. I listened. The waves went out from us as the rains moved in, sweeping the shore and eclipsing the light on the rocky headland. There was thunder, then lightning, and Father stirred, moaning with the dark that lived inside him.

I shook him, gently. Father, I said.

He opened his eyes.

❦

Apr 19, 5 o'clock—

I have seen to everything. It can do no harm now to write of it.

The carpet bag is packed and secreted beneath the bed, and I am alone, waiting for Bridget to return. She left the house at noon to pawn my wedding ring. With the money she will purchase two tickets for a north-bound train that will bring us to Walpole in the morning.

Tomorrow! I am frayed and shaking, a cord drawn taut. I can smell the old garden, the roses. The scent is more vivid in memory than it was in life, mingled with the perfume of soil and damp and that of the blooming linden. I close my eyes and hear the creek, sending up spray where it drops beneath the bridge, and remember the great clouds of dragonflies and the way they drew near us at dusk, wings flashing—

❦

Later—

I am locked in. The door is shut, the key turned fast.

Bridget has betrayed me. She now keeps watch outside, walking up and down the hallway and singing to herself in Irish. Moonlight spills in a fan across the floorboards, shining on broken glass and specks of hanging dust. I had time only to hide this diary before Mr Carr stormed inside with

Bridget following him meekly.

He was livid, incandescent with rage. He swept the bottles of my medicine from the dressing table and stomped down on the remnants, grinding the glass beneath his shoes.

Bridget retrieved the carpet-bag from under the bed. At first I thought she meant to spare it his fury, but instead, she merely placed it wordlessly into his hands. He snarled and tossed the bag on the fire. The fabric caught light, then the clothes inside, the blue silk Father loved—

I threw myself at the fireplace, but Mr Carr caught me by the wrists and pushed me to the floor at his feet. Throughout this time he said nothing, but his eyes were black and shrunken to points, like those of Mr Orne, when he ministered to me in the dark of that winter, or those of my mother when first she found us out in sin—

Mr Carr produced his ring from his coat-pocket and jammed it down the middle-finger of my left hand, forcing it past the joint so I knew I should not be free of it.

You made a promise, he said. To me, as I did to your mother. We mustn't forget that.

Come, he said to Bridget, and they were gone.

༒

Apr 21?

Mr Orne is here. He paces beyond the door. In his tread I hear the echo of steps from long ago and imagine the house in Walpole where I watch the faceless mourners come and go.

Some hold dresses or kitchen implements, bed-sheets caked with red and yellow filth. One man carries the charred remnants of my carpet bag while another walks with fistfuls of broken glass, blood dripping from his hands. They proceed with unearthly slowness and the gravity of pallbearers: rolling up the rugs, wheeling out the cradle, carrying off the materials of home like the seashell spoils of some god-conquering army.

Now the house stands empty. It is a ghost of itself, an absence made visible, like the clothes Father wore that morning, when he left the house, and which the Bosworth boy found above the falls. They were neatly laid out, the boy said, the pants folded in quarters, the wedding ring left in his shoe.

That ring, its smoothness on my skin. Whatever became of it? After the funeral, when the mourners had gone, Mother plucked the band from her own finger and flung it into the creek, as though to sink Father's memory with it, and now I am her cousin's wife.

The lamp is dim. Mr Carr's ring glitters. It casts a white smear on the wall, an inverted shadow which moves in time with the rhythm of my hand on the paper so that I think of the moon in Maine as it rose over the headland, dragging the waves behind it, water and light trapped in the song they sang between them until at last you woke and looked at me—

ह

Dusk when I reach Walpole. From the station I walk to the house, lifting my skirts and sprinting when I hear the singing creek.

I am too late. Little remains save rubble. The floors have been torn out, the walls collapsed into the cellar, and the garden, too, has been plowed under.

The flowers are gone, the rosebushes. Uprooted and piled on the brush heap. Burned. The smell of wood-smoke lodges like cotton in my throat, stopping the air in my lungs. I can't breathe—can't walk—a fever is on me—

It pulls like the spring current. It drags me through the ruined garden on hands and knees and down the path that leads to the footbridge. Here the water ripples, waves within waves. The creek is running high. Below the falls the waters teem with light, the glint of gold like the flash of drowned skin. Mother's ring—or yours—and my blue dress charred and floating—

This was where it happened, where they found you.

ह

Alfie is in the hall. I hear him scratching. I must

ह

The remaining pages are blank.

The next day I visited the hospital in Danvers and sought out the nurse who had sent the diary. She was younger than I had imagined, perhaps twenty-five. She thanked me for coming and for my kindness in reading the diary then showed me to the room in which the late Isabella Carr had lived out the final years of her life.

The nurse explained Mrs Carr had been committed to the State Hospital by her husband following an incident in their Beacon Hill home in which the family's Irish maid was nearly killed. Her uncle Edmund Ashe contested the committal on his niece's behalf but these efforts failed in court when evidence of her opium dependency came to light.

She spent ten years at Danvers and was never seen to write letters or keep a diary. She passed her days at her window, keeping watch, perhaps, or waiting for someone to come back for her. No one did. Aged twenty-eight she contracted pneumonia and died. The nurse cleaned out her room and found the diary inside her bed, concealed beneath the bolster where she had hidden it ten years before.

"It gave me chills," the nurse said. "For a moment I even imagined she meant for me to find it. Nonsense, of course. She wasn't well. Probably she had forgotten all about it. I should have mailed it to her mother, I suppose, but after reading it, learning what they did to her... well, it didn't seem right. And Edmund Ashe has been dead for three years."

"And she had no other family?"

"No," she replied. "She didn't." Her eyes moved over the empty walls and she was far away. "Though it emerged in court that Isabella had mothered a child some years previously, a little boy. She was unmarried at the time and it was all hushed up. Her mother and stepfather hid the pregnancy from their neighbors and married her off to Horace Carr. He was Mrs Orne's cousin, as you know, and it was rumored the marriage was never consummated."

"And the little boy? What became of the child?"

"He went to an orphanage. A woman came and carried him away. The poor child didn't see his first birthday. Cholera, I believe."

"What was his name?" I asked. "The baby's."

She did not answer me immediately. Instead, she went to the window and closed the curtains halfway, drawing a shadow across the bed then pausing in the doorway to address me a final time. "Alfred," she said. "The child's name was Alfred."

She disappeared into the hallway. Her footsteps retreated down the corridor. The sun broke through the parted curtains, and I was alone with my thoughts.

The Woman in the Wood

From the diary of James Addison Thorndike II (1828-1843?)

14th July. Thursday.

E vening. I spent to-day with my Aunt while Uncle Timothy was at work in the fields. His farm is the largest for miles around with hundreds of acres of hilly pasture. There are few trees save for a solitary stand of pine at the edge of his property & the wind is strong & constant. It comes down from the bare mountains & crosses the open fields.

Aunt Sarah is not at all what I expected. She is only a little older than myself though Uncle Timothy is older even than Father. She is his second wife, the sister of a traveling preacher. She speaks plainly & with an accent & is fond of quoting Scripture, as is my Uncle, though she is superstitious & shivers to hear the whippoor-wills passing overhead.

The baby Mary is not yet two. Aunt Sarah dotes on her. She carries the child with her all about the house, though she is only a small woman & expecting another besides.

I arrived in the village last night.

It was well past suppertime when the coach reached town & my Uncle was surprised to learn that my parents had permitted me to make the journey alone.

Later I heard them talking about me. My bedroom is next to theirs at the back of the house & I could hear them quite clearly.

A boy of his age? my Uncle asked. It isn't right.

Surely there's no harm in it, Aunt Sarah said. Traveling on his own.

He isn't yet fifteen.

Aunt Sarah laughed. She said: I weren't much older than that when you met me.

Yes, he said, a little sadly. I remember.

Then came a long pause before my Aunt spoke again. She asked: Is the boy truly ill? His father's letter says he does not sleep or eat—

Of course he isn't ill, my Uncle said. It's country air he needs, that's all.

č

[*The following passage is the first of several written in a rushed and nearly illegible script denoted here by the use of italics. The text was subsequently crossed out while the ink was wet, presumably by the diarist himself—ed.*]

& she's standing by the bed in her nightgown which she slides over her head, smiling as she reveals herself to me. She is white as milk & stinks of sin. Her belly bulges outward where the baby turns & kicks within her & below that the blackened mouth with its lips spread & dripping

č

15th July. Friday.

I found it in the fields near the pine-wood.

The beast was lying on its side & I thought perhaps it was sick. But I smelled the rot as I drew near & saw its blood splashed through the grass—

This morning it rained, though the skies were clear by noon. The day was hot so I wore my linen shirt & trousers. I ate sparingly of the dinner my Aunt had prepared (mutton roasted & charred) and afterward announced my intention to walk outside on my own as Father would never have permitted in Boston.

I walked the fields for the best part of an hour without seeing man or beast. Then I came over a rise & saw the great herd of them before me. They were grazing at the end of the stony pasture: dumb & grunting & caked in their own filth.

I went eastwards & climbed over a wall to the adjoining field where the land slopes down to the neighbors' property & the pinewood, which lies in a depression between so that none know for certain who owns it (or so my Uncle says).

The grass is higher there & that is where I found the ewe.

Uncle Timothy was at work in the pastures to the south. I ran toward him, waving & shouting & he came to meet me at a sprint. I told him what I had found & he sent me back to the house. Then he called to Auguste, one of the hired men.

Come, he said. And bring your gun.

I went back to the house & told Aunt Sarah that I had found a dead sheep. She said it was probably dogs or a wolf, but Uncle Timothy returned to the house at dusk & said it was likely a wildcat, though he hadn't heard of them coming so far south, especially in the summer.

Supper was strained & silent. Aunt Sarah was quiet where she sat opposite me & I could not meet her eye without thinking of the pasture & what I had found there.

I had no appetite. I asked my Uncle if I might be excused & he nodded.

So I came upstairs, thinking I might read *Wieland*, which had been Father's gift to me before leaving. But I could not touch my books & I passed the evening by the window, watching the clouds as they covered the moon & the stars.

~~without thinking of the beast where it lay in the grass with its mouth forced open, the jaws broken & the organs wrenched from out the shattered mouth: its heart & lungs & the ropes of its intestines, spread out on a slick of blood & the stench of shit coming from the mass of them where the sun's shone down through the day~~

ਵੇ

There is something else.

After I found the ewe, I turned & ran to fetch my Uncle & nearly collided with a woman in white who had, it seemed, emerged from the pine-wood. She was of much an age with my Aunt, though her dress & bonnet were as fine as anything Mother might wear to a Society Ball.

She smiled & stepped aside to let me pass, though she did not speak & appeared untroubled for all that she must have seen the fallen beast behind me & the long streaks of its blood in the grass.

ਵੇ

17th July. Sunday.

Church this morning—or "meeting," as they call it here. Uncle Timothy is a Calvinist of a kind, as is most of the village. The service lasted til well past noon with much of the town crowding into the low meetinghouse, apart from my Uncle's hired men (who are French-Canadian) and the woman I saw in the field.

My Uncle wore his Sunday suit while Aunt Sarah wrapped herself & the baby in a lacy shawl. There was little music but for some hymns & these were unaccompanied with the preacher (a Mr Gale) leading the congregation in a reedy voice.

He sang with great feeling of "the redeeming blood" & "the dear slaughtered lamb" & this though he is the town's butcher. There was black grit under his fingernails & dark flecks about his beard & lashes. I tried to listen but could not concentrate for the force of the thing inside me & when the bread was passed I would not touch nor taste of it.

Afterward we had our dinner on the town green. Uncle Timothy introduced me to Mr Gale & to his wife (a shy, slight creature) as well as to our nearest neighbors Mr Batchelder & his son, whose farm borders ours along the pine-wood.

He's my brother's boy, my Uncle said. Up for a taste of country living.

No mention was made of my sickness.

Soon the baby coughed & started to cry & I gathered she was hungry. Aunt Sarah excused herself, but later I saw her gossiping with Mrs Gale. The two women huddled together beneath a spreading oak & spoke with lowered voices.

They fell quiet when I approached. Mrs Gale was pale & frightened & she brushed past me as though I weren't there.

I wandered down the green & paused by the gate to the churchyard. I went inside & came upon the place where my Uncle's first wife is buried. Someone (my Uncle?) had placed cut herbs & wildflowers at the base of the stone & these I cleared away to read the words inscribed there.

Martha Jane Thorndike
Who was once well belov'd & who
vanish'd into the wood
19th Aug 1838

No one else was about & I cannot say how long I lingered there. But the light was dimming as I walked up the green & when I reached the steps of the meetinghouse Uncle Timothy rose & said it was time for us to go.

༄

watching as the blood seeped into it, turning the bread green & putrid. Corruption spilling from it, a dark fluid. The taste of it filling my mouth & nose & getting into my brain where the blood pulses, black & wild. Beating through the night so I do not sleep & then the woman comes for me, wearing her fine white dress with the skirts lifted up & the black mouth yawning beneath them, opening wide & then wider so her bones crack & break

༄

19th July. Tuesday.

I saw her again, the woman in white.

After breakfast, I went with Auguste to the village & helped him unload the ox-cart. We returned to the farm around noon & took our dinner in the empty cart.

Auguste's English is better than that of the other hired men. As we ate, he told me stories of Quebec & of the Cree Indians & of an evil spirit called the Witiko, which possesses sinful men & fills them with unnatural desires.

Then he asked me not to repeat anything I had heard.

It is your Uncle, he explained. He would not like it.

In the afternoon, I crossed the low fields on my own & walked north & east til I reached the edge of the Batchelders' property then climbed uphill along the winding stonewall til I had a view of my Uncle's farm. From there I looked down toward the pine-wood & spied a flutter in the grass where the woman walked, moving away toward the trees.

She wore the same dress as on Friday & her hair, I saw, was long & black, for to-day she wore no bonnet. Her steps she took slowly & with one white hand extended as though to hold the hand of another.

She turned around. The distance between us was great, but I distinctly thought that she smiled at me.

Just now I heard them talking, my Aunt & Uncle. They were discussing the dead sheep which I had found near the pine-wood.

That were no wild cat what did it, Aunt Sarah said. No catamount could do as Auguste described to me.

My Uncle said: You've been speaking to Auguste.

I knew you weren't telling me the truth, not all of it. I saw the boy, the way he was shaking—and no wonder. To have seen that poor beast, with the insides sucked out of it—

Quiet yourself, said Uncle Timothy. We shall speak no more of this madness.

It is no madness, she said, to believe the evidence of your own eyes.

ह

S's mouth clamped over my own. Her tongue pushes past my lips & wraps itself round mine, long & slick as an eel. I bite through it. I choke it down, the twitching weight of it. And then with the Witiko riding me devour her lips & nose, tearing the flesh from the skull til only those eyes remain, crusted round with blood & gazing into mine

ह

20th July. Wednesday.

My Uncle will not speak of his first wife.

This evening at supper, I mentioned I had visited her grave & read the words carved upon the stone. He did not respond but proceeded to cut his lamb into dry strips, the knife scraping on his plate. Mary slurped & suckled at her mother's breast.

I said: I do not understand. Was she never found?

Uncle Timothy set down his knife. His hands folded themselves into fists & I knew he was angry, though he is not one to show it.

He said: You saw her grave. You know as much as anyone.

And here he stood & stalked away from the table. My Aunt turned in her chair, as though to call him back & the babe's mouth slipped free of her breast, exposing the nipple, which was red & inflamed & with a dribble of milk hanging from it.

She was not embarrassed by this. She shifted the babe against her breast & covered herself with its mouth once more.

She said: Martha went to meet someone in the wood. Another man.

Oh, I said & was ashamed.

It's all right, she said. You weren't to know.

~

*and felt my teeth bite through the teat, my mouth filling with milk. The foul
taste of it, bitter as gall. I am*

~

21st July. Thursday.

Ninety degrees when I awoke. The barometer in the parlor read
thirty & rising. Uncle Timothy feared a storm & left before dawn to
fetch in the sheep.

In the kitchen Aunt Sarah floated between the counters & the
table with her hands dusted in flour, singing to Mary in the cradle.

I went outside. Even with my books & journal I could not bear
to be indoors. Again I walked to the edge of the Batchelders' property where it overlooks the pine-wood. The air was damp & sour &
there were clouds blowing in so I knew I should turn back but
didn't.

Then I smelled it: blood & rot & the odor of sheep's dung. There
were five beasts this time, arranged in the grass in a circle with their
heads pointing inward. The jawbones were cracked to pieces as
before & the steaming mess of their insides pulled out of them.

And I think I must have fainted because I remember nothing
more until the storm broke & I felt the first of the rain on my face.

I opened my eyes & saw the woman standing over me. The sky
sheared in two with a deafening roar. The storm was upon us but
she appeared as serene as the angels & wore the lightning about her
like a halo, though her lips were red where she had bit through
them.

She gathered her skirts into her fingers & lifted them above her
knees so I could see it all (*the black mouth yawning…*) and a drop of
blood from her mouth spattered her breast.

She walked off toward the wood.

Somehow I made it back to the farm. Auguste met me at the gate.
He sheltered me in his coat & ran with me to the house. By then

Uncle Timothy had returned but he left again at once.

He was a long time in returning & would not speak of the matter until after supper when I had been sent to bed. I heard them arguing in the room next door: Aunt Sarah's voice shrill & stabbing while Uncle Timothy tried to shout her down.

She said: That devil has come among us again.

Do not speak such foolishness. You'll frighten the boy.

Good, she said. He ought to be scared.

How do you mean?

Those horrible things he reads. That little book he's always writing in. He's terrified of something. Surely you saw the way—

Hush, Sarah. He is ill.

Ill? You said it were country air he needed.

And so it is. We'll go for a walk to-morrow, the four of us. Up Bald Hill if the weather allows for it.

But the sheep—

Auguste can see to them.

I could not make out her response to this. For a time, they were quiet, their argument over & later I heard noises from their room.

~~S moaning as she rides me, her face looming over me, ringed with light like the woman's in the field. A skull with the flesh peeled back, the eyes white & wide. Her fattened belly swinging, slapping against me at every thrust as to smash the child inside, its bones breaking as the dark pours out of her to cover us both~~

22nd July. Friday.

Rain again this morning & lasting through the day. We did not go up Bald Hill. Uncle Timothy forbade me going out-of-doors & I spent the morning in this room, watching from the window as rain-clouds drifted in the sky. I wanted to read but could scarcely touch the pages & found I could not concentrate for the images that crowded about me.

Around noon Aunt Sarah called me down for dinner. We ate together while Mary played beneath the table, murmuring to herself & ringing her bell. Presently she crawled away toward the parlor & my Aunt came to sit beside me. Her stomach bulged grossly beneath the plain dress she wore, but her voice was gentle & she did not try to touch me.

She said: The other night you asked us about Martha Thorndike. I told you she went to meet someone, a man. But that was only half the truth.

She leaned back against the chair & looked to the window. The world beyond had vanished into the haze of rain & wind & a long while passed before she continued.

There are things in this world, she said. Evil things, I suppose is what I mean. Timothy says I'm foolish to believe this but even the Word says it's so.

And here she quoted a line from Scripture: The Satyr shall cry to his fellow & the screech owl shall rest there & shall find for herself a quiet dwelling.

Five years ago (she continued), I was about your age. My brother Joshua was older than me by eight years & he used to take me with him when he traveled, preaching the Word to all with ears to hear. We arrived here in the summer, about this time, just before Martha Thorndike was taken. There were sheep-killings then, too.

My brother & I were in town three nights when Martha disappeared. Ran away with a man, Mr Batchelder said, a house-painter, but he was wrong. My brother was last to see her & it weren't a man she was with at all. Joshua was a holy man, God rest him, born with the Gift of Sight. Yet none believed him when he told what he had seen.

It was dusk & he saw Martha walking away toward the pine-wood with her hand out to one side as though it were being held by another though there were none walking beside her—only the old woman riding on her back.

Lilith. The screech owl, the woman in the wood. Old Virginia,

I've heard her called, though she isn't always old, for she has such powers over the eyes of men. She sees into your heart, the sin what's written there, and she makes herself out of it. Those she chooses she calls to the woods & rides them down into hell. Those like Martha Thorndike.

Timothy doesn't like to think of it—or of Martha. He believes she deserted him & maybe she did in a way. But he won't visit her grave & it falls to me to keep it tended & clean.

Aunt Sarah fell silent. Her story was finished, but I could think of no response. I told her nothing of what I've seen & experienced since coming here. I think it might have given me some solace, the same as this diary, but words spoken aloud cannot be crossed out or blotted away.

She said: You're trembling.

I did not reply.

She went to the basin & washed her hands, scrubbing the skin raw.

~

~~She could not see the table-knife in my hand or feel the weight of it. See me driving the tip through her belly again & again, though the edge is dull & jerks like a saw for to cut the babe from inside her. Then I hold the thing in my hands, still living: the slaughtered lamb, the Body & the Blood. Take, he said, and eat of it~~

~

It is not yet dawn.

I slept poorly for dreams of the fields beneath the storm. Again the sun beat down on me, wilting the grass & turning it yellow as I approached the circle where the beasts lay slaughtered, their bodies black & stinking in that heat.

The woman was there. The screech owl, Aunt Sarah called her.

She would not look at me but cradled something in her arms & sang to it as to a small child. Her voice was low & pretty though I

did not recognize the melody & soon could hear nothing for the roar
of the storm around us.

I came nearer to her. I saw the thing she carried.

ॐ

~~not a child but a lamb which she had pulled, half-formed, from its mother's~~
~~womb. The small bones were shattered & the face was missing, eaten away,~~
~~and the un-beating heart sucked out of it~~

ॐ

23rd July. Saturday.

The house is quiet. My Aunt & Uncle have not yet returned &
this room is empty of all but my thoughts. Visions swim out of the
dusk & I can hear her calling, singing to me as to the lamb of which
I dreamt—

The morning was clear, the barometer creeping up. Uncle
Timothy worked through the morning & in the afternoon we went
up Bald Hill. My Uncle was first up the path with Mary laughing on
his shoulders while Aunt Sarah followed behind with a mildewed
parasol.

The path bent sharply then followed the ridge over the valley.
The slopes had been cleared of trees years ago but there were some
berry bushes beside the path which blocked our view until we
reached the summit. Then the bushes fell away with the landscape
& the whole of the valley lay open before us, green & yellow &
misted with heat.

Uncle Timothy stopped to admire the view. There was a cliff
here & a long drop to the valley below, but Aunt Sarah joined him at
the edge, quite un-frightened. My Uncle looked back at me with the
wind rippling his beard & Mary's fingers twined in his hair.

Come & look, he said to me. But isn't this God's country?

Aunt Sarah asked if I might bring the picnic basket, which I did,
though I stopped short of the edge & would not approach any

closer. We sat in the grass. My Uncle said a grace. He thanked the Lord for the beauty of His creation & for His Son who saved us with His precious blood. We ate & afterward we lingered near the overlook.

Uncle Timothy produced a psalter from his pocket & proceeded to read some words of praise aloud. He meant them for his wife's ears, I think, though she wasn't listening. She stretched out alongside him with her eyes closed & the sweat glittering on her face.

And then I saw Mary. The child had made her way to the edge of the overlook. She stood there, swaying, about to fall & her curls blowing about in the wind.

I leapt up. I ran toward her.

My Uncle, alarmed, shouted for me to stop. I reached the child where she stood & gathered her into my arms even as Uncle Timothy came up behind me, his boots pounding in the grass. The child squirmed & kicked against me, crying out as I turned toward the valley—

And saw the whole of Creation awash in its impurity with man coupling with woman & child & beast & all while the sun poured down upon them, blisteringly hot, blackening the flesh & causing the fat to run, fusing all together in the moment of their ecstasy—a sea of open mouths—and still they did not cease from their depravities.

My parents were there & the Batchelders. My Aunt & Uncle & the baby Mary. And always the Woman passed among them, unnoticed, wearing white like the Lamb & making for the pine-wood. Once she looked back as to make sure I was following, and I was, and I saw the two of us as from a distance, walking hand-in-hand—

My Uncle was behind me.

I heard his breath come quick & gasping & glanced back over my shoulder. Aunt Sarah was on her knees, white with terror: the fear of what might happen, what I might do.

    I tried to explain. I said: I wanted to save her.

    I know, said Uncle Timothy.

    She was going to fall, I said.

    Please, James. Give her to me now.

ẽ

I ran from him & from the sunlit fields & did not stop until I reached the farmhouse where I collapsed at last, hot & panting & dripping with the stink. That was nearly an hour ago.

    Now it is nearly night. The cool of the pine-wood waits for me, the woman called Lilith, the screech owl. She knows the thing that is in me but still she beckons & I will go

Lucilla Barton (1857-1880)

From Quebec, Catholic Parish Registers, 1621-1979:

Lucille Marie St-Saveur
On the eighteenth of May eighteen-hundred and fifty-seven, we the undersigned (prêtre-vicaire, Saint-Gregoire) have baptized Lucille Marie St-Saveur born the day before of the legitimate marriage of Jean-Francois St-Saveur and Orpha Jeanne St-Saveur of this parish. [...] Father and mother declare they cannot sign.

From Quebec, Catholic Parish Registers, 1621-1979:

Jean-Francois St-Saveur
On the thirty-first of July eighteen-hundred and sixty-one, we the undersigned (prêtre-vicaire, Saint-Gregoire) have interred the remains of Jean-Francois St-Saveur in the cemetery of this parish. M. St-Saveur died in uncertain circumstances at an unknown date (suspected murder). Present were the undersigned and Joseph LaPrade of the Quebec Provincial Police. Mme. St-Saveur and child could not be located.

From the 1869 Town Report, Charlotte, Vermont:

The Town Farm at Thompson's Point sheltered 41 transients during the reporting period. Permanent residents of the Farm include Mrs. Pearl Livermore and daughter, aged seven [...] and Mrs. Orpha Savior and daughter, aged twelve.

☙

From The Burlington Democrat, Mar 16, 1870:

Consumption at the Poor Farm in Charlotte. Mrs. Savior is reportedly in the final stages of the illness.

☙

From Vermont Vital Records, 1760-1954:

DEATH - FEMALE

Full Name of Deceased		**Savior, Orpha**			
Color	Age	**35?** Yrs	Mos	Days	Single
Birthplace	**PQ**				Married
Date of Death	**1870**	Month **April**		Day **2**	Widowed **X**
Disease Causing Death		**Consumption**			Divorced
Contributing Factors					
Town		**Charlotte**			

☙

From the United States Census for the year 1870:

Bingham	Thomas	M	M	44	Overseer (Town Farm)
"	Dorothea	F	M	38	
Sutton	Stanley	M	S	29	Resident
Lavigne	Mary	F	S	71	"
"	Catherine	F	S	69	"
Livermore	Pearl	F	W	31	"
"	Elsie	F	S	8	"
Savior	Lucille	F	S	13	"

From The Burlington Free Press, Dec 15, 1870:

Overseer T.A. Bingham of Charlotte reports another death at the Town Farm after Mrs. Pearl Livermore fell sick with coughing on December 8. The disease progressed with astonishing rapidity and Mrs. Livermore expired of her illness in the early hours of December 10. She was buried at the Town Farm. A daughter, Elsie, will be placed with relatives in Burlington.

From The Charlotte Town Report, 1874:

Overseer reports [...] payment of $25 to Asa Irish for binding out of Lucilla Savior, aged 17, until she is of age [...]

From The Burlington Free Press, Mar 15, 1875:

Mrs. Asa Irish of Hinesburgh died early Wednesday of suspected pneumonic hemorrhage. Her husband noticed Mrs. Irish's absence Tuesday evening and found her outside beside the watering troth insensible. Mr. Irish carried his wife into the parlor where she recovered her senses and cried out in fright of an unknown woman no one else could see. A neighbor E.A. Barton ran for Dr. Pell, who tended the dying woman in her final hours.

๕

From Vermont Vital Records, 1760-1954:

MARRIAGE - BRIDE

Name of Bride	**Savior, Lucilla**
Name of Groom	**Barton, Eber Adam**
Residence of Bride	**Hinesburgh**
Date of Marriage	**Jun 5 1875**
Color	Age in Years **18**
No of Marriage	**1**
Occupation	**Domestic**
Father's Name	**Savior**
Birthplace	**PQ**
Mother's Name	**Orpha**
Birthplace	**PQ**
Town	**Hinesburgh**

๕

From The Burlington Democrat, Apr 22, 1876:

Defendants due in City Court: [...] E.A Barton; drunkenness; fined $15.

๕

From The Burlington Democrat, Aug 1, 1878:

Fines issued to multiple defendants including [...] Eber Barton, Hinesburgh, drunkenness.

From The Burlington Free Press, Nov 15, 1879:

[...]Eber Barton of Hinesburgh facing new charge of drunkenness after a young girl happened upon him in the woods while she was gathering beechnuts. Mr. Barton was delirious with drink and raved of ghosts or spirits in his house. The girl took fright and ran. Her father informed a Sheriff's Deputy leading to Barton's arrest—his third in as many years.

From The Burlington Free Press, Dec 5, 1879:

An infamous drunk assaulted his wife Saturday morning. Mr. Eber Barton had spent the previous night out of doors, unable to sleep, before returning to the house after daybreak. He entered the kitchen and attempted to bludgeon his wife with a hatchet, believing himself to be under the influence of "a witch's curse." Mrs. Barton escaped uninjured to a locked bedroom from which she called for help. The madman was subdued and taken into custody.

From the Montpelier Argus and Patriot, Dec 23 1879

DEATH OF AN INSANE MAN

The 6:55 from Burlington was waved to a halt Monday morning near Middlesex due to an obstruction on the line. One E.A. Barton of Hinesburgh was aboard, traveling to the hospital in Brattleboro in the company of a Sheriff's Deputy. Mr. Barton suffers from delirium tremens and reportedly became agitated upon realizing the train had stopped. He succeeded in escaping through the window of the car and sprinting down the bank to the Winooski River where he disappeared into the icy waters. His body was recovered the next day.

☙

From Vermont Vital Records, 1760-1954:

DEATH - MALE

Full Name of Deceased	**Barton, Eber**			
Color	Age **28** Yrs	**7** Mos	**3** Days	Single
Birthplace	**Hinesburgh**			Married **X**
Date of Death **1879**	Month **Dec**	Day **22**		Widowed
Disease **Misadventure**				Divorced
Causing Death **(Drowning)**				
Contributing Factors	**Insanity, Delirium**			
Town	**Middlesex**			

☙

From the United States Census for the year 1880:

Lucilla Barton	F	W	23	
Elsie Livermore	F	S	18	dom. servant

☙

From Vermont Vital Records, 1760-1954:

BIRTH - FEMALE

Name of Child	**Barton, Helen**	
Color **W**	No. of Child of Mother	**1**
Date of Birth **1880**	Month **August**	Day **18**
Maiden Name of Mother	**Lucilla Savior**	

Mother's Birthplace	**Canada**
Full Name of Father	**Eber A. Barton**
Condition of Child at Birth	Live **X**
Town	**Hinesburgh** Still

From the Burlington Free Press, Oct 15 1880

Less than a year since Eber Barton's death by drowning, a second tragedy has befallen the Barton family of Hinesburgh. Early Tuesday morning the body of Mrs. Lucilla Barton was discovered in a barn on her property. Suicide is suspected. Mrs. Barton was pregnant at the time of her husband's death last December and recently gave birth to a daughter. Eighteen year-old Elsie Livermore works at the house as a domestic and found her employer's body. Dr. H.A. Pell of Hinesburgh attended the scene with Chittenden County Deputy Sheriff J.S. Degree. A hearing will be held later today.

From The Burlington Free Press, Oct 18. 1880:

SUICIDE IN HINESBURGH
Young Mother Killed Herself, Hearing Concludes
Burial in Village Cemetery

An inquiry into the death of Mrs. Lucilla Barton of Hinesburgh determined the young mother ended her life by suicide on the evening of October 11.

The deceased was a widow of less than one year, aged twenty-three, and mother to an infant child. Her body was discovered early Tuesday by the hired girl she employed. Friday's hearing sought to establish the precise manner and circumstances of Mrs. Barton's death and to exclude any suspicions of foul play.

Justice Erasmus Smith opened the hearing at around one o'clock followed by testimony from the hired girl who discovered the body. Her statement is presented in full along with those of the various witnesses. Among these was Deputy Sheriff J.S. Degree who submitted into evidence a letter in Mrs. Barton's hand. The text of this letter is also reproduced below.

Elsie Livermore testified: I am eighteen years old; first met Lucilla Savior at the Town Farm in Charlotte; was sent there with my mother; remember very little of those days. Lucilla was five years older; very shy; spoke hardly at all. My mother loved her; took her in after Mrs. Savior's death from consumption. We were almost like sisters. Then mother died of consumption and I was adopted by a great-aunt; did not see Lucilla for 10 years.

Last spring I learned of a position in Hinesburgh with a young widow; arrived at the farm May 18th; recognized Lucilla straightaway. She remembered my mother and called me Miss Livermore; said I must call her Mrs. Barton.

My room was next to hers. I made the fires; dusted, swept, starched; baked the bread and cooked for her, though she rarely ate; could see the baby moving under her skin.

She was always formal, even cold; asked me once about my mother. I told her what I remembered; asked about her own mother but she wouldn't answer. The child came that night. I ran to fetch the midwife; helped with the birth and held the baby afterward.

Mrs. Barton couldn't bear to look at the child; was frightened, I thought; closed her eyes but was not asleep. I heard her rapid breathing.

The weeks went by. Summer turned to fall and she never sang to the baby; did not comfort her when she fussed; left Helen with me during the day but slept beside her in bed as though she worried what might happen.

The 11th was Monday. I was up at six to prepare breakfast; called to Mrs. Barton around seven. She put the baby in the cradle and went out; returned around mid-day. Helen heard her mother's voice and reached for her. Mrs Barton looked distressed; would not pick up Helen; asked me if I thought the baby loved her. I told her she did.

She went to her room; did not take supper; looked tired when I saw her again at eight o'clock. Goodnight, she said, and put Helen to bed. I did not hear her come out. Around ten o'clock I locked both doors and went to bed; did not sleep well; was disturbed by frequent coughing from Mrs. Barton's bedroom. The baby woke before dawn. I heard Mrs. Barton whispering but could not make out the words; heard Helen fall quiet, the bed creaking.

I slept until half-past-six; dressed and went toward the kitchen; passed Mrs. Barton's bedroom. Helen was asleep. The bedclothes were disordered, I noticed; assumed Mrs. Barton woke early and went out; proceeded to the kitchen and kindled a fire in the stove. The wood-box was nearly empty. I opened the back-door, which was bolted; believe the front door also locked; walked to the woodshed which overlooks the barn.

The doors were open; recalled Will [Barton] closing them; called out to Mrs. Barton but had no answer. I returned to the house briefly. Helen was not awake. I took down my coat; walked to the barn; went inside. Mrs. Barton, I said, and my own voice came back to me. I crossed the barn but did not see her; turned back toward the door as a shadow appeared at my feet; looked up. She hung from a beam high above me. Her arms were at her sides and head tilted; face black and swollen; hands the color of snow.

William Barton testified: Mrs. Barton was my brother's wife. Eber met Lucilla Savior when he worked for Asa Irish; took a liking to the girl, who was bonded there from the Farm; tried talking to her but she wouldn't respond; didn't speak to anyone except Mrs. Irish. The old woman died suddenly; had doted on Lucilla. They were going to send Lucilla back to the farm, but Eber said he'd marry her, if she were minded. She said she was.

The trouble started soon after. Eber thought the house was haunted; heard footsteps at night; voices in rooms that were empty. I lived close-by; worked for Mr. and Mrs. Barton; walked over most mornings from [Miles] Patrick's. Last winter I heard a commotion from the house and went inside. Eber had a hatchet, which I took from him. He had to go to Brattleboro, they said; died along the way.

I left Patrick's at half-past-seven on October 12; arrived at Barton's before eight. Elsie was outside with Helen; told me Mrs. Barton was dead; had killed herself. I walked down to the barn; found her hanging ten feet up; climbed to the hay-loft; stepped down to the beam she hung from; knelt to cut through her apron. The body dropped to the straw. Her limbs were stiff; skin cold; eyes open and staring. I covered her face with my coat; went back to the house where Elsie waited; told her to take the baby inside.

Miles Patrick of Hinesburgh testified: I own the next farm from Barton's; was on neighborly terms with Mrs. Barton; did not like her late-husband. My daughter came upon him once behind our house. He was drunk; claimed he was cursed; said a ghost was watching him.

Will Barton boards with me; works without pay for Mrs. Barton; came into the house at eight o'clock on October 12. I was having breakfast; could see he was upset. He had been to Barton's; told me what happened; said he had to get back to Elsie; asked me to go for help.

I readied the buggy; drove to Pell's. Pell said the Sheriff would need to be told; sent me to [Deputy Sheriff] Jonah Degree's with a message to meet at Barton's. I reached Degree's at nine o'clock; rode with him to Barton's; drew up at the barn and he got down.

I did not stay; did not enter the barn; did not see the body.

Dr. Horatius Pell testified: I attended the scene of Mrs. Barton's death on October 12; had no prior relationship with the deceased; met her once at Irish's when she was bonded there.

Miles Patrick pulled up at my house on Tuesday morning; informed me of Mrs. Barton's death; said it was likely suicide. I told him to fetch Jonah Degree; drove to Barton's. Will Barton met me outside; showed me to the barn.

Mrs. Barton lay on her back with face covered by a man's coat. I removed the coat; observed discoloration of the face and distortion of her features; loosened the noose; noted abrasions caused by the apron-strings. She had no other injuries. The neck was intact; skin cold; rigor pronounced.

I am of the opinion that the death occurred at around nine o'clock on the evening of October 11; that Mrs Barton died of strangulation; that she was a suicide.

Deputy Sheriff J.S. Degree testified: I have known the deceased for five years; arrested her husband on at least two occasions; was present at his drowning near Middlesex; could not save him.

Tuesday I drove with Miles [Patrick] to Barton's; arrived at half-past-nine; sent Miles home. Will Barton came out of the barn. I questioned him concerning the morning's events; examined the body in his presence; asked where he had found her. The beam in question was perhaps fifteen feet up. I climbed to the hayloft and over the railing; dropped down to the beam; found it easily done.

Will accompanied me to the house; stayed as I questioned Miss Livermore; held the baby while we talked. Miss Livermore stated she last saw Mrs. Barton at eight o'clock the night before; locked up at ten; confirmed both doors were locked when she awoke; claimed she heard her employer coughing in the night.

I proceeded to Mrs. Barton's bedroom; observed the bedclothes were disordered; identified a small depression near the center consistent with an infant and the outline of a second body to one side; called to Miss Livermore, who came in; inquired if she had made the bed on October 11. She replied she had; took offense when I suggested she was mistaken; insisted she had heard Mrs. Barton in her room as recently as five o'clock in the morning; that she herself was awake at the time; that she was not dreaming.

I dismissed Miss Livermore; examined the bedroom at length; discovered a letter underneath the bed surmising it had been fallen from the table. The note is in a woman's hand; unsigned; addressed to Miss Livermore.

Letter from Lucilla Barton to Elsie Livermore: Please don't think badly of me. I had no choice, no other means of escaping her jealousy. My father loved me and she killed him for it. Your mother too, and Mrs. Irish, and she drove my husband to his death in the river. Then Helen was born and I could not stop the child from loving me. I tried, God knows, but it made no difference. Tell Helen I'm sorry. Tell her I had to do it. This way she'll be free of her, and you, too, Elsie. I hope.

Miss Elsie Livermore recalled: The letter is in Mrs. Barton's hand. I have not seen it before; do not understand its meaning; do not know why it was left for me.

J.S. Degree's testimony, cont'd: I propose that Mrs. Barton put her daughter to bed at eight o'clock on October 11; that she wrote this letter to Miss Livermore which she placed on the table; that the letter fell beneath the bed delaying its discovery. She slipped outside unnoticed by Miss Livermore; proceeded to the barn and climbed to the hayloft; stepped onto to the beam; fastened noose to beam and jumped. The time was nine o'clock. At ten Miss Livermore locked up the house and retired to bed; heard the baby cry out in the night; dreamt or imagined she heard a voice from the bedroom.

The hearing concluded shortly after three o'clock. Justice Smith's final pronouncement echoed the opinions of Dr. Pell and Deputy Degree, and Mrs. Barton was found to have died by her own hand on the evening of October 11.

Lucilla Barton was laid to rest Saturday in the Village Cemetery. Will Barton attended the burial with Elsie Livermore, who held the orphaned child against the cold wind. Once the baby cried out and Miss Livermore was heard to sing to the infant until she quieted.

Miss Livermore is evidently a capable young woman. It is to be hoped young Helen Barton may yet avoid the orphanage.

☙

From Vermont Vital Records, 1760-1954:

DEATH - FEMALE

Full Name of Deceased **Barton, Lucilla Savior**

Color   Age **23** Yrs   Mos   Days   Single

Birthplace   Canada   Married

Date of Death **1880** Month **Oct** Day **11**   Widowed **X**

Disease   **Suicide**   Divorced
Causing Death

Contributing Factors   **Probable insanity**

Town   **Hinesburgh**

ॐ

From Vermont Vital Records, 1760-1954:

MARRIAGE - BRIDE

Name of Bride   **Livermore, Elsie**
Name of Groom   **Barton, William Charles**
Residence of Bride   **Hinesburgh**
Date of Marriage   **Dec 17 1880**
Color   Age in Years   **18**
No of Marriage   **1**
Occupation   **Domestic**
Father's Name   **Thomas Livermore**
Birthplace   **Charlotte**
Mother's Name   **Pearl (Stokes)**
Birthplace   **Charlotte**
Town   **Hinesburgh**

ॐ

From The Burlington Free Press, Dec 18, 1881:

Physician Horatius Pell reports four new cases of consumption in Hinesburgh. Mrs. W.C. Barton is not expected to survive.

☙

From Vermont Vital Records, 1760-1954:

DEATH - FEMALE

Full Name of Deceased		**Barton, Elsie L.**		
Color	Age **19** Yrs	**7** Mos **18** Days		Single
Birthplace	**Charlotte**			Married **X**
Date of Death **1882**	Month	**Jan**	Day **4**	Widowed
Disease Causing Death	**Consumption**			Divorced
Contributing Factors				
Town	**Hinesburgh**			

☙

From Vermont Vital Records, 1760-1954:

DEATH - MALE

Full Name of Deceased		**Barton, William C.**		
Color	Age **24** Yrs	**2** Mos **2** Days		Single
Birthplace	**Charlotte**			Married
Date of Death **1882**	Month	**April**	Day **19**	Widowed **X**
Disease Causing Death	**Consumption**			Divorced
Contributing Factors				
Town	**Hinesburgh**			

☙

From The Burlington Free Press, Jan 27 1888:

INSANITY OF A YOUNG GIRL

The New England Journal of Medicine describes an unusual case of inherited insanity at Burlington's Home for Destitute Children. The child in question came to the Home in 1882, aged about 1, following the deaths of her adoptive mother and father. She speaks only rarely and was at one time believed to be mute. Her birth-parents suffered from mental disease and her mother was a suicide. The girl does not smile or laugh and is only content on her own. She sits on her bed and talks to the walls in a language that might be French. "I am not alone," she says when questioned. "I am with Mother." A sad case.

Lilies

I.

I lost my parents when I was young. My sister raised me in their place but died in childbirth and the baby too. Her husband returned to Canada, and I was alone at twenty-one. I found work as a scrivener and took up lodgings outside Boston where I was staying when I received a letter from Edward Feathering, my last living relation.

I had met my uncle ten years before, at my father's funeral, where he had told me stories of Hannibal and the Punic Wars. He meant to comfort me, I think, but years later, I recalled little of our conversation save his ponderous manner and his voice like dry leaves rustling.

My uncle was a classicist and a recluse, a widower of more than four decades. In ten years, I had not received a single letter from him. Now he wrote to offer his condolences on my sister's passing and to invite me to visit him at his country house in Maine.

Come to Bittersweet Lodge, he wrote, and I accepted, though it would be half-a-year before I was able to make the journey.

In late August I embarked in Boston for the village of Westerly in Maine, changing trains in Portsmouth, where I purchased a newspaper on the platform. I expected a lonesome journey to Westerly and was surprised when a man and woman of my own age entered the parlor car and seated themselves near to me. The man was tall and handsome and carried with him the stale odor of pipe-smoke. His companion was plain by comparison with a narrow face reminiscent of a bird's. The train lurched into motion and the young man addressed me.

"You don't mind us sitting here, do you? We can take ourselves off if you'd rather be alone."

I lowered the paper. "No," I said. "Please don't."

"Excellent! A train journey can be such a bore."

I agreed this was so.

"You are traveling alone?"

I nodded. "From Boston. And you?"

"Concord. My sister and I travel together, though, so we have each other for company." He offered me his hand. "Justice St. James."

"Henry Feathering."

He introduced his companion. "And this is my sister Clemency."

The names puzzled me. "Your father was a lawyer?"

"A judge, actually," Justice said, "and something of an eccentric. A few years ago, Clem found a list of names he had scribbled in the family bible. 'Clemency' was there and 'Justice,' but there were others too."

"*Amicus* was one," Clemency said. "A boy's name."

"Prudence, too," her brother said. "And Pardon."

"You're forgetting Temperance. Father has always been a great one for legal virtue. I should be thankful, I suppose, I wasn't christened Impartiality."

"Why ever not?" Justice teased. "It has a certain ring."

"And you must concede," I said, "it is an improvement on, say, *Actus Reus.*"

She laughed. "But that would be a boy's name, surely."

"*Subpoena*, then."

"Or *Absentia!*"

"As your mother would have to be," I jested, "to consent to such a name."

She didn't laugh. She winced, looked away.

"Our mother died," Justice said, then held up his hand before I could respond. "You needn't apologize. You couldn't have known, and besides, it was years ago. She was ill for some time. The end, when it came, was something of a blessing."

I nodded. I recalled the stories I had heard of Jane Feathering, Edward's wife, and of the wasting disease that had killed her at age twenty.

"And your father?" I asked.

"The same as ever," Justice said. "Or so I imagine. Really, we rarely see him. He shuts himself inside his study where he spends the days and nights reviewing his old judgements."

"My uncle is much the same," I said. "He isn't a judge, though. Actually, I'm afraid it's rather worse than that."

"Oh?" Clemency asked.

"He's an historian."

I told them what little I remembered of my uncle, imitating his rasping voice to describe the Roman defeat at Cannae. I made a fool of myself, I'm sure. My only excuse is they put me at my ease. We talked of music and literature and I admitted even to my love of Poe and Hawthorne and to the escape I had found in romances of the darkest character.

Clemency leaned forward. Her eyes glittered, black and lustrous.

"I understand," she said, placing her hand over mine where they rested together in my lap. "Many nights I have longed to be at Prospero's Ball, and not in spite of my fear but because of it, as if in the extremes of terror I might leave this world behind and pass into a story and disappear forever—or at least an afternoon."

The train shuddered, slowing, and Clemency slipped her hand away even as the conductor called down the car for Westerly. I stood. Justice did too, then Clemency, and I realized we were disembarking at the same station.

"We're staying with our cousins," Justice said. "Edith and Phyllis Evans."

"Edward Feathering is my uncle, the historian. He's at Bittersweet Lodge."

Clemency asked, "Has he lived there long?"

"Forty years, I'm told. Do you know it, then?"

"Not really," she said, "but the house is visible from the road. I have often wondered about it. I thought it was abandoned."

"The place is a ruin," Justice said.

"Perhaps," Clemency said. "But I have always found it beautiful."

"Come for a visit," I said. "I'll speak with my uncle. I'm sure it would be alright."

Clemency glanced at Justice. An intimacy passed between them, a confidence between brother and sister into which I could not enter.

"Very well," Justice said, if somewhat stiffly.

Clemency said, "And you must come for dinner tomorrow."

"I would be delighted."

We descended from the platform. An open buggy waited in the street, a dusty figure slouched on the bench. My uncle's hired man, I assumed, sent down to fetch me from the station.

I made my farewells. I offered Justice my hand then bowed to Clemency.

"Until tomorrow," I said.

"Tomorrow," she said.

I climbed into the buggy. The old man whistled to the horse and we were away at a walk, cartwheels rattling. We neared the corner and I looked back to the station where Justice and Clemency lingered in the blinding sunlight, waiting for their cousins to collect them.

Justice appeared excited. He addressed his sister forcefully, gesticulating, but Clemency didn't respond. She shimmered, veiled in sunlight, her shadow sweeping the pavement as she turned from her brother toward the buggy, toward me, and lifted her hand.

II.

The sun passed behind the hills. Three miles from Westerly, the house loomed into view on a wooded hilltop, its windows bronzed with the last of the light.

The old cart-driver turned from the highway and whistled the horse uphill between two rows of ornamental cedars. Their branches twined together, forming a tunnel to Bittersweet Lodge. The house appeared as a study in slow decay with its roof-slates missing, brickwork half-collapsed, and the bittersweet vines over everything like a spreading cancer.

The buggy drew up at a side entrance. The air hummed with insect-life, crickets in the undergrowth. They sang to shake the bittersweet, which dropped its blooms like shedding skin.

"The door's unlocked," the old man said. "Mister Edward's in the study."

I went inside. The outer door opened to a narrow passage, unlit, awash in blue twilight. An open doorway led to a disused parlor with its rugs and furniture covered. I unlatched the shutters, let fall a flood of moonlight. The room swam in motes of silver dust.

Footsteps in the hall. I turned as my uncle appeared in the doorway, more haggard even than I remembered. His clothes were stained and moth-eaten and his gray beard hung down to his waist. He smelled of old books and mildew, creeping damp.

"Uncle Edward," I said.

I offered my hand, but he would not take it. "Henry, my boy," he said and stepped forward to draw me to his chest. "It is good to see you."

He released me. "You've had a long journey," he said. "You must be hungry. Shall we dine together?"

He showed me down the corridor to the kitchen, where a crude table was laid. The old buggy driver was there as well. Asaph, I learned, was his Christian name, and he was the only other resident of Bittersweet Lodge. He joined us at the table, sitting himself beside me and starting on the claret. My uncle didn't speak. He watched me from across the table with his eyes like fireflies dancing with the movement of our breath on the candle. Asaph finished his supper and licked his plate. He stood to go, and we were alone.

"How long has it been?" my uncle asked. "Since last we saw one another."

"Ten years," I said. "My father's funeral."

"You were just a boy. Now childish things are far behind you." He closed his eyes. "And what of me, Henry? Have I changed?"

"Not at all."

"No," he agreed. "I suppose not. To children even the youngest of men can seem ancient. And it is many years since I might be called young."

His eyes opened. "How long do you intend to stay?"

"I have made arrangements for the week."

He nodded. "I fear you may need to make your own amusement. The situation, sadly, cannot be avoided. You may know I am currently engaged on a study of the Teutoborg disaster and the fate of the lost legions, but the time is short, and there is much to do. However, I think you will find my library is not inconsiderable, while the property, too, is yours to wander."

I thanked him, cleared my throat. "I wonder, Uncle, if you are acquainted with the Evans sisters? Phyllis and Edith. They live in the village."

"The village," he repeated, then chuckled. "They may as well be in Carthage."

"I met their cousins on the train," I said. "Justice and Clemency St. James. I intend to call on them tomorrow, but thought, perhaps, they might visit here the day after?"

"Justice and Clemency," my uncle said. "A man and his wife?"

"Brother and sister."

"And there is nothing between the young lady and yourself?"

The question startled me. "No—of course not."

"Then please tell your friends they are most welcome." He withdrew his pocket watch. "As for me I must say goodnight. Quinctilius Varus has waited two millennia to see his reputation restored: I mustn't keep him waiting any longer. Asaph will show you to your room." He consulted his watch again. "You will find him in the pantry, I think."

The old manservant slumped against the racks of pickles, an empty bottle between his legs and a cheesecloth draped over his face. I said his name and he hauled himself up, cursing, to lead me down another narrow corridor to a bedroom at the rear of the house.

The atmosphere was stifling, feverish. I opened the windows, but I couldn't sleep, couldn't even read. Everything had changed. Until today the world had been to me a trackless wild, but now I saw the path before me, unwinding from my earliest memories of Edward to encompass Westerly and the Lodge and Clemency St. James.

I drifted off, then started awake at the sound of a woman's laughter from above. Clemency, I thought. My nightshirt dripped with sweat. I lay awake for some time but heard only frogs and crickets and rustling bittersweet. The laughter did not come again.

III.

Misses Phyllis and Edith Evans lived in a whitewashed cottage behind a high lilac hedge. The house was well hidden: I must have passed it three times before asking my way of a bespectacled gossip, who leaned in close to inquire if it was the young lady I had come to see?

It was, of course, but her brother opened the door to me. "Henry," he said, without much enthusiasm, and showed me into the parlor where two elderly women in black gowns sat sipping tea. "Cousin Edith," Justice said. "And Cousin Phyllis."

"Charmed," I said.

"You'll join us for dinner, I trust," Edith said. "Though I fear we dine rather early."

"I do hope," Phyllis said, "you will not hold our country ways against us."

"I wouldn't dream of it."

Clemency entered the room and flushed to see me. "Henry," she said, that was all, and I wondered how I had ever found her plain.

"I have spoken to my uncle," I said.

"I am relieved to hear it. I feared he had taken a vow of silence."

I swallowed. "I—which is to say, he—"

"Unless it was you, Henry, who swore the vow?"

"Clemency," Phyllis said, gently. "Don't tease."

I cleared my throat, continued. "He would be honored to welcome you and your brother as guests at Bittersweet Lodge."

Justice asked, "When are we expected?"

"Tomorrow," I said. "Unless that's too soon?"

"Not at all," Clemency said.

Justice fidgeted, consulted his pocket watch.

"Please, Justice," she said. "You will say yes."

He replaced his watch in his waistcoat. He nodded, said nothing.

"And you are certain," Clemency asked me, "the prospect is not a dreary one?"

"My uncle's property is… considerable. I am looking forward to our exploration."

Justice snorted. "*Exploration*? This is hardly darkest Africa."

"Excuse my brother," Clemency said. "He is inclined to play the cynic."

"Whereas you, Clem, must play the victim."

"Oh, yes?" she said. "And to whom have I fallen victim?"

"Yourself. You have always been the victim of your own romance."

He stalked out of the room and we heard his footfalls on the stair. He was angry, I thought, but Clemency only shook her head, as if bemused.

"A victim of romance," she said.

"A fair turn of phrase," I offered.

"Poe would have liked it."

"He would have liked Bittersweet Lodge, too, I think."

Clemency leaned forward. "Tell me everything."

I described a house of shuttered rooms and unlit hallways, and told her of the crickets' singing, how it echoed, until it seemed the very house was moaning, or screaming.

Clemency clapped, delighted. "Emily Bronte could not better it."

A bell sounded and Phyllis called us into the dining room. Justice pleaded illness, did not join us, and I was seated next to Miss Edith, who plied me mercilessly for details of life in Boston. I obliged her as well as I could though I believe she found my abstemious lifestyle to be, on the whole, rather disappointing. Phyllis and Edith cleared away the dinner-plates, and Clemency and I were left to ourselves, if only for a quarter of an hour.

We talked. That is all. We confided our griefs to each other and spoke of the comfort we had found in literature, recognizing ourselves in the romances of our childhood and later in poetry that gave voice to a loneliness we could not ourselves express.

"*From childhood's hour,*" I recited. "*I have not been as others were.*"

She recognized the verse. "*I have not seen as others saw,*" she quoted. "*I could not bring my passions from a common spring.*"

"Yes."

"I was much the same as a child," Clemency said. "Though I was never alone."

"Because of your brother, you mean."

She didn't respond, didn't need to explain. I understood, or thought I did, and I told her of my sister, who had died the year before. "She was ten years older than me and as a much of a mother as I could have wished. All the same, I was—lonely."

"And now, Henry?"

"Now?"

"Are you still that lonesome child?"

"I don't know," I said. "Once, perhaps. Not anymore."

She reached across the table, closed her hand on mine.

"Not anymore," she repeated, and we were quiet.

The others returned: Phyllis, first, then Edith, and even Justice, who seemed in better spirits. He escorted us to the parlor where Phyllis played at the spinet and we sang *Loch Lomond* and *Madam Will You Walk?* until the carriage clock struck eight.

Clemency walked me to the door, accompanied by Justice, his expression unreadable. We stood face-to-face but separated with less than two feet between us but unable to touch for her brother's gaze upon us.

"Goodnight," she said, and turned away, and Justice followed me outside. The weather was changing, clouds across the southern sky and a wind in the hedgerow, the smell of the sea.

Justice spoke. "You are not worthy of her."

"No," I admitted. "I am not."

"But you came here anyway."

"I could not stay away."

"A poor excuse."

"Perhaps," I said. "But there is no other."

"No," he said. "I suppose not."

He kicked at the ground and sent a flat stone skittering into the street. The gesture unnerved me, the violence of it, and he pressed his hands to his face, breathing hard.

"Please," I said. "I do not wish to quarrel. I have presumed too much, I know. I do not deserve your sister's affections—not now—but in time, I hope I might become worthy of her. Certainly, I will try. That much, at least, I can promise."

"You will try," he repeated, dully. "Of what use are such promises?"

"I can offer nothing more."

"You could scarcely offer less."

"What, then, would you ask of me?"

His hands fell away, making fists at his sides, and he stepped toward me with nostrils flaring and pupils like the heads of nails. "End it now," he said, "this… *flirtation.* Before any more harm is done. Send a letter, tell her we cannot come tomorrow. Invent some excuse."

"I cannot do that."

"Because you aren't a gentleman."

"No—because I am. I will send the letter, if you wish, but I will not deceive her."

"What would you write?"

"I do not know, but it would be the truth."

"You would tell her of this? What we have talked about."

"I would hide nothing."

Silence, then, the twilight humming. A mosquito settled on Justice's forehead and commenced to feed, stinging through his skin. Slowly, he reached up and crushed the insect between his fingers, then flicked it away, and laughed heartily, and clapped me on the back.

"Well, then," he said. "Until tomorrow."

"Tomorrow?"

"Bittersweet Lodge, Henry," he said. "We'll call at two."

He slammed the door. The sound echoed down the lane and I made my way back to my uncle's house. The Lodge was dark when I arrived: no lamps lit, no lights at all but a puddle of candlelight near my uncle's study. Edward stood at the window with his back to the door and a folio volume to hand. It was his habit to read in this manner, holding his book to the gap in the shutters so a sliver of moonlight swept down the page.

I wished him good evening. He glanced up from his book and squinted to make me out where I stood in the doorway. Probably he had spent the whole of the day inside the study.

"Ah, Henry. I didn't hear you. I thought you had gone up."

"I was in the village, actually."

"In Westerly?"

"Visiting with the Misses Evans."

He looked embarrassed. "Forgive me. I had forgotten." ·

"I saw their cousins as well," I said. "Justice and Clemency St. James. You'll recall they had hoped to call at the Lodge tomorrow."

"Yes, of course. Asaph will see to it."

The candle flared and spit, sent shadows up the walls. A woman's portrait hung over my uncle's writing desk. Its subject was about twenty years of age, aquiline and imperious, a figure from another time. Her gray eyes dazzled.

"She wore such a loveliness about her," my uncle said. "Such grace."

"You knew her, then?"

"A little," he replied, faintly, and turned toward the shutters, their lines of moonlight. "Too little," he said. "Even after we were married."

Jane Feathering. Edward's wife had died young, the victim of a wasting disease the doctors could not name or cure. The end approached and my uncle sent for my father, his brother, who kept vigil with Edward at the sickbed while Jane writhed and shook and fell silent.

There was nothing left of her, my father had told me. *Only those long fingers splayed on the bedding and that face like a skull in a cloud of black hair.*

Sunken eyes, skeletal hands. That was how I had always imagined her. I could not have guessed at her beauty or obvious intelligence or at a certain playfulness the portraitist had contrived to capture despite the apparent severity of his subject's expression.

Edward returned his attention to his book. He muttered to himself as he turned the pages, oblivious of my presence where I stood in the doorway, unmoving, unable to look away from the image of his late wife. The candle guttered, burning down, and Jane's face blurred into its shadow, as though she might yet turn toward me, smiling, or throw back her hair with a laugh. But my uncle coughed—the candle went out—and the dark crept over her like the stain.

IV.

They came early. At half-past-one the library door swung open and Asaph showed them inside: Clemency in white and her brother following in brown tweed. I fumbled at my collar and tie but Clemency took no notice of me. She looked about the library as in a dream.

Justice nodded to me. "Henry," he said.

"Justice."

Asaph coughed meaningfully. "Mister Edward's in his study," he said. "He said he wanted to meet his guests."

We found my uncle at his writing desk with his back to the shuttered windows and spectacles perched on the end of his nose. The desk was a mess of open books and piled-up papers covered with my uncle's cramped scrawl.

"Come in, come in," he said, rising.

Introductions were made. Edward questioned Justice concerning his archival work in Concord (I gather it involved the collation of court documents) affording me an opportunity to watch Clemency as she circled the study and to follow her gaze over the walls until it came to settle on the portrait of Jane Feathering, where it lingered.

My uncle addressed Clemency. "I understand you are this charming lad's sister?"

A flickering about her features. The color washed into her cheeks and she returned to herself as though from a great distance.

"His sister," she said. "Yes."

My uncle bowed from the waist. "Enchanted."

Clemency clutched her skirts and dropped to a curtsey, surprising us all, I think. "Likewise," she said. "Your nephew speaks highly of you."

Justice was at my uncle's desk. "Velleius Paterculus," he said, plucking a volume from among the chaos and examining the binding. "Burman the Elder. 1719. A treasure," he said, then turned to Edward. "You are to be congratulated."

"Nonsense," he replied. "It is far from being the jewel of my collection."

"You have others like it?"

"Many, yes. I should be glad of the opportunity to show them to you. Apart from texts in Latin and Greek I have in my possession the diaries of a local physician you are certain to find of professional interest. He performed numerous autopsies and served the village for decades as its Justice of the Peace. Shall we have a look?"

Justice hesitated, perhaps uncertain, but Edward took this silence for consent. He squired the younger man toward the door, pausing only to address Clemency. "And you, my dear?" he asked her. "Do you share your brother's interest in *old, unhappy, far-off things?*"

She shook her head. "Rather the opposite, I'm afraid."

"Is that so?"

"I would rather the past remain in the past. The present-day offers ample cause for unhappiness, doesn't it?"

"Quite."

I spoke up. "I had hoped to show Miss St. James about the property. I thought we might walk together while you were occupied in the library."

My uncle blinked and removed his spectacles. His gaze struck through me, searching, but he only nodded and waved us away, taking Justice by the arm and leading him toward the library.

Justice was furious. He glared at Clemency, then at me, but we were soon free of him. We slipped outside and descended the sloping lawn. The morning's damp clung, dripping, to the cedars, and a weak sun streaked the grass.

We talked of my uncle and the house, of Jane Feathering's portrait and the hold it exerted on us both. "Edward's wife," I explained. "She died young. My uncle never married again, never recovered from the loss. He was a different man, I gather, before she died."

"He must have been," she said, "to have wooed and won a woman like that."

"*A rare and radiant maiden,*" I quoted.

"Radiant, yes, but hardly a maiden. A wife."

We had reached the end of the lawn, where the rolled grass yielded to brush and evergreens, a line of firs broaching no light.

"Anyway," she said, "it's all nonsense. *This maiden she lived with no other thought than to love and be loved by me.* Such women exist only in Poe's imagination."

"Perhaps," I conceded. "But love is real enough."

"*A love that the winged seraphs of Heaven coveted?* I hardly think so."

"Now you sound like your brother."

"My brother?"

"Playing the cynic."

She shook her head. "You know *nothing* about it," she said with a voice like steel, cold and cutting, face half in shadow and the light behind her, gray eyes flashing to blue. She was beautiful and terrible, an army with banners, but I did not shrink away.

"It isn't nonsense," I said.

"You truly believe in it, Henry? *A love that is more than love?*"

"I do."

"And in that *kingdom by the sea?*"

"Of course."

She smiled. "And in covetous angels, too, I suppose."

"Naturally," I replied.

We reached the tree-line then turned to walk along it. The earth slumped to a long escarpment and we stumbled down it like children, running to keep our footing and laughing when we fell. We reached the bottom and ambled across an old field, wild with juniper, to reach the stone wall marking the boundary of my uncle's property.

Afternoon dwindled into dusk. We turned back toward the house, finding an old footpath that led us into a stand of young birch trees. Their green leaves crowding about us, layered shadows shifting underfoot. We emerged in a clearing formed by black locust trees, seven in all, wracked in twisting shapes like bodies in agony and older by far than the birches that surrounded them. Likely they had been planted here when all about was open field.

It was quiet but for the whisper of wind and leaves, no birds singing, and a gravestone marked the clearing's center like a sundial's gnomon, cut from dark slate and carved with a death's head and the words *memento mori.*

Clemency approached the stone and knelt to read the inscription. "*Lily Elspeth Stark. Twenty years, four months, two days. Et in Arcadia Ego.*"

"So young."

"My age," Clemency said.

"I'm reminded of *Wuthering Heights,*" I said. "The sleepers in that quiet earth."

"That's the worst of it, I think," she said. "The silence."

"I'm not certain I follow."

"My mother died when I was sixteen. She had been sick for years and I held her hand as she expired. The room was cold, and her last breath hung in the air like a cloud unraveling, dissolving into the silence. I loved my mother dearly. I even believed I knew her until the moment of death when she passed beyond all knowing to a place of endless quiet and I realized we were, in fact, strangers."

She turned toward me. Her eyes had dimmed and lost their color. "It's true of us as well," she said. "When I am in the ground, Henry, you will know no more of me than you do of Lily Stark. *Et in Arcadia ego.*"

"No," I said. "I will not believe that."

"Then you are deceiving yourself."

"You suggest we cannot know one another, not even in death, but you're wrong. I know you, Clemency, as I am known to you, and not in a glass darkly but face to face. The two of us together in this moment, this place, Arcadia."

The wind gusted. The locusts pitched and moaned. A leaf shook loose and drifted down to settle in her hair, where it remained, unnoticed, her eyes meeting mine and her face as empty as a chiseled angel's. She reached for my hand, squeezing it hard and pulling it to her breast and holding it there as my knees trembled and the pulse thundered in my temples.

"Clemency," I said.

I will not write of what followed. Some intimacies must remain sacred. Suffice it to say she consented to be my wife and that we passed together out of the locust trees.

Late August. Summer's lease had passed its date, but its warmth lingered on our shoulders as we walked together, hand-in-hand, our footprints like black glyphs in the earth or the first lines of a text known only to us, a story that began in Arcadia and led to Bittersweet Lodge, and then beyond, and had no ending.

V.

Justice and Edward were in the library.

They hunched over a high reading table with half-a-dozen volumes open before them, including legal texts and handwritten diaries, a treatise on botany.

Clemency and I had already agreed to say nothing of our engagement. She wished to speak with her brother in private, which I could understand, and I was likewise unsure of my uncle's reaction.

Justice looked up, unsmiling.

"Ah," he said, mockingly. "The prodigals return."

Clemency responded with the same forced cheer. "Where, then, is the feast, dear brother? The fatted calf? You've had hours to prepare."

"The whole of an afternoon, in fact."

"I fear I have kept your brother overlong," my uncle said, "but he was good enough to indulge this old man's vanity. I only hope I did not presume too much upon his kindness."

"Not at all," Justice said. "I found the experience… stimulating."
He glanced at Clemency. "My sister, I'm sure, would say much the
same."

His tone was acid, but Clemency only smiled.

"I would," she said. "Undoubtedly."

Seven o'clock. My uncle took his leave of us, muttering about
eagles and the Teutoborg. His words mingled with the patter of
rain on the windows, falling soft at first then harder for the wind
behind it, and Asaph ran to fetch the covered buggy. Clemency and
I had no chance of a proper goodbye. The old man drew up outside
and Justice rushed his sister to the buggy.

They vanished into a fog of rain, and I returned to the library
as the storm broke over the property. Lightning flickered in the
windows with thunder following close, as if the light itself would
shake the house to its foundations. I read, or tried to read, but the
hours crept past, and the storm still raged when I heard a tapping
at the door.

"Come in," I said.

My uncle entered. He moved as silently as a ghost, carrying a
candlestick with his hand cupped about the naked flame. My reflection shivered in the window glass, splintering to pieces of shadow
as Edward crossed the room with the light. He sat down opposite
me and set the candle on the table between us.

"It is time we talked," he said.

"Uncle?" I asked. "Is something the matter?"

"There is, yes. But not for much longer."

"Pardon?"

"I'm sleeping poorly," he said. "My dreams are troubled, and
every morning, I am weaker. One morning, I am told, I shall not
awaken at all, and that will be an end of things. Until then, however,
I must work. I must finish my manuscript if I am to be remembered.
No children will survive me. Jane is dead and Asaph is older than I
am. When you are gone, Henry, there will be no one left to think of
me."

"You mustn't talk in this way."

"I assure you that I must. Because I am dying. And because you are my heir."

Silence fell between us. I could not hear the rain.

Edward continued. "In exchange I ask of you one service. Publish my study of the Teutoborg when I am gone. Your grandfather was a man of means. He left his fortune to me, but I squandered it all on this house. A wedding present, you understand, but you may do with it as you will. I don't care. I was happy here, once, but that was long ago. Forty-four years. I remember every detail, cannot forget."

Lightning, thunder. The candle went out, and we were in the dark. Edward stood, as if to leave, and I reached across the table, finding his sleeve, his hand, his fingers all bone.

"Please," I said. "Wait."

"Henry?"

"I am engaged to be married."

Married. The word struck my uncle like a blow. He sagged, bracing himself with both hands against the table.

"Miss St. James," he said, weakly.

"I didn't realize what would happen," I said, "or how quickly. Please believe that. I had no intention of deceiving you."

He groaned and collapsed into the chair. Lightning flooded the library and his head was in his hands, fingers kneading his scalp.

"I'm sorry," I said.

"No, Henry," he said, lifting his head. "I should apologize to you. There is so much I should have told you before tonight, but I am, in the last analysis, a coward. Even at this late hour I had hoped I might avoid speaking of her. I see now that is impossible."

"Jane," I said.

But he shook his head. "There is a grave on the estate," he began, "that of a young woman. Lily Stark. She was the only child of the man who built this house. He was a ship's captain, a slave-trader, but his daughter was said to be as gentle as he was cruel. She planted the gardens and the vines that give this house its name. Then she died."

"How did it happen?"

"Suicide," he said. "They buried her in unconsecrated ground. Her father died and left the house to a cousin who sold it to me, but Lily is not at rest. She is as much a part of this house as the bittersweet vines she planted. Her presence pervades this house, her agony. The desperation of her final moments. Her rage. That above all."

"You seem to imply the house is—well, haunted."

"If you like. Something abides after such horror, whatever name we give it."

"You cannot be in earnest."

"Why not? Skepticism is a privilege afforded only to the young. I was your age when I married. Jane was younger even than Miss Clemency. An old woman called at the house soon after we arrived. She had worked for Cyrus Stark decades before and attempted to warn us away. We didn't believe her, naturally, but skepticism didn't save us. Jane sickened and could not eat. The doctors were of no use. Her innards rotted. The pain she experienced… the blankets caked in blood and filth… I was helpless even to understand. It was only when I learned the story of Lily Stark that I began to see. By then, it was too late."

The storm had passed: no more lightning, thunder fading into the sound of the rain. My uncle exhaled heavily and rose from the chair.

"The house is yours," he said. "But I will tell you now that you must sell it. Under no circumstances are you to bring Miss Clemency here. She will be your bride, Henry. Let that be enough. Marry her and take her back to Boston—and may your lives be filled with happiness."

VI.

The days passed and Clemency and I remained apart. It was for the best, she said, and perhaps it was, but the next week evaporated in a haze of summer heat and we were forced to content ourselves with words alone, hiding letters in the hedge outside her cousins' cottage.

I wrote to her of my uncle's bequest and of his warning to us, but she refused to treat his concerns with any seriousness, replying, *Surely you would not allow Death to spoil our Arcadia?*

The end of my stay approached, but I saw my uncle only rarely. He spent his days and nights writing, sleeping late then working into the early hours, taking meals in his study. One evening I chanced to encounter him in the hall outside the disused parlor. "Uncle?" I ventured, but he only patted my arm and said my name softly and passed into his study.

That same night, I walked to Westerly and found a letter from Clemency in the hedge outside the cottage. Her message was brief, a single line. *Justice knows*, it read, *Phyllis and Edith as well. Come for dinner tomorrow, won't you?*

I scribbled my response in pencil. *Of course I'll come*, I wrote, refolding the note and thrusting it behind the lilac leaves.

The moon was up. The road shone with its silver.

Outside of town, I turned back toward Westerly with its huddled cottages and plunging roofs and a lone lamp burning in an upper window. Clemency's, I thought, but it could have been any-one's. "Goodnight," I said.

The light wavered and went out.

The next afternoon, my last in Westerly, I returned to the village and knocked at the door of the Misses Evans. Phyllis and Edith met me in the doorway and welcomed me inside, taking it in turn to clutch me at their chests and offer their congratulations while Clemency looked on with no small amusement. Justice did not come down, not even at dinner, and Phyllis explained he had taken to his room. "A summer cold, he says. We've scarcely seen the boy."

Clemency and I had a few moments alone after dinner, and I asked after her brother's health, if he were truly ill?

She laughed. "Hardly."

"He is angry, then."

"No—he is frightened."

"Of what is he afraid?"

"Mother is dead," she replied. "Father has time only for his case studies. Soon Justice will have no one. You and I will be married and he will be alone. The prospect terrifies him."

"But surely he might find a wife?"

She shook her head. "Marriage is a state for which my brother has never shown the slightest inclination."

The cousins returned, and again, we passed a happy evening in the parlor. Around ten o'clock, I wished the cousins goodnight, and Clemency accompanied me outside, her elbow in mine as we stole behind the hedgerow.

We could not be married until the spring. Clemency would not receive her legacy from her mother until her twenty-first birthday while my own prospects were rather worse. At Clemency's urging, I had composed a letter to her father in which I described my expectations and asked for his blessing. "As promised," I said, producing the letter, but Clemency only glanced at it. She slipped it into her corset and took me in her arms.

I reached Bittersweet Lodge around midnight.

My uncle was accustomed to keeping late hours but that night, as I recall, the study was dark, and I wondered if he had, at the last, fallen asleep. I retired to my room but woke early the next morning that I might call on Edward before my train was due.

He wasn't in his study. The room curdled with a smell like sickness. I went in search of Asaph and found him at the table in the kitchen slurping watery porridge from a tin cup.

I inquired after my uncle.

"Sleeping," he replied. "He said I was to take you to the station." He squinted to see the clock on the wall. "The 8:05, is it?"

"Yes."

"Better be off, then."

He heaved himself from the chair and limped toward the door. I hesitated. I had hoped to speak with my uncle again, if only to thank him for his kindness, but it was half-past-seven, already, and my train would not wait.

The morning was crisp, autumnal. Asaph brought the buggy round and I took a seat beside him. He whistled to the horse and sent us clattering down the drive. I didn't look behind me, didn't want the backward view.

The wheels rattled. The seat shook beneath me, and I closed my eyes, recalling fog-damp fields and junipers, locust trees and Clemency, the smell of her hair. I slipped into dreaming and did not awaken till we reached the station.

Two weeks after my return to Boston, I received a letter from Clemency's father.

Opinion of the Court delivered by ST. JAMES, R. This is a petition by Henry Feathering of Boston, Massachusetts to wed Miss Clemency St. James of Concord, New Hampshire. Evidence supporting the petition was presented by Miss St. James herself and by Miss Phyllis Evans of Westerly, Maine. Evidence against the petitioner was presented by Mr. Justice St. James of Concord, New Hampshire, who voiced considerable misgivings concerning the petitioner's character and prospects. A telegram was sent to Mr. Edward Feathering of Westerly. His legal will was produced and submitted into evidence. Upon examination the will was determined to support the petitioner's case. PETITION GRANTED.

Clemency's letter came by the next post. Her father had given us his blessing, she said, but we must wait until after her twenty-first birthday in April. The wedding would be in Concord with Phyllis and Edith making the arrangements. Her father looked forward to making my acquaintance as well that of my uncle, as he believed the two men, anchorites alike, would have "much to discuss."

They were never to meet. My uncle died in his sleep on December 2nd. His condition had deteriorated in the months since my visit, and the end, when it came, was peaceful. The town was informed and Edward was interred in the village cemetery beside his wife.

Phyllis wrote to tell me of his passing. She herself hadn't learned of the death until after the burial when she chanced on Asaph sleeping propped against the cemetery fence.

I knelt beside him, Phyllis wrote. *The man reeked of rye whiskey and it was plain that he had drank himself into a stupor. I attempted to wake him before the constable might learn of his indisposition but succeeded only in dislodging him from the fence and dropping him hard upon the ground. His eyelids fluttered open. He must have recognized me as a relation of Clemency because he asked me to write to you. It seems your uncle experienced a premonition on the evening of his death and pleaded with his manservant to send you a message after his death. "Remember the lilies," he said. At least, I believe that was the message Asaph was intended to communicate, though I admit I had no little difficulty in understanding the man.*

I understood my uncle's meaning perfectly: not "lilies" but "Lily." He wanted me to remember Lily Stark, Jane Feathering, our final conversation. *The house is yours, but I will tell you now that you must sell it. Under no circumstances are you to bring Miss Clemency here.*

That same day I wrote to Clemency to express my misgivings, though I did not go so far as to suggest selling the Lodge as my uncle had urged. I thought instead we might rent the house while auctioning the remainder of the property. The proceeds of such a sale would suffice to support us in Boston or Concord or wherever we wished to make our home together.

Her response arrived the next evening.

I have read your letter, Henry, and it does you credit, but please try to remember your uncle was an old man at the end of his life. Our acquaintance was only brief, but even so, I sense your uncle's life was defined by love but limited by grief—and grief, as you know, can be a kind of madness.

Which brings us to Lily Stark. Phyllis has told me something of her story, and I am now entirely certain the woman is deserving only of our pity and understanding. Her life was a sad one, yes, but she is now at peace. You yourself must have felt something similar or you would not have been moved to quote from Miss Brontë: "How anyone could ever imagine unquiet slumbers, for the sleepers in that quiet earth."

I think of that day, the things you said, and it occurs to me that we

have a certain obligation to Lily's memory, and indeed, to the place
where she is buried. The stone leans badly and must be righted,
while the planting of white lilies strikes me as an appropriate
gesture. We will have need of a gardener, of course, but you
mustn't think of the expense; consider it instead a debt repaid.

Clemency's mind was quite made up: I did not press her. In April
I gave up the lease of my rooms in Boston and sent on my few
belongings to Westerly. Then I packed my best suit into a carpetbag
and traveled by train to Concord to present myself at the home of
Reginald St. James. Clemency met me in the doorway.

"Henry," she whispered.

Dinner was served, and afterward, I was granted an audience
with Clemency's father. The retired judge proved an even more
eccentric character than I had imagined and spoke in much the same
tedious manner as his letters.

Of my uncle's passing, he remarked, "This Court had hoped the
late Edward Feathering might present himself in person. As his
absence has become unavoidable, his correspondence with the Court
must serve as evidence of Mr. Feathering's integrity and character
as well as that of his nephew, Henry Feathering of Boston. The
opinion of Justice St. James will be disregarded."

But Justice's low opinion of me remained unaltered. He avoided
us that evening, and again at breakfast, and though he attended the
wedding, he would take no part in the service but sat with his father
in the box-pew glowering.

His anger did not ruin the day. We did not allow it.

Clemency and I exchanged rings and promises, and afterward,
we returned to the St. James house to find a veranda hung with
Chinese lanterns and a string quartet playing waltzes by Mozart
and Strauss. We danced into the dark of evening with everyone
watching though we looked only at one another or our own reflections in each other's eyes like fixed points in a world that spins and
will not cease from spinning.

VII.

We spent a fortnight in Concord and wired ahead to Westerly. Asaph met us outside the Lodge and helped us to unload our luggage from the hired buggy. It was late April, almost May, the air scented with new leaves and early apple blossom.

The buggy drove off. Asaph presented me with his keys on a heavy brass ring but lingered, awkwardly, waiting to be dismissed. He stood with his cap in both hands before him and head bowed, showing the pitted scalp.

"I'll go, then," he said, at last.

"Surely you aren't leaving us?" Clemency asked.

"I reckoned you'd have no need of me. Now Mr. Edward's gone."

"Then you reckoned wrongly," Clemency said, taking Asaph's cap from him and placing it back on his head. "Our need has never been greater. My husband may be younger by some years than his late uncle, but I assure you, he is no less hopeless."

Asaph nodded but didn't speak. I believe I made some feeble protest but they both ignored me, and Asaph tipped his cap to Clemency.

"I'll keep my room, then."

"Please," she said.

He snatched the keys out of my hands and went back inside. I shook my head and complained of his rudeness, but Clemency didn't hear me. She had turned from the house to the untended lawn and to the birch-woods beyond, the locust grove and Lily's grave.

She smiled, if a little sadly, and offered me her elbow.

"Shall we go in?"

We spent the rest of the day wandering the house, passing down galleries into shuttered rooms where we drew back the curtains and let in the light.

Near the top of the house, we happened upon an old nursery with bars across the windows. The wallpaper was black and crumpled, its pattern obscured, and there was no furniture inside except a child's rocking horse.

"My uncle's," I said, guessing. "When he was a child."

Clemency traced a line in the dust with her finger then drew another line across it to reveal the letter L scratched there by a child's hand.

"He must have earned a whipping for that," I said.

"A whipping?" Clemency said. "If she were lucky."

Then swiped at the horse with her sleeve and cleared the dust from the saddle. The rest of the name was visible. "Lily," I read, but Clemency wasn't there: her footsteps retreated down the gallery. I hurried after her, following the sound of her footfalls into a narrow staircase that reeked of mold before emerging into my uncle's study.

Clemency was at the window. She had unlatched the shutters, lifted the sash. Sunlight flooded the room. A pile of filthy china had accumulated near the desk and the chamber pot had not been emptied. It was obvious my uncle had taken to sleeping here during his last illness, burrowing into a nest of ragged blankets on the floor.

Edward's desk was a mess of coffee stains and candle-stubs, papers tied off with twine. His study of the Teutoborg must have run to a thousand pages covered front-and-back in his spidery hand with a dedication page reading, simply, *For J.F.*

Jane Feathering. The study was a mess but her portrait alone was free of dust or cobwebs: its colors blazed as brightly as on the day it was painted. Edward must have tended to his late wife's painting with a religious devotion though the rest of the house fell into decay.

The realization saddened me, as I thought only of my uncle's pain, but the sun moved over the portrait and I became aware of an answering light inside the portrait that animated Jane's features and leapt to her eyes as with the flaring of a candlewick.

She was dead, forty-four years gone, but in this portrait, she survived like a fragment of my uncle's own Arcadia, fixed in amber, so that I understood why Edward had lavished such care upon the image. He was, after all, an historian.

Clemency stood beneath the painting, looking up. I joined her there. "I thought at first the portrait might be taken down," I said. "But she belongs here, doesn't she?"

"She does," Clemency agreed and turned toward me, her hands in my hair as she drew me down to a kiss. "And so do we."

That evening Asaph prepared the guest room for us. The night was warm, the windows open, and I fell asleep with Clemency beside me and the wind in the bittersweet whispering—a soothing sound, but my sleep proved uneasy.

I dreamt I was outside the nursery. The door was open, but I didn't go in. Winter light streamed through the windows, glinting off wallpaper that was no longer black and crumpled but displayed a pattern of golden *fleur-de-lis*.

I closed the door and the world disappeared. Darkness surrounded me, a deadening cloud, in which I heard a woman sobbing, screeching, howling, her anguish like a disease that was catching until I, too, was sick with it. My throat burned, and I retched on the blackness that surrounded me, boiling out of my guts then spilling over, the same dark.

Until my vision cleared and I was in a different dream in an unused bedroom underneath the nursery. Everything was as I remembered, save that the bed was uncovered, the clothes kicked back to reveal a mess of dark stains. Old blood, I thought, and a jelly-like puddle had formed among the sheets, black and bottomless like the pupil of an eye.

VIII.

May became June. The lilacs withered into black husks as the bittersweet flowered and spilled its blossoms down the walls. We sent for masons and carpenters to repair the crumbling brickwork and hired day laborers to paint the interior and remove the damaged furniture.

Clemency had need of a sitting room, so I turned my attention to the second-floor bedroom of which I had dreamt. It was one of only a few habitable rooms on the upper floor and more suited to a sitting room than the old nursery. I examined the bed and found the sheets to be clean and quite unstained though the mattress teemed with vermin and could not be salvaged.

The workmen burned everything. They split the bedrails and piled them in the fire-pit with the featherbed then doused the lot with kerosene and set it alight. The smoke went up, a greasy plume, and I sent the men inside with instructions to whitewash the walls and floors and to paint the furniture and window-frames in the same brilliant shade.

They worked through the day and finished late in the afternoon when sun streamed through the south-facing windows and the white room caught its light and overflowed with it.

Clemency was in the garden. I opened the window and called down to her. She met me in the kitchen and followed me upstairs. I showed her into the sitting room then stood beside her in the light that filled the room, white and pure as the dawn after a snowfall.

She didn't speak. The sun blazed across her features, shining from them, but her eyes were closed, and I realized she was crying. Her tears cut long shimmering lines in her cheeks and throat then spattered the floor as she covered her face and fled.

"I'm afraid I'm being rather silly," she said, later, when I held her in my arms. "You mean well, I know, but you are far too kind to me."

"We won't speak of it," I said, and we didn't.

The summer drifted past: a dream of misty mornings and sweltering afternoons, of evening storms receding into nights of stars.

Late in August, I received a letter from Justice. Clemency was in Biddeford for the day and I was alone at the breakfast table when Asaph brought the mail. His letter was addressed to me, I noticed, rather than to Clemency, and I admit I delayed opening it until after luncheon for fear of what it might contain. I needn't have worried.

I know I presume overmuch in writing to you but feel it is my duty to apologize for my behavior of the last year. My relationship with Clem has always been close. Our mother died & Father retreated from the world so that we were together, always, the closest of companions. The prospect of losing her proved unbearable. Months later I realize my eyes were clouded by fear & that this same terror prevented me from wishing you the happiness you deserve. I only hope it is not too late to salvage something of our friendship & that

you might once more consider me
Your friend and brother
Justice St. James

His letter moved me, and I wasted no time in penning my response, extending forgiveness to him in no uncertain terms and inviting him to stay at the Lodge. I gave the letter to Asaph to mail then went outside with my notebook to roam over the property, sketching rows of trees we had not yet planted, a summerhouse we planned to build.

Clemency was late in returning. I was in the library, smoking my pipe and pacing the Turkish rug with *Edwin Drood* to hand when I heard the clop of hooves from outside and hastened to extinguish my pipe. Clemency disliked tobacco, the smell of it, and I had just emptied the bowl into the grate when she entered the library in her hat and coat and crossed the room to my chair. She perched herself on the arm.

"Smoking again," she teased.

I could hardly deny it.

"While your sainted wife was forced to tramp the dusty streets of Biddeford with only Beatrice for company. The dear girl is devoted but hardly an adequate conversationalist. *Yes, Madame. No, Madame.* Always the same two phrases. She has been in this country two years and I am not certain her knowledge of English extends much beyond them."

I withdrew Justice's letter from my pocket. "This came today."

"From Father?"

"No," I said. "But it is from Concord."

She unfolded the letter and began to read. She reached the end and folded the paper back upon itself before sliding from the chair and standing at the hearth with her back to me.

Dusk waned into darkness. The crickets sang.

At last she spoke. "Was there no message for me?"

"He sent only this letter which he addressed to me."

"Yes," she said, removing an iron from the rack. "I saw."

"You appear unsettled."

"Not at all," she said. "I am quite well." Then turned toward me, forcing a smile, saying, "but you must leave my brother to me. I will write a suitable response."

"I have already written to him, I'm afraid."

The smile disappeared. "And what did you tell him?"

"I—I invited him to stay."

She said nothing. Her knuckles knit fast about the iron.

"I hoped it would be a surprise," I said. "An agreeable one, that is."

The blood was in her throat and cheeks. The grate smoked behind her, where my tobacco remained alight. Blue wisps curled out of the ash, clawing upward.

"I thought you would be pleased," I said.

"Pleased," she repeated, dully, then swung the iron over her head, bringing it down hard upon the grate. The noise was dreadful, metal on metal. Ash whirled up about her and billowed into the room as she struck at the grate again and again until the rage went out of her. Her hands shook at her sides. The iron dropped to the rug and she wouldn't look at me.

"I will send another letter," I said. "I will say he cannot visit, that we are going away."

"No, you mustn't."

"Why ever not?"

"He cannot think—"

"What does it matter what he thinks?"

"He is my brother."

The ash settled, staining her skirts and the rug at her feet. She stooped and picked up the fireiron. "I have been very happy here," she said, replacing it in the rack, "but the world is such it cannot be ignored forever... as much as I wish it were otherwise."

Summer was spent, our Arcadia in ruin.

The next day, Clemency slipped from the house at dawn and I did not ask where she had gone. In truth, I hadn't the opportunity. She spent the evening in her sitting room and didn't come to bed until midnight or later when I was already asleep.

Justice's response arrived during breakfast. He had arranged with his employers to be away during the first week of October and hoped he might call on us in Westerly. I showed the letter to Clemency, who read it slowly, showing no emotion.

"He must come," she said. "If not now, then later—and better it be now."

Her footsteps echoed, fading. The front door opened, closed, and I went after her.

I followed her across the fields and through the birch trees to the locust grove where I had not been since my proposal of the previous year. The transformation was profound. Lily Stark's headstone was righted, no longer leaning, and ringed about with hundreds of white lilies in an arrangement recalling a cathedral labyrinth. Their blossoms shone.

A debt repaid, Clemency had said. This was unhallowed ground, the grave of a suicide, but by force of beauty alone had it been consecrated.

Early September: wind in the locusts, the lilies rippling, and Clemency kneeling over a dead girl's grave. She wrapped her arms about the stone and pressed her forehead to the inscription, an attitude of prayer. *Et in Arcadia Ego.*

I went to her. She showed no surprise at my presence and made no protest though I helped her to her feet. "Henry," she said, only that, and we walked back to the house.

IX.

I fell into a nightmare. No sound, no light, and again, the burning swam into my throat. I couldn't breathe, couldn't vomit. Blood like fire collected in my gut then burst the sphincter and spilled out from the orifice. I was choking, drowning in my own juices. A rush of hot fluid forced open my lips and streamed from my mouth, a darkness poured out endlessly.

Then a flicker of candlelight, the soft shaking into wakefulness. Clemency cradled my head in her lap and repeated the same three words over me like a spell of protection.

"Only a dream," she said. "Only a dream."

Morning came, and autumn too. The bittersweet turned dark. The rain proved unrelenting, and we were trapped inside. I prowled the house like an animal, scuttling down rain-dim galleries to shelter in the library or in my uncle's study with his dead wife's portrait on the wall and the cool light playing over it.

Jane Feathering had died at twenty, the same age as Lily Stark. My uncle believed Lily had taken possession of his wife, somehow, causing her illness, and I thought of Clemency, who was twenty-one, and of her daily pilgrimages to the locust grove, where she stayed for hours before returning to her sitting room and closing the door.

I went inside once, though I knew I wasn't wanted, and discovered her seated upright on the daybed with her knees at her chest. Her hair was tangled, unwashed, and she stared past me to the wall with its bars of shadow on sun. She didn't speak but gathered the silence about her like another room into which no words or light could penetrate.

September was a month of such silences: the days passed too slowly, and I longed for Justice's arrival. On October the fourth, he wired from Portsmouth and I arranged for Asaph to collect him from the station. He reached the Lodge at five o'clock. Asaph showed him into my uncle's study, but he halted in the doorway, as if afraid to approach.

Less than six months had elapsed since our wedding, but he appeared much older than in May. His clothing was dirty, unkempt, and he was terribly thin, besides. He stank of wine and shag tobacco and hadn't shaved in days.

"I am grateful to you for seeing me," he said. "My conduct toward you has been—unforgivable."

I rose and crossed the room and embraced him as a brother. "All is forgiven," I said, and meant it. "Thank God you have come."

We went outside. The day was cold and gray and deepening into twilight as we passed beneath the cedar-trees. I had thought to walk to the locust grove, but something stopped me. I do not know what. Instead we descended the drive, our footsteps crunching into the uneasy quiet that settled over us with the dusk as we reached the highway and turned back toward the house, and Justice spoke. "Tell me," he said, and I did.

I told him of the locust grove and of Lily Stark's suicide. He was already familiar with her story, which surprised me, until I recalled the afternoon he had spent with my uncle in the library. Edward had blamed Lily for his wife's illness, I explained, and recounted his final words of warning: *Remember Lily.*

"We were to sell the Lodge," I said.

"But you didn't."

"No."

"My sister's doing, I expect."

He was right, of course. I told him of Clemency's interest in Lily Stark and of her walks to the locust grove, of the hours she had spent there and the transformation that resulted. Her melancholia. Her anger.

Justice interrupted me. "As if she, too, were under the influence of Lily's spirit?

"Perhaps," I said, slightly embarrassed.

"May I speak plainly?"

"By all means."

"Your uncle may have believed in ghosts, Henry, but I do not, and neither should you. Where he might have seen actions of a malevolent spirit, I see instead the fevered workings of a disordered brain, that of a man broken by grief and decades of isolation."

"And Clemency?"

He exhaled heavily.

"My sister has long been disquieted in mind. You must have realized this. Consider her fascination with the strange, the ghoulish. Like your uncle she would see a ghost's influence where there is only illness. Unlike your uncle, however, she is not alone in her affliction."

I did not reply but thought of Poe's "Alone," which we had quoted to one another, and of the final lines that went unspoken.

And the cloud that took the form
(When the rest of Heaven was blue)
Of a demon in my view.

"Once," Justice continued, "when we were children, my mother came into the nursery where I was seated in the window-seat. She dragged me to the floor by my collar and thrashed me about the bottom while I blubbered and protested that I had done nothing wrong. I hadn't seen Clem in hours, but she had gone to our mother in tears and told her she had hidden from me in a cupboard and that I had broken the door to get to her. All lies, as it happens, but the cupboard was indeed broken. Clem had taken a hammer to it."

"Good Lord."

"She was a fantasist, Henry, as we all are in childhood. But a child's fantasy is madness in an adult. And Clemency is no longer a child."

"Madness," I said.

Wind, and the cedars rattling, raining down needles.

My voice was hoarse when I spoke again. "What is to be done?"

"I would speak with her," Justice said. "As her brother."

"Of course," I said.

"Alone," he said, and I nodded.

We returned to the house and a table laid for dinner. The cook struck the bell, but Clemency didn't join us, and Asaph admitted he hadn't seen her since the morning. I sent him upstairs to her sitting room, and he returned alone.

"Beatrice is there," he said. "She wouldn't let me in."

"Beatrice?" Justice asked.

"Clemency's maid," I explained.

"She told me the missus wasn't hungry. That she won't be coming down."

I waved him away. The cook entered with a platter of oysters and Justice and I passed a pleasant evening together. We did not talk of Clemency but of politics and philosophy until the last of the wine was poured. I sipped mine slowly, making it last, but the inevitable could not be delayed. Our cigars burned down, and we went upstairs.

Beatrice met us outside Clemency's sitting room. My wife's maid was a French-Canadian girl of about sixteen.

"Very sorry," she said. "No one is to enter, not even Monsieur Henry."

Justice spoke. "It's Beatrice, isn't it? Your loyalty to your mistress is to be commended, but I am Mrs. Feathering's brother. We have not been together since before the wedding. She is anxious to see me, no doubt, and would not wish for you to create further delay."

Beatrice's confidence wavered. "I do not know, monsieur."

"She won't be angry with you," Justice said. "I will make it perfectly plain that you followed her instructions to the letter." He produced a coin from his waistcoat. "In consideration of your service. All women should have such maids to attend to them."

Beatrice took the coin. She removed a brass key from her apron and placed it into Justice's hand. "Monsieur," she said and scurried off down the gallery.

Justice slotted the key to the lock.

"I'll return at eleven?" I asked.

"That should be sufficient, yes."

He turned the key, let himself in. The door closed, and I was alone in the half-light with the shadows like ghosts drawing near. Edward and Jane Feathering. Lily Stark. The girl was bones in the ground, nothing more, but she possessed a hold on Clemency I could not understand. Black shapes flitted down the gallery, and I recalled my own troubled dreams, and wondered, in a moment of fantasy, if these too were the influence of Lily's restless spirit.

But there were no ghosts at Bittersweet Lodge: there was only pain. Lily had taken her own life at twenty while Jane Feathering had died slowly and in agony. My uncle had needed to believe her illness wasn't meaningless, that it signified more than the world's indifference, much as I would believe in any fiction, no matter how outlandish, if it proved Clemency to be sane.

I paced the house. In the library, I took down Hawthorne's *Twice-Told Tales* and tried to read but could not fix my eyes upon the page. The lamp burned low and fitful and the windows were black and empty, openings to nowhere. The world beyond had vanished. No trees, no sky. My breath clouded on the glass and I wiped it away but did not move from the window until the clocks had struck eleven and I returned to Clemency's room as arranged.

Justice was letting himself out. He appeared noticeably shaken, breathless, his face flushed. He saw me but only shook his head before hurrying away down the gallery. I called after him, but he didn't look back.

The door was closed, locked. I heard movement from inside, then a sound like sobbing, but Clemency wouldn't come to the door and her brother had the key.

"Let me in," I pleaded but there was no response. My head fell forward, striking the door, and I listened, helpless, just as Clemency had listened at the grave of Lily Stark. But the door to her room—like that door into eternity—remained closed to me.

X.

Someone at the door. I stumbled out of bed and drew back the latch. Beatrice. The girl's hair was a mess, her eyes wild. The light wavered in her hand.

"You must come," she said. "Madame Clemency is ill."

Blood in my ears, then, a feeling of falling. The sweat prickled on my forehead and I steadied myself against the doorframe as Beatrice continued, saying, "She screams like she is in pain, but her room it is locked, and I do not have my key."

I swallowed, tasting bile. "Go and wake her brother," I told her. "Tell him he is to meet me at her sitting room with the key. Then send Asaph for the doctor. Do you understand?"

Beatrice nodded. She lifted her skirts and hastened to the guest room where Justice slept. I did not pause to strike a light but threw myself down the staircase, stumbling at the landing then regaining my feet and sprinting down the gallery.

Screams from the sitting room: a shrill, wordless howling, as of a beast in a cage-trap. I rattled the handle and battered the latch, but the door held. "Step aside," a voice said, and Justice was there beside me. He unlocked the door with Beatrice's key and we went inside.

The room smelled of blood and sickness, loosened bowels. Clemency thrashed about on the daybed, moaning, the blankets wound about like a shroud. The furniture was disordered, the end-table upturned. A wineglass had shattered on the floor and there were dark streaks about her mouth as she gasped and clawed at her stomach. Her eyes rolled white in her skull.

I ran to the daybed. I took hold of her arms and pinned them to her sides, but she spasmed and writhed and rose from the soiled bedding, her body twisting back on itself like the limbs of a locust tree. I climbed on top of her. Her fists flew up to bruise my face and head, but I held her down, somehow, and whispered into her ear such soothing phrases as I could remember, as though words alone might dispel the nightmare into which we had fallen.

She went limp. Her face relaxed, her eyes closed, and she was quiet. I inclined my ear to her breast and heard the flutter of a heartbeat.

"My God," Justice said, "she isn't…?"

"No."

"What is to be done?"

"Asaph is going for the doctor."

Justice nodded but appeared uncomfortable. "I'll see if he needs help." He excused himself. An hour passed, more, and he didn't return. The clocks struck three and the candlelight flickered on the wall, transforming the sparsely furnished sitting room into a shadow-play of swaying tree-limbs and blowing leaves, the silhouette of a woman leaning over the daybed: she touched her lips to Clemency's forehead.

"Henry."

Clemency was awake. The light made sparks of her eyes.

"Clem, I—"

"Don't," she said.

"Why did we ever come here? If only we had stayed away…"

"No," she said. "Your uncle was mistaken. He didn't know her, couldn't see—"

The breath failed her.

"Whom do you mean? I don't understand."

"No," she said, gently, and she was smiling. "I know you don't. Do you recall that day in the grove, what you said to me? That we could know each other. Face to face, as in Arcadia."

"I remember."

"This world," she said, still smiling. "It asks too much of us. Takes even more. But I regret nothing, Henry. You mustn't, either. Promise me."

I promised.

The doctor bustled in at dawn. He had been out on a call, attending to a birth in a neighboring village and guzzled a cup of strong coffee before performing his examination.

"Enteritis," he said. "Very bad, I'm afraid. There is nothing to be done."

Clemency died at ten past eight. The doctor closed her eyes, opened the curtains. Sunlight poured into the sitting room, white and blinding, an annihilating purity.

I ran. I fled to the library, but even there, her absence pursued me. The last dance at our wedding, how we whirled together with our faces in each other's eyes. The letters we exchanged, promises we made, and Clemency's arms about my neck, encircling like a halter. A woman in white, her lifted hand. Her face in death, its awful stillness.

An image, I thought. She would never be anything more.

The pain landed like a howitzer shell, punching through my chest and torching the blood that surged to my brain so body and mind were all one fire, one darkness, as in my nightmares of the house from which I could not awaken, even now, though I tore at my clothes and hair and hurled myself into the nearest bookcase. The shelf groaned and toppled over, shattering the window behind it. Glass was everywhere and blood on my bare feet as I kicked at the volumes, cracking their spines and splitting the binding. Cold air pushed into the room, sweeping the scattered pages from the rug and raining them over me, white and flapping, a storm of lilies.

Justice appeared.

His eyes were red, his skin ashen. We stood face to face with the torn leaves drifting between us, an illustration from "Ligea" of a woman reborn with hair *blacker than the raven wings of midnight*. The page twitched and lifted, catching the wind then floating away.

"Phyllis and Edith are here," he said.

"I cannot see them," I said. "Not now."

He nodded. "I will find something for them to do."

The two old women quickly proved themselves indispensable. They laid out Clemency in the parlor and sent word of her death to Concord while I was indisposed with grief and irrational. I wouldn't leave the library but spent the day gathering up glass in my hands and piecing together the books I had ruined. Sometime after midnight I collapsed in a chair by the fireplace and drifted into a dreamless sleep as night bayed and shrieked at the broken window.

Edith found me there in the morning.

"We must discuss the burial," she said, and I nodded. "As you know, your uncle is buried with his late wife in the village. The plot is wide and would suffice for Clemency as well, though Justice has also expressed an interest in removing the body to Concord."

"No," I said. "She must be buried here."

"In the village."

"In the locust grove."

"But that is unconsecrated ground—"

"Then find someone to consecrate it!"

Edith turned and left. I feared I had offended her, but she did exactly as I had asked, traveling by train to Biddeford where she found a minister willing to preside at the burial, returning with him on the morning of the wake. Clemency lay in the parlor as the mourners came and went, but I waited outside, wishing to remember her only as she was in life, not death, and because I had no likeness of her: no portrait, not even a photograph.

Afterward Asaph screwed down the coffin lid, and Edith's minister led the procession to the locust grove, where Clemency's gravesite had been prepared beside that of Lily Stark. The day was fine and warm for autumn. Dead lilies rustled under our feet, brown and trodden where they had once been white. Words were said, the body consigned. The first shovelfuls of dirt were cast into the grave and the mourners returned to the house.

I did not join them.

"It's a pretty spot," Phyllis said.

Her presence surprised me. I had thought I was alone.

She continued, "My dear sister had doubts concerning the place you had chosen for our cousin to rest, and Justice, too, had hoped to bring his sister home. But being here now I believe this was the right decision."

"I asked her to be my wife here."

"Is that so? I didn't realize."

"We were walking and chanced to stumble on this place. Her grave."

"Lily Stark," Phyllis said.

"You know her story, don't you? Clemency mentioned you had told it to her."

Phyllis pulled her shawl about her shoulders. "I do," she said.

"Will you tell it to me?"

"It's a sad story," she said. "Could we leave it for another day?"

"Please," I said, and she relented.

"Long before your uncle lived here," she said, "this house was owned by a family called Stark. The father, Cyrus, was a brute, who had earned his money in the slave trade and subjected his family and servants to the same treatment he had learned at sea. His wife died of consumption as did his three eldest children. Only Lily survived to adulthood. He loved her, it was said, but there is no doubt that he was cruel to her. There were rumors of abuse and, really, the most shocking things were said.

"All of this I heard from my mother, who was a young girl at the time. Her father was a doctor here in town and a frequent guest of the Lodge and my mother had met the older Lily on many occasions. I believe she admired her—worshiped her, even—and Lily was unquestionably a remarkable girl, blessed with a talent for living things. She kept the kitchen garden where she grew all manner of exotic plants and even built a hothouse round the back where she cultivated flowers, seedlings, fruit trees."

"My uncle told me she had planted the bittersweet."

"A gift for life, as I said. Perhaps that's why it happened."

"Pardon?"

"She fell in love. Hard, the way some girls do. The man worked on a neighboring farm. He was young and undoubtedly poor. A freedman, I have also heard, and maybe that was true, because Cyrus put an end to it. Most say he bought the boy off, though some believed they fought and the boy fled only for fear of his life. He left, anyway, and Cyrus arranged for his daughter to marry a business partner. But it never happened."

"She killed herself," I said.

Phyllis nodded. "If the girl had any sense, she would have cut her own throat or drowned herself in the ocean. But, no, she mixed up a poison from such plants as she grew and drank down the bottle. It burned up her insides. Her father found her in her bedroom with the blood pouring out of her. He sent for my grandfather, the doctor, who was also Justice of the Peace, but Lily was dead when he arrived. He couldn't help her but was able to determine what had happened, how she'd done it. Cyrus blamed himself, naturally, and died soon afterward. A cousin inherited the property and sold it to your uncle, who lost his wife to illness, and now Miss Clemency…"

Phyllis shivered, adjusted her shawl. "This place has seen too much tragedy."

"Yes," I said.

She took me by the elbow. "Come along," she said. "I believe the weather's turning cold."

☙

Justice was dead by March. His father heard a gunshot and rushed to the nursery of the house in Concord where he discovered his son curled up inside a broken cupboard. The revolver was still in his hand, smoking, but he left no note and no indication as to motive.

Edward Feathering's study of the Teutoborg appeared in print the following month. Notices weren't kind. My uncle's knowledge was described as superficial, his style tedious, but in publishing the book, I had secured my freedom: I sold Bittersweet Lodge to a New York banker and returned to Boston, the life of a bachelor.

Little more is left to say. My story is ended, but I can offer no explanation for the events I have related. Lily Stark's grave. My aunt's long illness. Clemency's death and Justice's suicide. These are to me like the strands of a story that can never be knitted, but I have learned to accept this. Life, as it is lived, rarely conforms to the shapes prescribed by literature.

Forty-four years later and Clemency hasn't left me. I live alone but for the lack of her, married to her absence. Her voice I hear only in dreams and faint for the gulf which divides us, which always separated us, even in life.

I regret nothing, she says. *You mustn't, either.*

I am sixty-six years old.

I have not kept my promise.

The Lake

August 1997. Samuel is twelve, almost thirteen, but looks younger. He despises himself, his thin limbs, hairless body. His best friend Jason is a Boy Scout and an athlete, pitcher for the town's Little League team. The boys are neighbors, have known each other for years.

It's early evening, not yet suppertime. Most days in summer the boys ride bikes to the dam, but tonight, they are waiting for Nick, watching for him from the windows of Samuel's living room. Nick lives in the next town and attends a different middle school. He met the other boys at church camp, where Samuel's father is pastor.

A truck pulls up outside. The red body gleams, waxed and shining, its hubcaps like silver sunbursts. The driver is visible through the windshield, dark glasses hiding his eyes. Nick's father. His skin is shockingly pale, his hands white where they grip the steering wheel.

Nick dismounts from the cabin and totters up the lawn. He is pale and heavy, asthmatic. He wheezes when he runs, breasts bouncing in the shirts he wears to swim.

His father pulls out, gunning the engine, and the boys dash outside. They meet Nick on the porch and set off with him, following the road along the lakeshore with its floating docks and ranks of summer cottages. Samuel and Jason go first, nearly running, while Nick trails behind, panting, pleading with them to slow down, to wait.

They reach the dam. The site is long disused, its sluices blocked with rust, concrete chipped and pitted. The boys remove their shoes and socks. They scale the hemlock which overhangs the dam and lower themselves to the ledge.

Jason goes first, then Samuel, then Nick, who trembles as he releases his grip on the hemlock and stands unsupported on the dam. A motorboat passes, startling the gulls from a nearby thicket. The noise of the engine tails off to a drone then silence though the waves continue to move in its absence, spreading over the lake like the cracks in a mirror.

The ledge is slick, wet with spray from the lake five feet below. Samuel, cautious, steps carefully over the dam, hooking his toes in the crumbling concrete. He goes from pockmark to crater, listening all the while for Nick's breath behind him: the catch in the other boy's throat, the occasional wheeze.

Jason is far ahead of them. He walks the ledge with an acrobat's grace, slowing only as he nears the center of the dam. Samuel has not been out so far, has never dared, but Nick is behind him and he doesn't want to appear afraid, says nothing.

They reach the dam's center where the ledge is highest. Behind them an old streambed runs downhill past a shuttered cottage before bending out of sight beyond a stand of hemlocks. The dark trees shimmer. The day's rain webs their foliage, hangs from branch and needle. The lake is calm, all waves dissipated. Samuel looks down at his reflection far below.

Jason strips off his shirt. The muscles show in his arms and shoulders as he raises his hands, joining them together over his head. He turns his wrists one against the other and stretches, bending himself from side to side.

Samuel asks: "What are you doing?"

"Limbering up."

"Why?"

"We're going to dive."

"Here? It's too high."

"Ten feet, maybe. No more than that. Same as the diving board at the Y."

"I don't know."

"Don't dive, then. I'll do it alone."

Jason drops to a squat. His legs tense. He straightens, readying himself for the jump.

Nick says: "Wait."

Samuel wheels around. He watches dumbly as Nick snorts from his inhaler and shuffles forward past him. The fat bunches at his elbows. His nipples show through his tee shirt.

He says: "I'll jump with you."

Jason grins. "Okay, then," he says.

Samuel reddens and retreats down the ledge. He turns his back on the others, faces the boarded-up cottage. The windows are shut, the doors padlocked.

Behind him Jason and Nick line up at the edge of the dam. He hears them, their breathing. Jason counting down from three. "One."

They jump. Samuel glances behind him, sees Jason fall with his back curved in upon itself and hands thrust out even as Nick steps forward timidly and drops from the ledge feet-first.

The air rushes up toward Nick, unbalancing him as he falls and flipping him onto his back. His tee shirt inflates, rides up, revealing his chest: the breasts like lumps of dough, the lines of yellow bruising near the waistband of his trunks. He strikes the water and plunges toward the bottom. Samuel's reflection unravels with the impact, shattered in the whorl of rising bubbles.

Jason breaches the water. He is some distance from the dam and making for the lake's center. His strokes are perfect: he cleaves the water like a boat's prow, the long wake rippling behind him.

Samuel waits. Nick does not resurface.

The water re-knits itself, becoming smooth as glass. Samuel's face floats within it, a perfect image: the lines round his mouth, the lips wide as he yells for help. His throat yawns before him, black with the shadow from a dying eddy.

His voice is broken, shrill, but it is enough. Jason hears him and turns round. He swims back toward the dam, shouting to Samuel as he draws near. He urges Samuel to jump in, to help, but Samuel can't. His legs refuse to move, his eyes to close.

Jason dives, surfaces. There are weeds in his hair, water streaming down his face.

"Where is he?" he demands. "Can you see him?"

But the lake is a mirror, obscuring all but Samuel's own pinched face, the tongue flapping uselessly against the dark of his throat. Jason swears and forces himself under again—longer this time though he comes up gasping, alone. He treads water briefly, breathing hard. Two deep breaths and he submerges himself for a third time, disappearing behind Samuel's reflection.

At last he resurfaces, Nick's head lolling on his shoulder. The other boy is limp in his arms, pressed close to his chest as he holds him up, kicking them both toward shore.

Samuel runs to meet them. He sheds his paralysis and sprints along the dam, forgetting his earlier caution. His bare feet sting as they slap the concrete.

Jason reaches the rocks near the end of the dam and pulls himself from the water. He drags himself forward with one hand then turns to haul up Nick behind him.

There is blood in the boy's scalp and his tee shirt hangs loosely from his neck. His exposed chest appears soft, rubbery, white but for the bruises at his waist. They form a mottled line, purple and yellow, which disappears into his underwear.

Samuel sees them first, then Jason.

They look at each other, look away.

Jason takes Nick's wrist in hand and listens for the pulse. He cradles the boy's neck between his legs and leans forward, covering Nick's lips with his mouth.

He breathes in, out.

Nick startles and coughs. Jason exhales heavily, falling back. The strength drains from Samuel's legs, and he drops to his knees.

The coughing subsides. Nick's eyelids flutter and open.

His eyes are bulging, wild and white.

☙

Samuel tells no one what happened that day. Jason, too, is silent but only because Samuel begs him not to tell. His fear still eats at him, his shame or something more.

Fall comes and school, eighth grade. Nick disappears from their lives, and it is winter, January, when Samuel sees him again.

Early morning: sun coming up, gray smudges on thick cloud cover. Samuel sits in his mother's car at the end of the driveway, waiting for the school bus.

The morning is cold, below zero. The heat vents rattle. Samuel's head rests against the window, his breath misting on the pane.

Through that fog he watches the red pickup truck come barreling down the road, driving too quickly for the ice on the roads. Nick's father. Samuel recognizes the black glasses, the pale hands on the wheel, and then the truck is past them.

A face at the rear windshield: Nick. He is as pale as his father and his mouth is open, a black circle.

The years pass and Samuel is seventeen, a senior in high school. In the spring he gets his license and takes to driving the lake-roads at night, circling it round and round.

Most nights, Jason rides with him, the water-pipe in hand and the windows down, the night-air breaking like waves around them. Jason offers the pipe to Samuel but always he refuses, thinking of his father's disapproval, and weeks pass in this way before he caves.

Tonight they trade hits from Jason's water-pipe and park below the dam. "Leave the music on," Jason says, and Modest Mouse is playing as they climb out, slam the doors.

The car's headlights shine on the wall of the dam before them, the hemlock-branches through which they climb. They reach the dam and lower themselves down. Stand side-by-side on the ledge, their shadows stretching ahead of them into the water.

The night is clear. The stars are out, the bow of the Milky Way. It joins with its reflection on the water to form an ellipse, an open mouth.

"Well, shit," Jason say. "That's really something."

Samuel is slow to respond. When he does he says it's like the future that's waiting for them, ready to swallow them whole. He is thinking of the coming autumn, when Jason will leave for college, but Jason, laughing, tells him he is stoned.

They talk of other things: Boy Scouts and church camp and summers spent swimming at the dam. One morning in particular when they donned goggles and snorkels and swam out to the center of the lake which marked the boundary between two towns. They crossed the border, Samuel remembers, then turned round and swam back to shore.

Jason asks: "You think you still have those snorkels?"

"Sure. Back at the house."

"What do you say we try them out?"

"Tonight?"

"Yeah."

"Alright."

It is after midnight. They walk back to the house and let themselves into the mudroom. The snorkels are in the closet along with two sets of goggles, the lenses gray with dust and spider silk. Samuel hands one set to Jason and takes the other for himself.

Silently, then, they slip outside, drawing the door shut behind them. They return to the dam and strip to their boxer shorts, climb the hemlock. Jason squats down, leaning forward to rinse his snorkel in the lake-water. Samuel follows suit then takes the mouthpiece between his lips. He gags at the taste: mud, mildew, puddled snowmelt.

Jason laughs, his face hidden behind his goggles. Samuel turns from him and looks out toward the lake, its center. His breath moans in the snorkel.

The moon is waning. The stars cut brighter for the ranks of darkened cottages all around, and the Milky Way is on the water, rippling, opening from itself to receive them as they step forward and drop from the edge.

Samuel hits the water. The lake closes over him, colder than he expected. It sloshes over the snorkel-top and fills his mouth so that he comes up coughing, blind where the lake has seeped into his goggles.

He treads water. "Jason?" he manages.

A voice drifts back to him. "Yeah?"

Jason is ten feet away, nearer the shore, where the lake is shallow enough for him to stand. His bare chest is visible where it thrusts from the water with its web of stars.

Samuel says: "Nothing."

Jason leans forward and submerges his head. He wades along the shore, parting the water before him with his hands.

Samuel empties his goggles and snorkel and begins to swim. The lake-bottom rises out of the blackness as he nears the shallows, the shore.

His toes touch mud and he continues at a walk, wading as Jason did with his goggles submerged in the water. Beyond the glass the lake-bottom appears as a moonscape, lit by stars and cratered where his feet break through it, raising plumes of muddy debris.

He rotates his head toward the lake's center, the line dividing his town from Nick's. The water is deepest there, he knows, and before him the darkness draws itself into thin bands interspersed with beams of light, stars shining through from above.

All is quiet. Samuel is conscious of no sound save the whistle of air in the snorkel, the slow and even lapping of the lake. The weeds ripple beyond his goggles, the mud blossoming before him at each step. He spreads his arms and brings his hands together, dividing stars from darkness from whirling mud.

The silence is broken.

Samuel hears a heavy splash behind him, as though someone else has fallen from the dam. Panting, grunting. The sounds of frantic swimming.

He spins round, startled. He tears the goggles from his head.

Jason is halfway out of the water, running. He reaches the rocks and scrambles up them, and he must have lost his boxers somehow, because Samuel sees that he is naked, his buttocks showing, white and wiry. He vanishes over the lip of the dam.

Samuel goes after him. He thrashes a path through the shallows and bolts up the wet rocks. He falls once, twice, cutting open his foot. He reaches the dam and vaults over the edge, swinging himself down from the hemlock.

Jason is in the car. The passenger-side door is open and he has draped himself in a red gingham picnic blanket. He holds the pipe between his teeth with the lighter in one hand and the other hand cupped round, trying to coax a spark.

"It's nothing," he says, mumbling. "Freaked myself out, that's all."

"All? You scared me."

"Thought I saw something. In the water."

"What did you see?"

Jason shakes his head, will say nothing more.

Samuel retrieves their clothes from the dam. When he returns to the car, he finds Jason seated with eyes closed and pipe lit, smoke curling up from his open mouth.

Samuel starts the car, pulls out. Jason dresses himself in the dark while Samuel averts his gaze, watching the road unfold in the glare of the high-beams.

Jason's breathing is unnaturally loud to him. Samuel turns on the radio.

Jason's house. Jason crosses the lawn with his hands in his pockets and mounts the steps to the screened-in porch. Samuel watches. The headlights strike through the screens, making shadows like nets which close over him, catching Jason as he turns, waves, disappears inside.

☙

The separation happens slowly, by degrees. On Friday, Samuel calls Jason's house and speaks to his mother. She tells him Jason is out. "Lauren came by and picked him up."

Lauren? The name means nothing to him. Samuel spends the night in bed with his headphones on and his face to the ceiling, the fan-blades going around.

The weekend passes with no word from Jason. Sunday night, Samuel goes out walking. His footfalls carry him up hill to the lake, the dam—and that's where he sees them, seated together on the ledge. Jason with his back bent forward, his head in his hands. The girl beside him with her arm extended, hand spread across his back. She is speaking to him softly, almost whispering. Jason's shoulders shake.

Samuel skulks back to the house, says nothing of what he saw. In school the boys continue to greet each other, passing in the hallway, but Jason takes to spending the weekends with Lauren and weeknights, too, once summer arrives.

In the autumn Jason leaves for college on a baseball scholarship and Samuel goes to work for his uncle, who owns a contracting business. He sees Jason around the holidays, but only then, and soon they lose touch altogether.

Samuel is twenty-one, twenty-two. Sometimes, at night, he remembers the lake as it was on that night in May with the stars in its folds and the Milky Way on its surface, yawning, joining its reflection to receive him as he fell.

In dreams he stands on the dam, cold concrete between his toes. He hears his own breathing, strained and whistling, and Nick's face is in the water below. It shimmers in place, floating on the dark that whirls up from beneath.

The image stays with him on waking, a trapped melody. One night, late, he staggers out of bed and tiptoes downstairs to his father's office. He digs the address book out of the desk and flips through it until he finds Nick's number.

He takes down the phone and dials the number. He raises the receiver to his ear and waits for a ringing from the other side. He has no idea what he will say, how he will begin.

Four beeps in sequence. A woman's recorded voice.

The number has been disconnected.

2012. Samuel is a manager in his uncle's contracting business, a youth pastor in his father's church. He teaches Sunday School, arranges field trips to the lake in summertime. He lives alone. His apartment is in the next town but he drives up to the lake on

Sundays for dinner with his parents. From them he learns that Jason is engaged. His mother says: "He's coming home for the wedding. They're getting married at the lake."

He doesn't expect an invitation, doesn't receive one. At dusk on the night of the wedding he cruises round the lake at twenty miles per hour, watching for signs. He spies one, slows. *Jason + Amanda,* it says, the words in green letters on a yellow background. An arrow points up a driveway to a big house on the water, rented for the occasion.

A tent has been erected on the lawn, tables laid with champagne flutes and electric candles. The wedding, it seems, is over, but the dancing continues, men and women whirling together beneath strings of Christmas lights. They are beautiful, achingly so, wearing their best clothes and dancing, pairing off to music he can't hear and always the lake behind them, its awful stillness. The water is calm, un-rippled. Purple with the reflection of a sky that isn't there, not really, and he thinks of his childhood, the years since high school. The surface of his life and the memories it hides. The bruises at Nick's waist. His father's black glasses.

Jason's voice. *Thought I saw something. In the water.*

Samuel backs out into the road. He straightens the wheel and depresses the gas pedal, anxious to be away. Thirty-five, forty. He rounds the northwest corner of the lake just as a pickup truck pulls out from a side-street, cutting him off.

He slams the brakes. Taps the horn as he approaches, but the truck does not increase its speed. Twenty miles per hour. He is ten feet from the other vehicle, less. The tailgate flaps up, down—groaning, broken—and the truck itself is filthy and decrepit.

Samuel strains his eyes. He leans into the glow of his headlights but cannot discern the color of the pickup for the layers of rust and mud. The license plate is similarly indistinct, a gray rectangle, while the truck's rear windshield is fogged over, opaque but for a swath where someone has wiped it clear from inside.

Samuel glimpses movement in the cabin, the flutter of something white. He flashes his high-beams. Glimpses a face at the window, a boy.

The child's eyes are black, or appear so, as is the mouth that drops open, crying out, screaming for help while the tailgate bangs up and down.

Samuel brakes, hard. His car shudders, screeches. Stops.

The truck drives away.

Samuel's mouth is dry. His hands shake as he fumbles for the stick-switch, his brights. He sees it again: that face at the window, an open mouth. Screaming even as the truck vanishes beyond the cone of his headlights, leaving the empty road, the windblown trees. The leaves and the patterns they make like ripples in water.

He stomps down on the accelerator. The engine responds, pushing up toward forty. The lake drops away to his left, the north shore visible through a lattice of birch-branch and pine, and again the pickup is before him.

The tailgate falls open, releasing a cloud of dust from the truck-bed. It rears up before him, white and fine where his headlights strike through, illuminating the interior of the cabin. The driver's head is visible, a shimmering in the truck's rear-view, but only for a moment before it is gone, eclipsed by a hand at the back windshield: a child's hand, the fingers spread.

Samuel slows, his bumper five feet from the truck's tailgate.

He turns on his high-beams, flooding the pickup's interior, revealing the dark stains on the dashboard and headrests, the mold sprouting from the upholstery. The cabin swims with damp, trapped breath whirling like smoke before the light.

The hand vanishes, reappears.

It feebly thumps the glass.

The truck accelerates. The chassis shakes as the driver up-shifts, shedding flecks of paint or rust which spatter Samuel's windshield and skitter away into the night.

Samuel speeds up to maintain his distance, punching his horn all the while. He flashes his brights, but the truck will not slow, will not pull over, and together they follow the road as it curves to the south, away from the lake, dark trees yielding to fences and farm-fields.

He presses down the gas pedal. The speedometer jumps to fifty-five, sixty, bringing him within two car-lengths of the truck. The road ahead of them is clear. He jerks the wheel sharply to the left and pulls into the other lane. He continues to accelerate, draws level with the cabin.

The driver-side door is rusted out, sealed over. The window is misted with breath, smeared with fingerprints. The windshield, too, is completely obscured, though the truck continues to accelerate, pushing seventy as they approach the straightaway.

Samuel rolls down his window. He shouts across the seat, but the other driver pays no heed. With the window down, Samuel hears a thudding from the truck and sees the boy's face at the window. There are bruises about the mouth and neck but the features are familiar, somehow, the eyes, though in this moment, he cannot be sure if it is Nick's face, or Jason's, or his own—and then the road is sliding out from under him.

He hits the ditch. Flips, keeps rolling. Tumbles end-over-end through the hay-fields. The airbag explodes from the steering column and he hears a sound like waters churning, sees the stars come rushing toward him: the Milky Way, its open jaws.

౷

He survives. A young woman, driving behind him, witnesses the accident and phones for help. Later, in her statement, she says that Samuel was driving erratically: changing lanes, shouting out his window. She doesn't mention a second vehicle.

He is in the hospital. The days pass, and he is discharged, sent home to recover. Home: his parents' house, where he is treated like a sickly child. His mother hovers by the bedside, reading passages aloud from the Bible or *Reader's Digest.* His father kneels by the bed with his hand folded round Samuel's, offering up prayers for his recovery.

Some of his Sunday School students come to visit, three boys in tee shirts and swimsuits. They linger in the doorway, their limbs white and hairless. One boy is heavier than the others, the fat forming dimples where it overhangs his knees. They sing songs from church, their faces like masks showing nothing, and afterward, the fat boy says they are going swimming.

"Off to the beach, then?" Samuel's father asks.

"No," the boy says. "We'll probably just go up to the dam."

The final song is sung—*let the lower lights be burning, send a gleam across the wave*—and his father ushers them from the room. Samuel listens for their voices as they retreat downstairs, the door closing behind them.

The boys are gone.

He heaves himself onto his side, turns his face to the wall.

A Shadow Passing

*M*arch 15th, 1937. *These things he remembers.*

The light is green, then gold. The elms are waving, and he is a child again, feverish and chilled. He smells smoke, leaf-mold in the gutters. His mother's eau de cologne.

She lingers in the doorway, dressed in widow's black with kid gloves buttoned to her sleeves and her hair in a bun with no strand out of place.

I'm going out, she says.

She speaks these words to no one. The others are upstairs (his grandfather, his aunt), and she does not see him where he crouches behind the settee, listening as the doors fall shut: the inner, the outer.

He leaps to his feet, running, and watches from the window as she rounds the far corner. Her shadow dwindles down the pavement, vanishing with the light through the elm trees.

He waits.

Later, his aunt finds him curled up in the window-seat, shivering as his fever climbs. Minutes or hours have passed, and his mother has not returned.

Poor child, she says. *You needn't worry about her.*

And he does not reply because he knows better. Because his mother has come to him at night when the fires have gone out and told him of the shapes that dwell between the buildings, the winged shadows she calls *them.*

His aunt helps him up. She places her hand across his forehead, sighs, and leads him to the kitchen that is her sanctum. It is warmer here, the flames kindled high and licking round the copper kettle. She sits him down at the table and sees to his supper in silence, as is her way, unspeaking unless spoken to and he has nothing to say.

The kitchen is quiet but for the rasp of her breathing. His aunt makes herself coffee and rolls out the dough for her teacakes, which she keeps in a tin with the President's face on it and the words *Remember the Maine* inscribed below. This tin is forbidden him, as are so many things, and his aunt keeps it on a shelf where he cannot reach.

Six o'clock. His aunt claps her hands to rid them of flour and lights the kerosene lamp. The wick she turns down to a glowering—orange like the windows that look west to the street. She will not use the gas. She is thrifty, as is her sister, who lives near Boston with her husband and saves her hair in jars to use as stuffing for her cushions.

His grandfather does not join them. There will be no stories tonight, no tales of djinns and princesses such as his grandfather is fond of telling. They eat alone in the paneled dining room with the vast expanse of table between them and the lamp placed near its center, the flame burning low as the hour stretches, and the windows are black past the lamplight when he hears the doors slam shut: the outer door, the inner.

His mother enters. Her hands are bare, the gloves discarded so her knuckles show, the long fingers. Her eyes are blank, hair windblown and wild.

His aunt, rising, takes his mother by the arm before she can speak and walks with her down the hallway to the stair. It is some time before his aunt returns, and the boy is alone with the darkness gathering into shapes like wings all round him, beating out of the shadows.

Afterward, when supper is finished, he sneaks a candle from the tallboy and brings it to his bedroom upstairs. His aunt would disapprove, as would his mother, but he strikes a match and lights the candle and quickly falls asleep.

He is shaken awake. His mother looms over him, white and ghostly in the half-dark.

She says: *I saw them again. They came out of the canal, rising in a smoke where the sun makes patterns from the floating leaves. I ran. I fled over the bridge, up the hill. I was making for the church—I thought I'd be safe there—but the alleys swarmed with them, hundreds of them, with bodies made of corners so you see them only where they block the light. I lost my hatpin, my gloves, but still I did not stop, not until I reached the church on the hill. I fell down, gasping, but they would come no nearer. They unfolded their bodies, forming rings around me. The church was at my back, its black spire, and I thought—*

Her lips are wet, her breathing strained and rapid.

She says: *It's raining.*

The elms are dripping, a gentle music. An arabber drags his cart down the street, whistling down the damp.

Then his mother notices the pilfered candle, and her face changes, her voice. Her mouth curls in on itself so that he scarcely recognizes her, this creature with a voice like the frost and the spittle flying from her lips.

You wicked thief, she says. *You stole this from downstairs, didn't you?*

She slaps him once across the face. She calls him ugly and selfish and cursed with his father's temperament. She snuffs the light and carries it with her when she goes.

His aunt is waiting in the hall. The two sisters argue in whispers, as not to wake his grandfather, who is sleeping in the room next door.

The rain continues.

The boy lies awake with the blankets pulled to his face, the nerves vibrating in his gut. An omnibus, passing, drags the puddles behind it, and he recalls the first time she saw them.

Like winged shadows, she said. *But with hooks for teeth and long arms to reach.*

Beyond that, she would not describe them, or perhaps could not, for she said she spied them only from the edges of her vision, in the angles where two roof-lines met, or where a tall man's shadow divided on a slab of uneven paving.

In his dreams tonight, they surface out of the Moshassuck, with wings spread and mouths open, gums and lips flapping. They breach the water and hover in plumes above the river, coiled in darkness and merging with it before scattering themselves over the city with the rain that strikes the window, calling him from sleep.

It is Sunday morning, the curtains slightly parted. He fumbles at the bedside, fingers closing round the pocket-watch that belonged to his late father, whom he never knew.

Nine o'clock. Church bells sound throughout the city.

He dresses himself and descends the stairs, passing the parlor, where he is surprised to hear his aunt's voice. She is not at church, then, but is talking with her father, his grandfather, and with his other aunt, visiting from Boston, the door closed and fastened.

There is no one in the kitchen. The boy lingers over the hearth where the coals smolder in the grate. He looks west toward the street, the rows of gray buildings washed clean by rain, sending back the bells in echoes.

His mother has gone out—early this time. He imagines her foot-steps, heels striking pavement then soundless where they drop like rain amongst the muddied leaves.

And silent in the same way he tiptoes down the hall to the parlor, where his aunts are arguing now, their voices indistinguishable from one another.

It cannot continue. Not like this.

So young. And such a fragile thing—

Not as fragile as his mother.

But surely that is the point.

His grandfather's voice: queer and creaking, scarcely audible.

Too much, he says. *Sent away.*

With these words, the fear settles over the boy. Terror fixes the bones inside him, binding the muscles so he cannot move, though footsteps cross the parlor and the door swings open to reveal his married aunt, who keeps her hair in tins beneath the bed.

She scowls. *Listening at keyholes now?* she says.

He turns and runs and throws himself into the window-seat. He pulls the blanket over him and presses his face to the window. The old glass vibrates with every bell from outside, blurring the light with the drips from the eaves and the elms beyond like yellow flags waving—and still his mother does not return.

An hour passes. He watches the married aunt depart with her umbrella, making for her hotel. She proceeds quickly, cheeks flushed and head down and so she does not see him.

His aunt enters the hall and lingers over the window-seat, wreathed in the smells of coffee and pipe-smoke. He lowers the blanket. She extends her hand to him with the palm open, a tea-cake nestled in the thatch of wrinkle and bone.

Take it, she says, and he does, and chokes it down quickly for fear that she might take it away or that his mother might see him with the sugar smeared about his lips.

His aunt nods, satisfied, and continues to the kitchen.

The boy retreats to his bedroom. He wraps the blanket round him like a shawl as to ward off the chill, returning now with his fever as the afternoon passes. He loses himself in the books he has borrowed from his grandfather's study, rereading the stories of heroes and dryads and gods from the sea. He is working on a tale of his own, a story of a ship. He opens his notebook—a gift from his grandfather—but finds he cannot focus on the page for thoughts of his mother and of the things that follow her.

Hours later, with night approaching, he hears the doors open and shut and listens for her step outside his bedroom. It does not come. He closes the notebook and steals across the hall to the carved railing that overlooks the staircase. His mother sits on the landing, marooned in a mess of skirt and crinoline and with her head held in her hands.

She lifts her gaze. Her eyes are dry and empty and she sees through him where he stands with his fingers round the railing and the terror bursting over him once more.

Too much, his grandfather said. *Sent away.*

His mother says: *They waited so long. I walked for hours and miles and still they didn't show themselves. It was dusk before they came for me.*

I watched them approach. I waited with hands held out, expectant. They gathered themselves into clouds, which whirled and spun beyond my grasp for all I begged them to touch me, to take me. They parted with a ripple of wings, and I saw the hill beyond them. The church was clearly visible, and I knew at once what was required of me.

His mother hears footsteps, is quiet. His aunt emerges from the kitchen with a ladle in hand and her lips pressed together, a thin line.

His aunt says: *You were gone all day.*

His mother shrugs.

You might at least have told us where you were going.

Nowhere, his mother says.

Our sister has come from Boston. She wanted to see you.

His mother laughs. *Is that so? She's staying at a hotel, isn't she?*

We talked to Father. You've left us no other choice.

Father, she says, dully.

About your—sickness.

I am perfectly well.

Please, you must think of the child—

He is my child, she says. *Not yours.*

Anyway, Father is in agreement. The doctor is coming tomorrow.

Doctor. The word drops like a thunderclap between them and his mother is on her feet, yelling and flailing out. The boy bolts down the hall to his room and slams the door on the noise from downstairs. The leaves of his story rise up in a storm from the desk and then float down softly, landing face-down on the floor.

He burrows deep into the bedclothes and closes his eyes as the shadows loom over him, slanted with the streetlamps through the curtains. He sees winged creatures with legs like thin cables and arms arrayed in writhing masses. A church spire long and sharp where it wounds the sky, the clouds pouring down blood. His mother surfacing out of the river. She grins, horribly, showing steel hooks for teeth. He does not go down for supper.

Midnight comes, and his mother enters the bedroom, souring the air with her perfume. He pretends to sleep. She places the candle on the nightstand and sits down beside the bed. She says nothing, makes no attempt to wake him, and he does not stir, though an hour passes or more until at last she rises and goes out, her perfume fading.

Hours later, he wakes with the same fever, familiar now. His legs ache, and his head is like crown glass. There will be no school today.

His mother is downstairs in the parlor. She is sleeping on the daybed while the glow makes patterns on her face: light through leaves and the leaf-shadows overlying it. Her brow is relaxed, hands falling open, her fingers half-curled like the smile on her lips.

He finds his aunt in the kitchen, leant up against the countertop with a teacup clasped in both hands and her gaze fixed on nowhere, the curtains drawn across the windows. She nods at him as he enters and wordlessly boils him an egg. As usual she takes no breakfast herself but merely watches him eat while sipping her coffee to the dregs, and her voice is hoarse and brittle when, finally, she speaks.

She says: *Your Grandfather is asking after you.*

She breathes out sharply, fumbles in her apron for her pipe.

She says: *There is something you should know about. My sister reckons you're too young, but Father and I—well, we think maybe you're old enough.*

She lights her pipe, waves him away.

Go on, she says. *He's in his study waiting.*

The door to the study is ajar, though the boy pauses at the threshold. His grandfather is slumped at the desk with his back to the door and his head bowed forward. The breath whistles from him, doubling the sound of the wind in the casement.

Come and sit down, his grandfather says.

The boy shuffles inside with head bowed and eyes averted, saying nothing as the old man's gaze strikes across him: his ugliness, his shame. He sits on the rug beside his grandfather's chair and crosses his legs.

His grandfather looks out toward the street, and his gaze lingers there a spell, as though watching for a long-awaited guest. He opens his mouth then hesitates, closing his eyes—and with eyes closed, he tells a story. This time he does not take down a book from the shelf behind him but speaks instead from memory or imagination with the words and phrases trailing one another, a halting procession.

Once in Baghdad, he says, *there lived a princess, who was the Caliph's daughter. Her hair was darkly luminous, as is the new moon, while her smile was coy and lovely as the crescent. She had many suitors, princes of Syria and Jordan, but the Caliph loved her more than life itself and could not bear to be parted from her. He turned them all away, princes and poets alike, and the princess withdrew into her loneliness.*

Around this time a young man arrived in the city. This boy was the son of a magician and carried with him a sealed bottle, which his father had left him, though he had warned the boy against opening it. For within this bottle there dwelt a djinn, who was cunning and cruel, as are all such spirits. One night, at dusk, this young man chanced to spy the princess on her balcony and a kind of madness overcame him. He unstoppered the bottle.

The djinn issued in a vapor from the bottle's narrow neck and unfolded himself to stand in a cloud high over the boy. The spirit was tall as the tallest man and black as an eclipsing sun and curved the night about himself in the same way. The djinn proposed to him a bargain. If the boy would but break the bottle, giving the djinn his freedom, the djinn would grant the child his heart's innermost desire.

Now this young man could have had anything, but he was afflicted with love and thought of nothing save the princess. He wished for one night alone with her beauty, which was to him, the boy said, as pale and bright as the stars in winter. Saying this, he smashed the bottle.

The djinn kept his bargain. He gathered the boy and the princess into his arms and whisked them away to a mountain far from the city, to a place where no living thing grew and the snows lay deep and white as the Milky Way overhead.

The djinn departed. He laughed as he rode the night winds, leaving the two lovers alone in that place of winter, just as the boy had desired, with the cold stars shining over them. There was nothing to eat, no wood with which to make a fire, and the young man, despairing, leapt to his death.

But the princess was the Caliph's daughter: she was born with iron in her heart. The tears froze inside her eyes but she trusted in her father and waited through the night for the rescue she knew must come.

His grandfather halts. The old man's voice trails off to a strangled pitch, his breathing slow and labored. His eyes stray to the window overlooking the street, where a coach has pulled up beside the house. A man alights from inside, wearing a black cloak and top-hat.

His grandfather says: *And in the end he, too, betrayed her.*

These last words circle the boy, unheard for the heat of his illness and the blood that pulses in his ears. The old man lowers his head to the desk once more. His story is over, will never be finished, and the leaves outside are shearing from the elm trees, burying roads and walkways. The doorbell sounds.

His aunt responds from the kitchen. *Coming,* she says.

The boy, standing, backs up toward the hallway, terrified by the thought of the cloaked visitor and the fate which has come for him.

His mother appears. She sweeps toward him down the corridor, dressed in black with her hair pinned up beneath a wide hat. Her face betrays excitement, relief.

This way, she says, and takes his hand in hers. She drags him down the corridor to the back door and outside onto the lawn.

She says: *They are waiting for us. We mustn't be late.*

And so they run. He flies with her down an adjoining alleyway, his hand folded in hers and her skirts billowing out behind. The folds engulf him, wrapping round his face and eyes so he follows blindly, their steps carrying them downhill and at such a pace that the speed of it threatens to lift him from the ground and send him sailing up behind her, a tethered balloon.

They reach the canal, the bridge, and the sea-wind blows her skirts free of him as they cross over. A teamster curses and draws up his horses, their hooves flashing over him as his mother pulls him hard to the right and the road turns to climb toward the top of the hill.

The church is ahead of them, the black spire of which she has often spoke. The street is empty with the trees in rows to either side, branches stripped by the winds and their leaves upon the ground: crimson and yellow and brown about the edges with the mud from the weekend's rain. The paving is slick, yielding. The boy's feet slip, give way, and his hand slides from her grasp. He strikes the paving with his knees then his hands and heaves onto his side as the light shifts and changes, sun compassing sky so the shadows swing toward him from the trees and alleys and from the doors of the church, left open to receive her.

The bare trees rattle. The shadows writhe and stretch and bend upon themselves, turning to fragments when his mother reaches the church and hurtles through the doorway, visible to him in that instant as she spreads wide her arms and the wind encircles her with its roaring. Her mourning dress shreds, spins loose from her body. Her corset next so the pale limbs show, her nakedness, though this, too, dissolves with the whirling shards of fabric and flesh that twist and circle, ringing the center which is her illness: a churning chaos.

The wind recedes, releasing itself.

The doors fall shut and his mother is gone. The pieces of her move away down the street like flapping leaves: shadows of the coming winter, a mountain he cannot reach.

A hansom pulls up. His grandfather is seated within, slumped against the far door with a handkerchief to his mouth. Beside him rides the man in the cloak and top-hat with a doctor's bag placed between his feet.

It's alright, the doctor says and offers his hand.

The carriage brings them back to the house, where all is quiet and cold. His mother is nowhere to be found and his aunt paces in the kitchen, pipe-smoke drifting from beneath the closed door. By now his fever is worse, and his grandfather carries him upstairs to his bedroom, gasping with the strain.

Evening. There are shadows on the wall, wings and hooks retreating with the elms that toss and sway. His grandfather departs but returns with a kerosene lamp. He lights the wick, sets it burning by the bedside. Then waits with the boy for the fever to break and for the sickness to go out of him, a shadow passing.

Dream Children

The cats are at the door. The black, first, with a white blaze at her breast. Then the gray tom, wiry fur, tail like a curling feather. He stands on hind-paws, bats at the glass. Beside him the kitten with stripes and one eye, blue, the other sealed by scar tissue.

I slide back the door, scatter kibble on the rug. They eat. When they are finished, the tom lifts his tail to spray the wall then slips outside, the black cat following. The floodlight sends their shadows ahead of them into the dark.

Nearly dawn. The sky is souring, purple and red.

The kitten lingers. I kneel before him, but he backs away, making for the sliding door, watching me all the while. His blue eye shines out of the dark.

❧

7 am, Thursday. I turn on my phone.

One new voicemail, a man. His name's Mark Karimi, he says. He's worried about his wife, believes she might be missing. Can I call him back?

I look him up. Karimi is an architect, junior partner in a downtown firm. I find his photograph on the firm's website. His jaw-line prominent, hair close and black. He's smiling.

The phone rings and rings.

"Hello?" his voice slurred with sleep.

I'm returning his call, I say. "Your wife is missing?"

"Yes. Well—I'm not sure. She's gone, anyway."

"Have you contacted the police?"

"They think she's left me. That she's gone off with someone else."

"But you don't think so."

A burst of static. His breath on the receiver.

He says: "Can we meet?"

He provides his address, a street across town in the North End.

"I'll be there in an hour," I say.

☙

The house is new and modern: big windows, copper siding. A two-car garage in the same style with concrete flooring inside. Twin SUVs, both black, washed and gleaming.

Mark shows me in. We pass through a living room with a flatscreen on one wall and a piano against the other. The table in the dining room is zinc, blurred with a watery patina. French doors open to a covered patio, a lawn adrift in unraked leaves.

Mark sits opposite me with hands round a coffee mug, face wreathed in steam.

Music is playing. Slow beats, heavy bass, a woman's voice.

"Do you mind?" he asks, meaning the music.

"No."

"Just—it helps to keep me calm."

"You don't need to explain yourself."

"Only it feels wrong somehow. Fiona always hated stuff like this."

"Maybe you should tell me what's happened."

He explains. He was out of town on Monday, performing a site survey. He spent that night at a hotel in Springfield and spoke with his wife on the phone as usual. Tuesday morning he tried calling her again from the car, driving back, but received no answer.

"Was that unusual?"

"Not really," he says. "She wouldn't pick up when she was practicing."

"Practicing?"

"The piano," he says. "She's always played."

He went straight to work, wasn't home til dinnertime. There was no one in the house. Her car was in the garage but he wasn't worried. Mornings, Fiona practiced yoga or played the piano. In the afternoon, she walked the nearby bike path, north past Leddy Beach with her earbuds in, stopping sometimes to look at the lake. He assumed this was where she'd gone. Then he noticed her phone on the table. A note with it, handwritten on her favorite stationery.

I have to go to him, it read. *I can't wait any longer.*

He drains his coffee mug, knits his fingers. Lets them rest folded on the table before him. "I contacted the police, showed them the note. I told them about the car, how she'd left it, but it was obvious what they thought."

"That her lover picked her up."

"It isn't like that, though. *She* isn't like that."

"What is she like?"

He produces his phone. Swipes to unlock the screen and shows me his background. A photo of them together, their arms wrapped round each other. Behind them the lake at nightfall, a row of trees with leaves of the same sunset color.

Fiona is tall, her husband's height, with eyes spaced close but of a pleasing color, more green than blue. Her hair is long and straight and very fair.

"This was on Friday," he says. "That warm night we had. She was excited. Something was different somehow. We've been trying for a baby, you see, and it's been more than a year since we started. Last Monday she had an appointment with an OB/GYN."

"And?"

"All good news, Fi said. This weekend she seemed happy."

More questions. They are thirty-three and thirty-four, married three years. They met when Fiona was working downtown as a restaurant hostess, when she was still Fiona Peale. Her mother is dead, her father estranged. She grew up in Maine but moved to Burlington for school. She studied music at UVM, piano performance, but dropped out in her third year.

"Health issues," Mark says. "That was the reason she gave. She used to drink."

"Used to?"

"She gave it up. Around the time I met her."

"You said she saw a doctor last week."

"She wanted a child so badly—we both did—but it wasn't happening. That was hard. So she went to the doctor just to make sure everything was okay. And it was. Like I said, she's been happier lately. I thought things were getting better."

Wind in the yard. Leaves in whorls and rising.

I stand up. He stands too.

I say, "You mentioned she left her phone behind."

He nods.

"Can I borrow it? It might help."

He goes upstairs. Footsteps on the ceiling. Rain on the French doors.

I go back to the living room. Sit at the piano, touch my fingers to the keyboard.

Sheet music on the stand: Elgar, *Dream Children*, the first movement. Andante in G Minor. The book appears new or at least little used, its spine uncreased.

"Do you play?" Mark asks. He holds out her phone.

I shake my head, swipe the screen. Nothing.

"It's dead," he says. "The battery went last night."

"You've tried contacting her friends?

"Yes, but she doesn't have many. I called Kate. Kate Spear. They've known each other since college."

"And she hasn't heard anything?"

"No," he says. "No one has."

❦

I say goodbye, walk to the car. Close the doors, connect her phone to the stereo. Let it charge as I drive home down Riverside Ave and park at my apartment.

The screen illuminates. No new voicemails, no new texts.

I open her calendar, recent appointments. A doctor's visit last Monday. Yoga on Tuesday morning. Coffee with Kate after yoga.

Thursday afternoon: a piano recital at the University. Dinner with Mark on Friday.

Then nothing. I scroll back further. Dentist's appointments, Pilates, weekly meetings with Kate. A red X to mark her periods.

Recent calls. Most are from her husband but there are a few missed calls from Kate since last Tuesday, an outgoing call on Wednesday to a Burlington number. Duration: 3 min 16 sec.

Rain on the windshield, running down the hood. The wipers thump, thump.

I call Kate Spear. No answer. I hang up, unplug the phone, bring it inside. I'm just through the doorway when it vibrates in my hand.

Kate. A photo of a woman in her thirties: dark hair, silver earrings, sunglasses.

"I already told Mark," she says. "I don't know where she is."

"I realize that."

"She's probably gone off somewhere, God knows."

"Mark doesn't think so."

"Listen," she says. "I'm at work. Come meet me. City Hall Park. Twenty minutes."

~

We sit together. Kate's dressed all in black, skirt, blazer, and tights. Red leather shoes with heels and a floral-print umbrella wide enough to cover us both. Rain pours from it. Bare trees blur together, brick faces of the buildings opposite.

"We met at UVM," Kate says. "Freshman year we were on the same floor and in our second year we roomed together on campus. The year after that we moved in together. We had an apartment downtown with two other girls."

"It must have been around this time Fiona dropped out?"

"Her third year, yeah. Midway through the fall semester. Her grades had been slipping for a while. She drank too much. We all did."

"But you stayed close."

"After graduation I moved away for law school but we kept in touch. Just chatting online, talking on the phone, that kind of thing. She told me how she met Mark, how she stopped drinking. Then last year I got a job in Burlington and moved back."

"You reconnected."

"We used to get coffee, talk about our lives. She was different, of course. The years had changed her as much as they changed me, but lately she seemed moody, depressed. I knew something was wrong but I didn't want to press her."

"Is this what you talked about on Tuesday?"

"They were trying for a baby. Nothing else mattered to her. It'd been months and months and no luck. I told her she should go to the doctor, make sure everything was as it should be."

"And?"

She hesitates. Then says: "I assumed the worst, the way she spoke to me."

"I'm not sure I understand."

"It doesn't matter," she says. "Let's just say she turned on me. We argued. She said—awful—things. I got up, stormed away. Told her to sort herself out. I tried calling later to apologize but she wouldn't pick up. She's like that sometimes."

Sunlight through rain. Colors like oil in the puddle at our feet.

"And you believe that's where she's gone? To sort herself out?"

"Maybe," she says. "I don't know."

She says goodbye. Stands and shakes out the umbrella. Side-steps the puddle, her red shoes shining.

Fiona's phone is in my hand, her music in my headphones. Webern. Scriabin. Schoenberg. I draw up a timeline of the last ten days.

Mon, 11/30. Her doctor's appointment.
Tues, 12/1. Her meeting with Kate. Their argument.
Wed, 12/2. 10:34 am. She dials a Burlington number.
Thurs, 12/3. Piano recital at UVM.
Fri, 12/4. Dinner with her husband. Her apparent happiness,

the setting sun behind them.

Tues, 12/8. *I have to go to him.*

Recent calls. I flip back to Wednesday, 10:34 am. Turn off her music, press redial.

A woman answers. "Abernathy Clinic."

"I'm calling to confirm my appointment," I say.

"Under what name?"

"Karimi."

"I'm sorry," she says. "You have the wrong number."

She hangs up. The line is dead.

I try again but there's no response.

I drive to the North End. Leave the car at Leddy Park and walk down the bike path with her phone in my hand, her music playing softly. Alban Berg, Violin Concerto. The music is strange, atonal. Strings squeal and scrape, mix with my footsteps in the leaves, a dry scratching.

Dusk is at hand, the cold night nearing. I follow the path where it bends along the lakeshore, walking north, Fiona's route. Past an apartment complex, a condo development. A row of brick townhouses with windows facing west.

In one window, the third, an old man in a white coat sips liquid from a Dixie cup. His glasses are mirrored, the lake before him streaked red and blue.

The music stops. Water-sounds. Tree-sounds. Leaves slipping loose with the wind that shakes them. I turn round in the dark, walk back toward Leddy.

Home again, and the black cat is waiting. She sits in the glare of the floodlight with the kitten beside her, its one blue eye. In her mouth: a savaged bird.

Morning, and the cats come and go.

I sit at the computer. Look up Elgar's *Dream Children*. Fiona left the sheet music on the stand. Played it, maybe, before leaving the house. Most recordings are orchestral, but I find an arrangement for solo piano, press play. The melody is slow and wistful, haunting. It hangs in the air, circles the room. Nothing at all like Berg or Webern.

I open the University's website. Search by date til I find last Thursday's recital. "Solo piano with University Distinguished Lecturer Eugene Salterton." Link to the program. Debussy. Chopin. The recital concludes with "Selections from Elgar, arranged for solo piano."

Eugene Salterton. I find his bio. He's from Newburyport, Massachusetts, has taught piano performance at UVM since 1998. There's a photo of a gray-haired man in his sixties. Jaw pointed. Nose long and thin. His smile appears forced, teeth white and prominent.

His office is in the music building. Southwick Hall: named for a woman who never married, who died young. I park nearby and let myself in by a side-door. Salterton's office is locked, but a work-study student points me toward the performance hall.

Rows of chairs, all empty, and the man from the photo on-stage. He sits before the grand piano, dressed in a tweed blazer and paisley bowtie. His posture is perfect, his playing forceful. Struck chords echo from the paneled walls, down the deserted aisles.

I sit in the first row, nearest the stage. The piece concludes and the old man stands and slaps his hands together. Sweat flies from them. He steps to the edge of the stage, looks down at me. "May I be of some assistance to you, dear child?"

His speech is clipped, slightly accented. Boston Brahmin.

I say, "I hoped to speak to you about Fiona Karimi."

"Karimi? The name, alas, is unfamiliar."

"You would have known her as Fiona Peale."

He smiles. "Ah, yes. Dear Fiona. Very gifted. Fond of the Second Viennese School, as I recall. Curiously fond, I always thought."

"She was your pupil?"

"At one time, yes. Though she was ultimately unable to complete her studies."

"She dropped out."

"An awful waste. There were—issues."

"She drank," I say. "Is that what you mean?"

"As you say," he replies, waving the words away. "But all this was many years ago. And I am likely an old fool, but I cannot pretend to understand your interest in poor Fiona. Are you acting on Miss Peale's behalf?"

"Her husband's, actually."

"Ah. That would be Mr. Karimi."

"Fiona's left him. Monday night she walked out. Or maybe Tuesday morning."

His smile unslipping. "Dear child, I fail to comprehend how any of this is my concern."

"She came to see you."

"Me? I really fear you are mistaken."

"Last week. She was at your recital."

"Was she? If you are right I consider myself deeply flattered by the implicit compliment. All the more because she never much cared for my style of playing."

"And why is that?"

"Why—because I am a Romantic."

"And she wasn't."

"Plainly not," he says. "She preferred Schoenberg and his ilk. Or do you truly know so little about her?"

The stage-lights beat at the bald spot in his scalp. He wipes his sleeve cross his forehead.

I ask, "You didn't see her in the audience?"

"I possessed no inkling of her presence whatsoever. Scout's Honor."

"And she didn't approach you afterward?"

"Good heavens, child, why would she do that? Poor Fiona. She was not exactly a happy girl when I knew her. I should hardly think she'd wish to revisit that particular chapter of her past, do you? Good day."

❧

It's colder now. Sky like glass, no clouds, sun cutting shadows down the sidewalk. I unlock my car, slide into the seat. Start the engine and drive past Southwick.

An old man crosses in front of me. He hurries along with coat zipped, collar up, but the light flashes from his glasses and I can see the sleeves of a white coat at his cuffs.

The man I saw from the bike path. White-coated and drinking out of a Dixie cup. Seated in the window of a brick townhouse, the third window.

He rounds the corner, goes into Southwick. I pull over by a dorm-building, where there's students outside smoking, dressed in tall boots and little jackets.

I take out my phone. Open up Maps, zoom to the North End. Find the bike path and follow it north past Leddy. I turn on Satellite imagery, swipe past roofs of condos and duplexes til I find a brick townhouse. Switch back to maps, street-names.

Lakeshore Terrace.

❧

I park out of sight, approach on foot. Three doors up: I try the handle. Locked. A camera over the door, its red-light blinking. I ring the doorbell, wait, rap on the glass with my knuckles. I unlock Fiona's phone and call the Abernathy Clinic. I hear a phone ringing inside but no one answers.

Back to the car. I'm nearly there when I hear a door close behind me. Look back to see a young woman step out of Number 3. She is twenty or so, smallish and blonde. Wrapped in a wool sweater with a yellow scarf at her throat.

She sees me, crosses the street. I go after her.

"Can I talk to you?"

She ignores me.

"They wouldn't let me in," I say.

She lowers head, keeps walking.

"Please," I say. "It could be important."

She wheels round to face me. Her hair is unwashed and she sounds angry, tired. Smells of cigarettes and stale beer. "What do you want?"

"I'm acting on behalf of a friend."

"So?"

"You just came from the Abernathy Clinic, didn't you?"

Her expression unreadable. "They turned me away again. Said I wasn't ready."

"Again? Were you here last Wednesday?"

"I was. Friday too. Both times they sent me away."

I show her Fiona's phone. The photo: Fiona, Mark, the sunset behind them.

"Do you recognize her?"

"She was here, yeah. Wednesday. She wanted to talk to me but the nurse made her leave. She knew about Salterton. She was the same as me, she said. I didn't ask what she meant."

"Eugene Salterton? The music teacher?"

She doesn't look at me, won't.

"My professor," she says. "He's very—persuasive. I was stupid."

"He made your appointment for you?"

"He did, but Abernathy turned me away. Today they wouldn't even let me see him. The nurse sent me home. Come back in a week, she said."

We're at the car. "Can I give you a ride anywhere?"

"I'd rather walk, thanks. As long as the sun's out."

"Won't be too many more days like this."

"No," she says. "There won't."

❧

I dial up Kate. Voicemail.

"Call me," I say. "Please."

Redstone Campus. Southwick Hall. The shadows lengthen: black lines, black paving. I park near Southwick with lights off, the engine idle.

Full-on night when Salterton appears. He's bundled against the cold with a briefcase under his arm. He passes the parking lot, descends the hill on foot.

I kill the engine. Run to catch up then follow at a distance. His pace is brisk, long legs swinging shadows under the streetlights. He turns right off Prospect then right again into the driveway of a white Victorian with a fenced-in yard. He lifts the gate and steps to the door. Unlocks it, goes in. A light switches on, lamplight, yellow on the curtains.

I linger by the fence, shelter in its shadow. Inside a piano is playing. The gate is open. Its hinges creak. I slip through it, then sideways along the fence, circling round to the back of the house. A basement window. I kneel, press my face to the glass.

The room beyond is dusty and dim. I can just make out a sofa, a record player with LPs stacked alongside it. Sheet music, rolls of it fanned on the floor. A hand-vacuum. A length of rubber hose. A large fish-tank, empty.

My phone vibrates. Kate.

I scuttle from the house, make my escape while the piano plays.

I pick up. "I wanted to ask you something," I say.

"Ask it, then."

"It's about the Abernathy Clinic."

Silence. I lower the phone, glance at the screen. The call is active. Finally, she says, "Can you meet me?"

"Where?"

"God, I don't know. Anywhere with a bar."

I meet her in a Bank Street brewpub, sit down across from her. Our booth is lit by votive lights, her hair black and immaculate, pale face reflected in the scotch glass she holds. She drains it, orders another. Sips from the second glass and tells me about the clinic.

"Fi asked me to drive her. To wait for her there."

"This was in your third year?"

"2003. Around the time she dropped out. Just before, actually."

"Salterton made her appointment?"

"He said it was his 'responsibility.' Said he knew someone who would take care of it."

"Doctor Abernathy."

"I guess. I never met him. An old guy, she said."

"But you drove her to the North End?"

"The North End?" she asks, surprised.

"To the clinic."

The glass is at her lips. She shakes her head.

"I went with her, yes, but the clinic was downtown. Not far from here, actually, in one of those office blocks off Church Street. I'm not sure I could find it again."

Her glass strikes the table. Empty.

She says: "I remember the smell, though."

"You went inside."

"Only as far as the waiting room. The floors were white-tile, walls painted the same shade of white. There was no wallpaper, nothing hanging up. Everything was spotless, sterile, swept clean."

"And the smell?"

"Fresh paint. Air freshener, antiseptic. But there was another smell too. Something earthy, bitter, burnt. I can't describe it."

She looks down at the table. Her face disappears into her hair, its shadows, the flash of a fire-truck's lights on the window behind her.

"Fi rang the bell," she says, "and a nurse came out. A big woman in purple scrubs. She seemed to be expecting us. She didn't speak but motioned for Fi to follow her. I offered to go along with her, but Fi said it was okay. *She'd* be okay, she said, and so I let her go."

"What did you do?"

"I waited. As long as I could stand it, anyway. The smell was making me sick so I left a note on the desk and went out. I wanted to clear my head, but it was raining, and the rain had that same dirty smell about it. After a while I went back inside."

"How long did you have to wait?"

"Two hours. Maybe three. It took longer than I expected and Fi was alone when she came out. She was walking slowly. Shuffling, really. She was incoherent, mumbling to herself. The anesthetic, I guess. I took her by the arm and walked with her to the car."

She pauses. Fidgets with her napkin, tears it into strips.

"When we got home, I turned on some music, that weird old stuff she likes. Her jeans were wet so I helped her into the bath-room. I took off her sneakers, her pants, and she was laughing because of the drugs they'd given her. God knows she needed them."

"How do you mean?"

"She was bandaged up to her belly button. It was just supposed to be a minor procedure, no big deal, but this looked like real surgery. She was giggling to herself all the time I cleaned her up. She lowered her voice, whispered in my ear. 'Complications,' she said, and laughed and fell back against the toilet-seat. She laughed until she was crying. She cried for an hour before she fell asleep on the toilet. I shook her awake. Helped her back to the couch and covered her with a blanket. She slept through the day, most of the night. When she woke up she acted like everything was okay. I thought it was. We didn't talk about it, though. Not for years."

"Until you told her to go to a doctor."

"That word. 'Complications.' I wondered."

"What happened last Tuesday?"

"I asked about her appointment. She got angry. Blamed me for everything. I should have helped her, she said, should have taken her away from that place. She was right, too."

She stands up, shaky. The napkin balled and shredded in her hand. Two glasses before her, emptied of all but candlelight, red moons on their rims.

"You said she went to the doctor, that everything was fine."

"That's what she told Mark."

"It wasn't, though, was it?"

☙

11 pm. No cats tonight, snow drifting down. Fine flakes like rain form clouds about the floodlights. The wind howls in the mouth of the Winooski.

I make tea, carry the mug into the living room. Sit before the sliding door. Watch for the cats as snowfall accumulates, blows, drifts. My breath on the glass like mist. It joins with steam from my mug to blot out my reflection.

Revisit the timeline.

2003. F goes to Abernathy Clinic.
Mon, 11/30. OB/GYN appointment. Lies to her husband afterward.
Tues, 12/1, morning. Meeting with Kate. Their argument.
Tues, 12/1, afternoon (?). Walks on the bike-path. Sees Abernathy?
Wed, 12/2. 10:34 am. F calls the clinic. Goes there, talks to student.
Thurs, 12/3. Salterton's recital.
Fri, 12/4. Warm night. Dinner with Mark.
Tues, 12/8. Gone. *I can't wait any longer.*

Midnight. All quiet except for passing plows, the slush they drag behind them. I take down the phone book, flip to *S*. Salterton's number is listed, his address in the Hill Section.

He picks up. "I assume this is not a social call?"

"You were sleeping with her."

"Was I?" He chuckles. "Call me an old Don Juan, but you really must be more specific when making such accusations."

"Fiona Peale. She was your student."

"Yes, and rather a brilliant pupil as well—as I believe I have said already. One does not necessarily follow from the other."

"You got her pregnant. Your friend Abernathy helped you to get rid of it. The procedure was supposed to be simple, but it didn't go to plan."

"Oh, dear. This is getting much too sordid."

"Last week Fiona had an appointment with an OB. She found out just how badly Abernathy had botched it. He's moved his clinic, but she happened to see him from the bike path. And she always knew where she could find you."

"Is this all by way of suggesting I was being—heaven help me!—blackmailed?"

"She could have exposed you. Abernathy too."

He doesn't reply, but I can hear the piano. Elgar, *Dream Children*. The first movement, Andante in G minor. I think of Salterton's recital, the program I found online. *Selections from Elgar.* "You played that at your recital," I say.

"Naturally! It has long been a favorite of mine."

"Fiona was practicing it before she disappeared."

He stops playing. "Really? Now that *is* interesting. She had little time for Elgar when I was her teacher. Disliked him intensely, in fact, but only because she did not understand him. She was too young, you understand. Not even 21! What could she know of regret? Of guilt? And Elgar—not only English, but a Catholic! Well, you see what I mean."

"The sheet music was new. She'd hardly played it."

"Mm. I don't follow, I'm afraid."

"She was at your recital. She heard you play it and then acquired a copy for herself."

"Yes, it's possible, certainly. It's a lovely piece, quite evocative, and she must be in her thirties now, yes? Old enough to find some meaning in it."

"What *does* it mean? *Dream Children?*"

"An allusion," he says, playing again but with one hand, picking out the theme. "Are you familiar with Charles Lamb? No, I rather thought not. He has an essay by that title. A reverie, he calls it, in which he imagines the children he never had. In the end he surfaces out of the dream to find himself in his 'bachelor armchair' with his poor, mad murderess of a sister beside him. Lamb was like me, you see. He never married. However, I like to believe he would have shared my appreciation for womanhood in its first and briefest manifestation."

"How many students were there? How many procedures did you and Abernathy arrange?"

"Oh, dear. I don't think I appreciate what you're implying."

"Convince me I'm wrong, then."

"Of what possible benefit would that be to either of us? Your opinion of me is not exactly charitable, yes? You are unlikely to change your mind. Why, then, should I make what would almost surely amount to a futile effort?"

"Because I intend to contact the police."

"The police? How exciting." He switches to scales, both hands now, the low notes like heavy footfalls. "And if I were to suggest an alternative course of action? If you were to come to my house tomorrow morning—you do know it, yes? Yes, I supposed as much—I believe we may be able to settle the matter to our mutual satisfaction."

"I'm not interested."

"Oh, I don't propose to pay you. Is that what you thought? Good Lord, no. For all of my failings, let it never be said that I am not a man of honor. But if you were to provide me with twenty minutes of your time, I feel certain I could show you where poor Fiona has gone."

"Make it tonight, then. If you're so certain."

"Look outside, child. The snow! It's positively deadly out there. And, in any case, I'm afraid it really must be tomorrow morning. Early. Shall we make it five o'clock?"

I wake to the alarm clock, turn on the lights.

Outside, the snow has drifted six inches high against the sliding door. The gray tom appears out of the snow, more white than gray, and the kitten beside him, red flecks in its whiskers. They sniff at the kibble without interest and curl up together by the heater. The gray tom cleans the kitten's face, licks the blood from its whiskers and chops. They sleep.

I go outside, start the car. Drive across town.

Salterton's house. I park and pass through the gate, trudging through new-fallen snow.

The door swings open. Salterton. He's dressed in a heavy coat, a furry bomber cap tugged down over his ears. "Ah, there you are.

Splendid. Might I trouble you to join me in the garage?"

He holds up his hands. Mittened. Empty.

"You needn't worry," he says. "You are quite safe with me."

I follow. Back through the fence-gate then next door to a converted carriage house.

He pulls up the garage door. Inside there's a pickup truck with a tarp thrown over the bed, secured with nylon cord. Salterton approaches the driver's side, climbs in. The engine starts. The heat vents rattle. His face appears in the wing-mirror.

"My dear child," he says. "We must be quick. Did I not say? Our time is short."

"What's in the truck-bed?"

"Let's call it a surprise. You shall find out soon enough, I assure you."

"I'd rather look now."

"By all means," he says. "If you absolutely insist."

"I do," I say and lift the tarp.

Sweet stench of rot. Black eyes in the dark. A deer carcass.

"You needn't pretend to be shocked," Salterton says. "It is hunting season, yes? My friend Julian rather fancies himself a sportsman. Dr. Abernathy, as you know him."

I lower the tarp, re-knot the cords.

Salterton says: "Haste, child! Haste."

I join him in the truck's cabin. He backs out.

Main Street to Battery then north along the lake. Past the old Catholic orphanage and left at the high school toward North Beach, a mile from Leddy, walking distance from the Karimis'.

The gates are closed, padlocked for the season. Salterton dismounts from the cab, removes the lock with a key from his parka. He returns to the truck, and we nose forward, pushing through the gates. Salterton drives down to the beach, pulls up shy of the water. The sand is winter-hard, iced with the last night's snowfall. He gets out, flashlight in hand. I step down. Lower my head to the wind as it rips at my face, my hands.

Salterton opens the hatch, unknots the tarp. He wrestles with the doe's corpse and drags it from the truck. It strikes the ground, heavy. Undressed, organs still intact. Salterton pants, hauls the carcass by its hind-legs to the water. I join him there, the waves at our boots.

"My apologies for the smell," he says, "but death is often a fragrant business. I do hope you are not too disquieted by Julian's handiwork."

"What are we doing here?"

"Waiting."

He stomps his feet, rubs his hands together.

"For what?" I ask.

"Why—for this."

First light. The lake catches its reflection, the color of it: blue-violet and gleaming with the ice that's forming there. Salterton checks his watch, hands me the flashlight. He grabs the deer by the throat and splashes into the shallows, towing the body behind him.

Out to the edge of the light. He's waist-deep when the water heaves up, roiling, seething with white shapes like small hands, grasping fingers, teeth. They tear at the doe's body, darkening the water to a black spume through which the pale bodies surface and plunge, feeding, white then red where the flashlight catches them.

The carcass is gone.

Salterton returns to shore, splashes onto the beach. His pants are bloody and sopping.

"Oh, dear," he says. "And now I fear I *have* disquieted you."

My voice is dry, choking. "What are they?"

He doesn't answer, changes the subject.

"You must believe me," he says, "when I tell you I have nothing but compassion in my heart for poor Fiona. A kind of love, even. She was so brilliant, so talented. And so very, very lovely. I admit it freely: I succumbed. She was the first of my young ladies, but Julian's techniques were as yet—imprecise. There were consequences."

"Complications."

"If you will. You were right that she came to see me last week. I am sorry to have been dishonest with you on this point, but one never knows to whom one is speaking, yes? Fiona told me she had been to the new clinic, that she had met another of my young ladies."

"She threatened you."

"Yes, but you mustn't think she was after anything so common as money. She was not that kind of person, the poor dear."

"What, then?"

"She wanted an apology. Which I was only too happy to give her. I have always regretted the way things ended between us. More than that, though, she expected a promise of future—well, 'good behavior,' shall we say? Fortunately for both of us I was able to offer her something in exchange which proved far more agreeable."

He looks at me. "Would you mind terribly turning off the light? Much obliged. Even old men have their vanity."

In the dark he strips off his parka, sweater, shirt. His pants, too, his underwear. Stands naked on the sand, a thin silhouette with the chill wind tearing at him.

He continues. "You see, I was able to offer Fiona the one thing she wanted most in the world. A son. Our son. The child she thought she'd lost."

"There was no child," I say. "Abernathy took care of that."

Salterton looks offended, even hurt. "He did no such thing, I assure you. The man is an outstanding surgeon, a neonatologist of international reputation, and you would persist in likening him to a mere *abortionist?* For shame, shame."

"What did you tell Fiona?"

"The truth, of course. How she might find him, our little one. How they might be together again. I can only imagine she came here."

"And then?"

Salterton doesn't reply. He removes his wristwatch, folds his clothes and coat together. Places his watch on top, his keys.

I press him. "What happened to her?"

Click on the flashlight. The light glances off his face, eyes like flints as he turns away.

He speaks in a voice that's barely audible. "Dear child," he says. Gently, almost sadly.

"I really wouldn't presume to say."

He walks down to the water. The clouds lighten but the lake stays dark, starred with ice-flecks when the flashlight sweeps across it. Salterton's outline, just visible. His wiry spine and shoulders, arms spread as the water surges round him.

Pale limbs, hands. Black eyes like his.

He rolls onto his back, swims beyond the flashlight's beam.

༶

The city shakes off sleep, snow, sets cars skidding.

I reach my apartment, let myself in. The tomcat pushes past me, followed by the kitten. They leave fine hairs on my trouser-legs, gray and white mingled.

Dream Children. I search YouTube, press play. Picture Fiona at the piano, her hands on the keys. Andante in G Minor: music to conjure loneliness, longing. Her yearning for a child in the days since she saw Salterton, the child she never had.

I can't wait any longer.

North Beach. December 8, early. Fiona sits in the sand, knees at her chest. Light in the sky when the children surface, treading water, and her son among them with eyes like black glass. She wades in, swims out, doesn't slow though the water boils and churns: a mouth with teeth and closing, closed.

The lake settles, mirroring light. The silence she leaves, left.

I grab for her phone.

Press down home but there's nothing there: screen dark, battery dead.

༶

I return the phone to Mark.

"I couldn't find her," I say. "I'm sorry."

The snow is gone by noon. Home again, I spy the black cat in the yard. Dead. She sprawls on her side with her belly torn open.

I bury her in the yard and go back inside. Evening, and the

floodlights turn on. I hear them like moths at the glass: the gray tom, the kitten. They're hungry.

"Come in," I say, and open the door.

To the memory of Joseph S. Pulver, Sr

Lincoln Hill

SPRING

A man came limping down the track between the ribs of Lincoln Hill. He passed beyond the lumber mill, a woman on his broken back—with child, yes, but thin with lack, where he was seventy and ill, but still he carried her until they vanished in the tamaracks.

The snow looked ashy in that light, then crimson in the place they died. We found them frozen hard and white but heard a wailing out of sight, as if a lamb were caught outside... its faint cry faded with the night.

SUMMER

The season passed and lilies grew to fill the empty clearing where we buried them with muttered prayers, and where Elise and Abbie flew to pull the bramble and the blooms they wore like gemstones in their hair.

Elise, eighteen, stripped herself bare to meet a boy nobody knew. Her sister came home terrified to find me kneeling at the stove and begged for me to come outside. Elise made no attempt to hide but waited, waking, in the grove—but with such dreams behind her eyes.

Fall

The wind was in the naked trees the night he knocked upon our door and shouted to the upper floor that he had come back for Elise.

He brought with him the winter's freeze. We huddled in our coats and furs and wept to hear the holy words they whispered as the chimney breathed.

My daughter wore the cotton plain her mother made to jump the broom, and even now, it bore the stains of blood and love and loving's pain, as when she cried out in her room, and silence answered, and the rain.

Winter

The days like decades dimmed the glow.

He guttered like a dying coal then winter stripped away the soul and left him changed, a balding crow. My daughter had to watch him go to pieces as the year turned cold. The roof-beams creaked and could not hold the weight of years, the drag of snow.

That night, the gusts came high and shrill into our house and howling round, and Abbie, dreaming, watched until her sister danced him past the mill and whirled the old man from the ground to join the wind on Lincoln Hill.

A Sleeping Life

Zero

The sack surrounds me, a room of no light. I float, weightless. Breathe without breath where my lungs are empty. The scalpel slices, saws. The room opens to spill me into the blankets and the air bursts to my lips as the cord is stretched and severed.

Her flesh on mine, the heat of it. Her milk in my mouth.

One

Her hair falls over me, black and thick like veils against the brightness of the house. Windows open, the curtains half-drawn. A smell of oil and smoke, drone of old words spoken over me in my fever. Her chest rises, falls, and so do I, til a voice breaks on our darkness and the breast is withdrawn, the veil parted. A hand traces shapes upon my forehead. Her breathing hums in the walls of her chest, a soothing sound but falling away as I am lifted, lowered. The cold—

Two

The light. A man's face haloed by it. He wears gold-rimmed spectacles, sports a gray-black moustache. I close my eyes. He taps at my knees, draws the needle-tip down my feet. He inclines his ear to my chest and listens.

"Good," he says, and his finger is in my eye. He hooks the lid with his nail and lifts to expose the white. His other hand holds a reflecting glass, which he angles to the window, directing the sun into my brain. The light pierces, searing. The nerves spark and fire and the doctor chuckles.

"You see?" he says. "You hear how the little lad screams? All will soon be well."

THREE

"And all manner of things be well."

These words they sing and with their faces to the pulpit while Mother holds me on her knee, dressed in her frock and white ribbon and my uncle beside her in his Sunday best.

The song is finished. The priest cries to the echoes that linger and speaks with thunder of Christ's humility. He says: "All Jerusalem came to greet Him. The people wished to make of Him a king but Christ rode upon an ass and washed the feet of his disciples. Is there any among us who would refuse the crown? No. For his humility was a thing of heaven rather than of earth and greater still was his obedience. We mustn't forget how he allowed himself to be led without protest to the hill of his crucifixion. He went willingly, lovingly, meekly as a lamb."

My uncle is a killer of horses. He prays, his head in his hands. Beside him Mother watches the sun swing behind the west windows, sweeping color through the glass.

FOUR

To turn the country into light.

The town is below us, the square with its shops and houses and the medieval wall encircling. The railway station with its tracks running to north and west through farm-fields gold with wheat at harvest and all glimpsed through the face of the city clock.

We are in the clock-tower, the great bells hanging over us: one to mark the hour, another to summon the fire brigade. The latter is rung with a rope and counterweight. The bell-pull forms coils all around us where Mother kneels beside me, breathless.

"You cannot know," she says, gasping. "How I have prayed for this."

She holds me, presses me to her chest. "Doctor Leibenhauer said it was hopeless. Even Father Johannes despaired, but I know you, Child. You are like me. The world is before you in its glory. Of course you would wish to see."

Her eyes are open: I see myself in them, but briefly. Then the clock advances and the counterweight descends—

FIVE

The blow shakes the darks of sleep, sets points of light behind my eyes like stars exploding. My uncle looms over me with bloodied hands and there's fluid in my mouth as at my birthing—and teeth. I swallow them, choking, and cough with the pain that rakes my throat.

"Well, well," my uncle says, snarling. "You're awake now, aren't you?"

He pulls me up by my shirt-collar, strikes me again with a closed fist. I tumble backward, bruising my head so the stars brighten and nova.

My uncle leans over me. He says my name. There is red spittle on his cheeks and brow and I can see that he is frightened.

He holds her portrait in his hands. It is edged in black, the glass smeared with finger-marks: mine, his. Her hair spreads blackly on the coffin-pillow, and her eyes are closed, hands folded together, a white ribbon cinched about her wrists.

SIX

It twitches in my hands: a length of rope and the old mare beside me limping. We cross the yard together, stepping over wheel-tracks frozen into ridges and hoof-prints dusted white with frost. The horse's head bobs, eyes downcast. Her shoes strike stone, resound.

My uncle stands with the mare's owner, a rich man in silks and fur with a top hat and jeweled watch-chain. He is a landowner and nobleman, an officer in the army. He speaks of war and horses but my uncle is only half-listening, the pipe in his mouth, gun broken over his elbow.

My uncle finishes the pipe as we approach. He inverts the bowl, strikes it with his hand's heel. The ashes blow to dust to catch the blowing wind, and the nobleman is quiet, thoughtful.

He asks: "This boy is your nephew?"

My uncle grunts. The pipe disappears into his pocket.

The other man dons an eyeglass. He studies me with interest. "You will know, of course, his condition is a subject of much speculation in town. My dear friend Doctor Leibenhauer has examined your nephew on many occasions. Could it be the boy is sleepwalking even now?"

My uncle does not answer. He touches his hand to the mare's head, strokes her ears and mane. "Poor old girl," he whispers. "One thing to be done for you."

SEVEN

"All she did for you. For me. She was a saint if such things can be and like a saint she suffered. Her heart was weak and she was always strange, always talking to herself or to God. She was twenty when she went to Ulm. We had a cousin there she stayed with, and she worked in a milliner's shop. That's how she met him. He was a writer of some kind. He took—liberties. She yielded herself, knowing no better, and was pregnant before I learned what had happened. I went to Ulm. I chased him off, her fiancé. I brought her back here, but it was no use. She wouldn't eat. She was so frail I thought she was sure to die in her laboring through all the long hours that passed before she spit you out sleeping in the sack. She didn't, though, and you wouldn't wake for all she tried, til that morning she sneaked you up the clock-tower. She should never have done it: her heart couldn't stand the strain and she was breathless and wheezing when I found her up there. 'He looked at me,' she said. 'He smiled.' It was all she longed for in this world and maybe there was more than that too but Lord forgive me I wasn't listening. I was too scared. I could see she was dying. She couldn't move for the pain in her chest and her breath wouldn't come right. I tried to carry her down the steps, but she wouldn't let you go, and you howled and kicked against her in your sleep while the bells went on and on—"

Eight

The rain sheets down, relentless. It pools beneath my uncle's body where he lies face-down, unmoving. It mingles with his blood, rippling with the wind.

The stallion circles the courtyard, screaming for his shattered leg. His eyes bulge. The reins trail behind him and his prints are dark and red.

A man is shouting at me. The horse's owner, a tenant farmer. He shelters behind the courtyard gate while the lamed horse stamps and shrieks.

"The gun!" he says, gesticulating wildly.

The shotgun is trapped beneath my uncle's body, but I do not move to pick it up. Already the horse is tiring. His strength wanes, his pace. He falls. The breath heaves and is gone.

The farmer unlatches the gate. He sprints toward me and kneels before my uncle. Takes hold of the coat, rolls over the body.

The eyes open, staring. Rain strikes them, sets them quivering in their sockets. Lightning silvers the courtyard, but the thunder is far-off yet, too distant to be heard.

Nine

In the silence we are made to stand, sixty boys at two long troths and Father Johannes at the lectern. He clears his throat. He reads to us from Proverbs though we are starved and sickening and the food-troths are before us, steaming. One boy collapses, weak with fever. He is pulled to his feet and the reading is finished, the Grace spoken.

"And now I must entreat you to remain standing," Johannes says. "Tonight Freiherr Von Steinfeld has deigned to join us at our table. He is among the most generous of your benefactors, my boys. Let us make him welcome."

The doors swing open to admit a man in jewels and fur: the nobleman who once brought a mare to my uncle. He smiles broadly, beneficently. He circles the room unspeaking, inspects our clothes and teeth. He pauses before the troth. He inclines his head over it, sniffing.

Charred potatoes. Stewed cabbage in shreds. He samples both, grinning wide to suck the grease from his gloves. The taste is in our mouths, the smell.

TEN

Sweetness of rot and mud: a grave opened by lantern-light, Old Heinz's teeth green and shining. My limbs are weak for hours spent shoveling and my hands are clamped about the dead boy's ankles. Heinz secures the armpits. Sackcloth conceals the corpse's face, but the feet protrude, colorless, and we descend into the pit.

Father Johannes is here. He stands over us, Doctor Leibenhauer beside him. Their shadows join together, stretching to cover the open grave with its dozens of sacks under our feet like a world laid to rest in its afterbirth. We squelch, sink.

Leibenhauer says: "He is a strange one, isn't he? His mother too. You're a better man than I am, Father, to have taken him."

"His condition has proved useful to us. That is all."

"And he will remember nothing of this?"

"He is asleep. He has no life but dreaming."

"Remarkable. And is the Freiherr aware of the boy's involvement?"

"My dear man," the priest says, "the idea was Steinfeld's own."

We lay the body down. Heinz grunts, and we climb to the lantern's light.

ELEVEN

Then falling, not falling. The pavement strikes my knees, hard. My head snaps back, and a blond-haired boy stands over me grinning.

Two others hold my arms while a third boy, younger than the others, opens my coat and fishes the parcel from inside. He hands it to the blond boy, who steps back toward the gate of a fine house. Summer's stillness. Moonlight streams through gaps in the iron pailing and only the shadows move.

The boy rips open the parcel, whistles.

"Our luck is in, boys," he says. "There must be fifty marks in here."

A man's voice: "Nearer five hundred, in fact."

He appears at the gate behind the blond boy. He wears a silk evening jacket and smells of women's perfume. Von Steinfeld.

"Freiherr!" the blond boy says, frightened.

"Hans Müller, is it? Yes, I thought I recognized you. What would your dear departed mother have to say of such behavior?"

The boy looks down, says nothing.

Von Steinfeld continues: "And to think she had such hopes for your prospects. She used to speak of you, little Hans, when I had her crushed up against a wall or bent down in front of me. But I see you have not inherited her obliging nature. Indeed, you have not even apologized."

Müller is shaking. "I'm sorry, sir."

"Ah, never mind. But I believe you have something that belongs to me?"

Müller relinquishes the parcel, takes off running. The other boys scatter and Von Steinfeld slips the money into his jacket.

He takes my hand, pulls me to my feet. He watches me closely, glass affixed.

Behind him the moonlight breaches the iron pailing. It clothes him with its chill, a blaze of silver, and my eyes fall shut.

TWELVE

He opens them. Jams in his thumbs, forces up the lids. Hans Müller. He is a school-boy now, a favorite of Father Johannes. He wears the orphanage school's uniform with rows of badges down the front and has taken to carrying a knife.

He produces the blade, holds it at my throat.

"You *are* awake," he says. "I knew it."

We are in the outhouse, the floor carpeted in yellowed newspapers, stained brown with filth and the light itself is muddy where it streams through gaps in the roof.

A boy of six or seven lies nearby, sobbing.

Müller spits behind him. "Shut up, will you?"

The boy sniffles. His front teeth are in a pool in front of him, broken from the jaw. They glisten, faintly. Müller returns his attention to me. His breath is hot and rapid.

"Listen to me," he says. "You don't want to tell anyone what you've seen here, understand? Or I might just have to tell the Freiherr you've been pretending all this time. What will happen then, you think? I reckon there's plenty of room for you in that pit, don't you?"

He sheathes the knife, pushes me away. I strike the door, plunge backward through it. My teeth snap shut, and there is blood on my lips.

THIRTEEN

"How she kissed my wounds. Her brother had taken my eye and would have taken more if she hadn't clung to me so tightly. She pleaded with him for my life, which he granted me, just as she begged me, afterward, to let her go—and I did—though no word of hers could have served to persuade me had I known. But, then, I had no means of reaching her. She never wrote to me. My own letters were written and went unsent, accumulating for years til one night I burned them all. Until last year when Ostermann offered me a position at the paper. I knew this was where she had lived and hoped, somehow, that I might see her again. I went to the town hall first, and it was the clerk there who told me she had died. He pointed me to your uncle's house, abandoned these four years, but the neighbors told me there had been a child, a boy—"

A pillow under my head.

Light flickers on the ceiling and there's a man in a chair beside me. He is tall and thin, his complexion dark. He falls silent, stands to see me stir. The candle is in his hand, shining on his face. His left eye is sightless, slitted, sealed with scarring, and his nose is bent where it's been broken, but his voice, when he speaks, is gentle, low.

"Please," he says. "Easy," he says. "You are safe here."

The candle held higher.

"You are so much like her," he says, wonderingly.

The light wavers at his breath. The clock-tower is nearby. The bells strike once, twice.

Fourteen

Startlingly close.

I wake with the peal to a room framed in rods and wire. Father sits opposite me. His eye fires with the gaslight inside it.

"Good," he says. "Very good."

In his hands he holds a slate on which some letters are inscribed. He points to these each in turn. The air murmurs in my throat, my voice, I hear myself speak the names of the letters to which he points. He nods, erases the slate. The dark closes round, a drawn shutter, and again the bells are ringing in my ears, deafening.

"Yes," Father says. "That's it. Come back to me."

Hands to my face.

My head is enclosed in a steel framework. Fishing line has been drawn between each joint and pulled taut as to vibrate with every movement of my head. The line is knotted in multiple places and secured with hooks to a pair of bells which nestle in my ears. Each bell is hand-cast, perfectly fitted to the cavity in which it sits.

My head drops. The lines twitch to set the bells ringing and I am awake. My father smiles, encouraging. These words he has written on the slate:

"In the beginning."

The months pass and I can read, write. The words are in my head, the shape of them written. The letters join one with another like light with the dark or a rope to be climbed, hand over hand, til my weight exceeds the counter and the bells sound in my ears, even as my pencil moves to catch the scattered words, to capture sound and shape before it's gone.

"God created the heavens and the earth."

I sleep through the day, rising when the dusk falls and Father returns from the paper. We sup on rolls and black coffee. Afterward he teaches me Hebrew, Russian. We read from Nietzsche and Freud and talk over my lessons til the sky turns gray and Father un-straps the frame from my head. I sleep, awaken, sleep, and today, I am four-teen. For my birthday Father presents me with a gift, a journal.

"You must write in it," he says. "Tell me of yourself. All that you remember."

FIFTEEN

The sack of birth, its softness. My mother's hair spread over me. Her warmth. Her voice. Her eyes closed in the portrait I remember, at peace where she lay within the coffin.

My uncle. The pipe-smoke on his breath. Hymns he sang, horses he shot: their screaming. His body with its broken skull, eyes quivering with the rain which dropped in them.

A boy like me. Half-dead from starvation and the priest murmuring over him. Johannes leans forward over the bed, places his hand upon the lad's brow. Other boys like him, dozens. Their prayers in the dark and dying as Leibenhauer passes by. Graves opened in the night. The stench of bodies heaped half-rotting in the mud.

Father Johannes: "The idea was Steinfeld's own."

Von Steinfeld in his silks and top hat. "Nearer five hundred."

Father exhales.

The journal is in his hands, the whole of my sleeping life made to waken in its words. He sits at the window, reading, while the clock-tower looms over us to darken the room and no sound but the turning pages, the softness of his sobbing.

The night is past: the day is near.

Father rises from the chair. He looks at me, looks through me. He shakes his head but does not speak then dons his hat and coat and slips away.

SIXTEEN

He does not return. Night falls. Spring snow turns to slush in the street and I am alone at the window with the clock-tower striking eight.

Downstairs.

The door gives onto an empty boulevard where the snow lies heavy on the lamps and telephone wires. I slip down an alley toward the town hall, reaching the square just as a group of young men in school uniforms depart from it, laughing.

Hans Müller is among them. He wears the gaslight about him like a cloak, but I am unnoticed. The town hall is shuttered, the square deserted save for shadows and blowing trash.

The day's paper. My father's name appears below the headline, some words just legible for the gleam of gas-lamps on the snow. *ORPHANAGE-SCHOOL CONSPIRACY. EVIDENCE OF LIFE INSURANCE FRAUD. A LIST OF THOSE IMPLICATED.*

Father's voice. I hear him calling to me from across the square, find him lying in the muck behind a fruit-seller's cart, his forehead gashed open.

"Those men," he says. Dazed. Concussed. "The priest's boys."

I help him up. He mutters to himself as we stumble home.

"The same as before," he says. "His hands on me. That spoon which took my eye. Those things they called me. Nothing changes in this world, but somehow, I am changed. This time—"

SEVENTEEN

The shadows are different, deeper for the moon which fills the parlor. Herr Ostermann's house. His wife Anna is beside me, tea and saucer cupped in her trembling hands. The sun is down, the lamps unlit. We do not speak or stir.

Ostermann is on the stair. He storms into the room and halts halfway across the rug. He stands awkwardly, fidgeting with his hat. He stinks of sweat and hair-grease and will not meet my eye.

Anna speaks. "The trial. It is done?"

Ostermann nods. "Guilty."

"And the sentence?"

"Three years."

He collapses on the settee. He hooks his thumbs in his watch-chain, curses under his breath. A train's whistle sounds, shattering the twilight.

"Tell us," Anna says.

"Anna…"

"He deserves to know what happened."

Ostermann looks down at the rug.

"Your father is a brave man," he tells me. "Always you must remember that. Today he showed more courage than any man I have known. He faced his accusers. He testified on his behalf. But the judge was a fiend. He is Steinfeld's man—you may depend on it—and so too the witnesses they called. Such lies they told! Leibenhauer. That crooked priest. What a nightmare we inhabit to have such men among us."

Anna says: "But your witness, the insurance clerk—"

Ostermann shakes his head. "Dead."

"Dead!"

"Suicide, they say. It happened last night. The devils!"

"Friedrich," she says, gently.

He closes his eyes. "They have seen to everything."

Again the whistle howls down the line. The windows hum, the engine drawing near.

Eighteen

The trains are at the station. August, and the young men form columns in the square. They are dressed in gray with rifles at their shoulders, flowers bound in wreaths about their necks and the town's women surrounding to see them off.

Müller is a sergeant now. He barks an order and the men fix bayonets, present their guns to the officers as they ride past, resplendent in boots and cuirasses. Von Steinfeld leads the procession, his saber bared and upraised so the sunlight pours from it.

Doctor Leibenhauer rides behind. His spectacles gleam, reflective, cutting circles where his eyes should be.

Von Steinfeld calls the officers to a halt. A figure in black appears among the women. Father Johannes. He steps from the crowd and the men incline their heads to hear his prayers for victory. The horses stamp, whinny. The prayer is done. Von Steinfeld nods to Müller, who shouts the men into motion while the women, watching, weep for pride or fear.

The horses first and the young men follow, marching as though asleep with the flowers raining down before them and their mothers screaming Fatherland. The men do not break step. Their faces betray nothing as they are led to the trains and the war and all to be buried in their sacks while their fathers count the profits.

Your father is a brave man. Always you must remember that.

I sprint back to the square, up the steps of the town hall. Father Johannes appears in the doorway, but I am taller than him now. I cast him down, leap over him as he falls.

Upstairs. I follow the winding flight to the clock-tower and draw the bolt to seal myself inside. The fire-bell hangs over me, suspended in its swinging frame. Through the clock I watch the troop trains loading, hear the ocean in the crowd's roar.

I jump for the bell-pull. Catch hold of the rope and drag it down. The bell sounds. I rise as the counterweight drops, hurtling upward, then falling with the pull as the bell strikes again, deafening, and there are voices at the locked door now, fists beating against it.

The bell sounds again and again. Blood trickles from my ears and still the soldiers file into the waiting cars like horses to the slaughter and I lose my grip upon the rope. The first of the trains moves forward, gathering speed, soundless on its rails of grease while the whole of this darkening day crashes down with me, and all is silence, sleep.

NINETEEN

"Fourteen years. You say he slept throughout that time? Until his father adopted him—and his condition improved? How remarkable.

His father must have been an ingenious man. Yes, quite ingenious, though I see he has since died in prison. A shame. No doubt it was the shock of it all which caused the patient's relapse. I trust you have recovered fully, Father? Good, good. Of course it's all very sad, but you were right to entrust him to my care. You may be aware I possess some expertise in the area of hypnosis, which is known to produce miracles in cases such as this. For isn't obedience the inner-most wish of all men? To serve a master? To be of use? You really mustn't worry, Father. He will soon be well. I shall find for him a purpose."

Arena

The sun is behind him. His shadow lengthens, sweeps the blood-ied earth.

He is broad-shouldered and tall, his bronze helm flecked with crimson and crowned by a lunging sea-serpent: Leviathan coiled at the bottom of the world.

His steps are slow and regular, unhurried though the crowd roars to urge him toward me. Their voices blur into echoes, a sound like rushing water.

The fountain to which the centurion sent us. My brother accompanied me, and we carried the clay jug between us. A holy man was there, a prophet dressed in the rags of a beggar, and he lifted his hands above his head, as though to compass the sun where it sat within the sky. The crowd swelled, thickened. The blind, the broken, the diseased: their wasted bodies pressed close, their dead hands lapping at us.

We were caught up. My brother, two years younger, clung to my arm as to drifting wreckage while the holy man blessed us with a voice like a slow-moving river: tranquil in aspect, inexorable in force. The square fell silent. Even the stones listened as he spoke of the passing of this age and of a kingdom still to come.

A judgment was coming, he said. The first would be last and the last would be first: the slave become master, the master made slave. He would break our chains. We would be free.

He said: "For I am not sent to bring peace, but a sword."

The words cut. I felt myself un-tethered, falling inside myself. Beside me, my brother wept, though for sorrow or joy, I could not tell. The kingdom was near, quickening inside of us, and from the realization we took flight, running. We reached the house and burst inside, panting—and only then did we recall the reason for our errand and the vessel we had left behind us, unfilled.

☙

Fifteen paces, ten. He stops. Holds the sword level with his hip, the blade turned slightly so the fluid runs from it, mingling with his own blood on the ground.

Already, he is wounded. His side is pierced and pulsing, half-concealed by the buckler he carries at his breast. Its once-ornate design has vanished, battered into obscurity by his previous opponents: two net-men, both dead.

The first lies on his back near the center of the arena, his trunk slashed open across the stomach. His innards show. The second man is nearby. He has also been gutted, the right arm hacked off at the shoulder. The sinews trail from it like water weeds.

All around us the crowd jeers and thumps their feet, a jagged rhythm. Women are chanting, but I cannot make out the words. My opponent raps his sword against his buckler. The blood flies loose in drops that catch the sun like red fires winking, going out.

He bows his head. The great helm dips toward me, as if in recognition, but he doesn't speak, and now he is in motion.

☙

Moving with the sun. Circling the post to which I was chained, while my brother, kneeling, scrubbed my blood from the stones.

The centurion had made his judgment: we were to pay with our bodies for the jug we had lost. Its cost had been counted against our ration and the days had passed without food and with little water until I chanced to drop the master's helm and was whipped for it.

The day was hellish, hot. My brother went without tunic and the post-

shadow fell like the rod across his back. I tried to speak, but my throat was dry, and the brush moved rhythmically in his hand, back and forth over the stones, back and forth, a soothing sound.

The sun went out.

Sight returned, and pain.

Hours had passed. It was late afternoon, the sun high and riding. My brother lay before me, collapsed. His back was blistered, scored with dark lines, and he would not move for all I shouted, crying out to him, to anyone. I screamed my throat raw but none would come for us, not til evening, and later, in the night's agony, I watched the moonlight creep across the floor. A new kingdom, the holy man had promised, and in the thirst of my grief, I panted after it.

In dreams the heavens dimmed and turned black, the color of cooked flesh. The clouds caught fire and rained down plumes of flame like bolts of cloth unfurling. The seas boiled, over-heaving the ocean's banks, and the centurion, drowning, cried to heaven. But all were guilty, all consigned, and the sword that was promised felled all before it like fields of wheat at harvest.

He crashes toward me. His sword raised, buckler swinging. I brace myself. I drop the net behind me and grasp the trident with both hands, thrusting it out before me.

His strength is immense: his charge, the weight of it. His buckler strikes the trident to one side, wrenching the weapon from my hand and driving it point-first into the ground.

I stumble backward, unbalanced by the shock of the blow, and his sword is falling toward me, a closing arc like the moon in its waning. I lose my footing. The blade whistles past, cleaving light from sky and casting back the gleam: dazzling, white.

I catch myself, remain standing. My right hand is useless, numb from the shield-blow, but I gather the net from the ground with my left and throw it at my opponent's feet.

He retreats from it. I hurl myself forward, grabbing at the trident where it juts out of the dust. My left hand closes round it and I bring it up hard, turning with it to meet the next attack.

The trident catches his buckler. It caves in the iron round his fist and knocks him back. His sword goes wide, shearing open my shoulder and scraping the collarbone.

Heat runs down my chest, filling my navel, but there is no pain, not yet, and my opponent is winded, breathing hard. The air whistles in his helm. His wounded side pulses, spitting gouts of bright red fluid. He is losing blood, and quickly.

I press him. With the trident I strike to left and right only to meet the buckler again and again as we cross the arena, drawing near the dead men, their butchered bodies. Our shadows join and pass through one another, dancing, and the crowd thumps and cheers, keeping time.

෪

His footsteps woke me. The other slaves were asleep but the old cook came and knelt before me, the damp standing in his eyes.

"You were at the fountain," he said. "You heard the teacher speak."

"Yes."

"You must not mourn," he said. "Your brother is dead, but the teacher has promised the just will be reborn. Even the teacher himself, it is said, will die to come again in glory. He has promised this much: his blood, though spilled, will serve to hasten the coming kingdom."

I asked: "Why do you tell me this?"

"Your grief," he said. "Your anger. You must leave it behind you as he told the fishermen to leave their nets."

I shook my head. "What is a fisherman without a net?"

And the cook told of how the teacher had sighted the fishermen from the shore and called to them to leave their nets and follow him. The teacher said: "I will make you fishers of men."

Fishers of men. The phrase haunted me. I whispered it to myself when seeing to my work, and in the night, when sleep deserted me, I imagined the breaking of water, the sound, and saw the nets hauled up dripping with his naked shape inside.

The centurion. He was stripped of robes and armor, white and twitch-

ing like a fish. His mouth worked soundlessly as I split him groin to throat, plunging my hands into the blood-hot viscera. The intestines in ropes. The bags of his lungs.

And always the eyes and mouth open, lips gibbering.

ॐ

The clangor of iron. Trident ringing off shield and helm as I beat my opponent back toward the far wall. His footing is careful, even as he withdraws, sidestepping the long washes of blood. His head remains upright. His eyes are hidden but locked on mine, probing me as to anticipate my every assault. The feeling returns to my right side, and I wield the trident with both hands now, driving him across the arena like an ox before the goad.

We reach the far wall.

He stands with his back against it, sword low, shield ready.

I jab at his neck, two rapid strokes that catch the buckler. He raises his shield to guard against a third attack and I lunge forward, this time aiming low.

He is too quick. His sword whips down across the trident, deflecting the blow. His buckler, upraised, swings out across his chest to smash into my temple.

Hearing deserts me, the sight in my right eye. My lips split open over my teeth, and the blood fills my mouth and throat. I gasp, reel back.

He surges forward to hack at my neck, but I dodge to the side, somehow, and now I am in retreat, stepping backward, guarding against his attacks with the trident.

The fluid moves in my deafened ear. In my skull, I hear the ocean.

ॐ

Like the waves of their shouting. Men and women filled the streets, jeering as the condemned were led to the place of execution.

From an upper window, I saw the soldiers pass in two bristling ranks.

The mob yielded, clearing the road, and I glimpsed the centurion alongside his men, cracking his whip at those who failed to let pass. His tall plumes swayed.

The shouts grew louder. The condemned appeared.

Their clothes were torn and stained, dripping where the lash-wounds had soaked through. Two of the men were plainly thieves, but behind them limped the one whom cook had called teacher, the holy man whom we had seen at the fountain.

His blood, though spilled. *I recalled the old cook's words and wondered at their prophecy while below me the whole of the city cheered the holy man's death.*

He struggled forward, saying nothing. His wounds left black trails in the dust behind him.

The centurion's whip cracked and snarled, biting.

☙

He is relentless. The sword streaks toward me, alternating with the swing of his shield, and already, I am near to fainting. My ears ring, the blood in me a struck bell chiming ceaselessly, louder for the din of sword and trident.

His shield glances off my cheek, breaking teeth.

The sword blurs about my head.

I am nauseated, half-blind. I must act. I shift my footing to anchor the base of the trident against the ground. He takes aim at my head and I dodge to one side, catching the sword between the weapon's prongs. I twist with both hands, stomp down hard.

The sword snaps.

His buckler, cutting sideways, collides with my skull.

The air blows out of my lungs, and the broken sword, jabbing, strikes me through the side, plunging to the hilt. He pulls it free. He rips me open along its edge.

I do not fall. His helm gleams, sun-touched and glowering. The bronze serpent regards me, eyes round and black with dried blood.

☙

The sun eclipsed. Leviathan, leaping, swallowed the light, and all was made dark, as in my dreams, if only for a time. The day returned and later the true night fell.

The old cook, returning to the house, told of how the teacher had expired. The end had come quickly, he said, a mercy. The women had anointed the dead man's wounds with oil and laid the body to rest in the tomb, and a great stone was rolled across the entrance to seal it off that none might violate it.

"It is finished," the cook said. He exhaled heavily. To me he appeared older than ever before. He said: "Your kingdom come."

They were hopeful words, but he would not meet my gaze, and afterward, he tottered off to the kitchen to sleep, to wait. I waited too but only until the hour before dawn when the whole of the house was sleeping and none awake to see me go.

The kingdom was imminent. I felt its coming in my blood and in the beating at my ears as I scaled the outer wall to the centurion's bedchamber. He was asleep. He snored and blubbered, drunk on wine or the day's cruelties. He did not stir and made no sound even as his own sword struck him through the chest. His eyes fluttered open, fell shut.

I wrenched out the blade, tearing wide the wound and spattering my face and hands. Beside him the sleeping woman woke, one of the lady's handmaids.

She saw me. She opened her mouth.

The wounds belch and spurt: his, mine. I thrust my left hand to my side and fumble at the ragged flaps of skin and muscle. I press down hard to dam the flow and stagger backward before his attacks. Five paces more and the net is at my feet.

My opponent advances, sword raised.

I release the pressure on my side. Warmth spills out, wetting my leg, and the arena starts to spin. I transfer the trident to my left hand and allow my right to drop behind me, fingers spread, straining at the fallen net.

He raps his fists together. Broken shield, broken blade.

Breaking stone. The noise of hammers underground. We were chained ankle to ankle, seeking for veins in the stone, for the glimmer of ore by the overseer's torch. A lifetime had passed since I fled the city of my birth but here the din of breaking sufficed to stretch time and swallow years until the day the heretic was sent to us.

The boy was too young to have known the teacher but even so he claimed discipleship, denying the facts of the holy man's death and of our subsequent abandonment. He spoke of the kingdom as though it were a place nearby, close enough to taste. In chains he pretended to freedom, and his eyes, luminous, caught the torch-light.

"The kingdom is here," he said. "It surrounds you and still you do not see."

Later, when the day's work was done, I heard him whispering to himself. He was praying for me or my deliverance. His hands were pressed together, raised to his mouth to catch the words, the softness of his voice. His eyes glimmered. The hammer, sweat-slick, slipped in my hands.

My fingers in the netting.

He is close, less than three paces away. He protects himself with the buckler and chops at my left arm where it holds the trident.

With my right hand, I sweep the net from the ground. The ends twine round his shoulders. His elbow, netted, strikes his side, and his hand opens to release the sword.

I must be quick. I jam the trident into the ground then use both hands to pull fast on the net. My opponent stumbles forward and I sidestep to avoid his fall. He strikes the ground, stiff as a felled trunk with the net wound about him. I pull at the ropes with what strength is left to me, trapping his arms to his body, then reach with my left hand for the trident.

His breath is low and murmuring, his face upturned.

Eyes flash wetly in his helm.

Open doors. A light beyond all imagining the first time they prodded me out of the darkness and into the arena. Nothing was known of my past crimes save that I had murdered a man in the mines and now must face the judgment.

The heat dizzied me. The air itself was corrupt, tainted by the stink of torn bodies. Excrement. Organ-meat. They pushed me out toward the center of the arena while the surrounding crowd screeched for my death as they had for the teacher's long ago, and I, too, was naked, with only a net and spear to defend myself.

The arena's champion bore down on me, wielding a maul and clanking in his armor. He was taller than me, a giant of a man, but he died the same as the others while always the crowds roared their approval, cheering me on through the months and years in which I revenged myself on the hell of this creation, netting men like fish and piercing them, body and spirit.

I gutted the sun: I drank my fill of heaven.

ૐ

Blood in my mouth. I swallow and choke on it, gasping after breath.

My opponent grasps at the cords that bind him. His hands are wet and cannot find purchase. I clench my fist and draw the ropes taut. I raise the trident, prepare to strike.

His fingers close. He has the net. He pulls hard, unbalancing me. My legs buckle and give and the trident impacts the ground. I fall across it, trapping it under my weight.

He stands and jerks upon the net, tearing it from my hands. He casts it over me.

I attempt to free myself, but he is too strong, the cords too tight about me. His foot connects with my ribs, a crunching sound. He rolls me onto my back then stands over me with one foot on the net, his outline looming cross a blue sky without cloud.

The ropes hold. They bite through flesh like chains but I fight against them, rising. I cannot hear the crowd, only the breath in his helm. I am on my knees.

ૐ

The tomb before me, the kingdom at hand. Soon their bodies will be found: the centurion, the handmaid. The soldiers will come for me and still I wait.

Dawn approaches. The tomb is sealed, as the cook has said, but I watch the boulder to see it rolled away. My shadow appears and lengthens to cover the ground at my feet. I hear birds, smell cooking fires from the city below. The night is spent.

Desperate, I scrabble at the side of the boulder. My hands are greased and slick, but I haul myself up by broken nails until I reach the gap between the stone and the hillside. I thrust my face to the earth and peer into the chamber beyond.

See nothing, nothingness. Darkness deeper than shadow in the place where no light penetrates. The teacher lies within, hidden beyond sight or rescue, his soul chained to bone and sinew as I too am shackled, even here, with the centurion's blood cracked and drying on my hands. Smoke rises from the city, visible now. My master's face fades with the daybreak to be replaced by another as the skies fire and lighten and morning blights the hillside.

෧

He removes his helm. The eyes are familiar, the voice: the memory of rivers become river itself. I am drowning. My lungs fill. I pant after air that will not come even as the blood continues to pump from his wounded side, poured out without cease.

He says: "Did I not promise you I would return? That you would be free?"

The ropes strain, binding me.

His sword is raised. Red hilt, red hand, and falling.

Canticle

Marginalia discovered in a Spanish breviary

"Where have You hidden Yourself,
And abandoned me in my groaning, O my Beloved?
You have fled like the hart,
Having wounded me.
I ran after You, crying; but You were gone."

My mother is weeping. She hides her face, but the tears run down between her fingers. They wet the dry blood on her hands, staining them crimson. Her shoulders shake. She makes no sound and does not hear me though I call upon her. Mother, I say. The word slips from me, a thin sound, and I am awake. My eyes open on this narrow room, cramped and filthy and no shapes visible but the outline of the high window through which the water drips and puddles on the stone floor. It is not yet Lauds. This house is still, emptied of all but dreaming and the rain.

Three seasons have passed in this prison. Winter and the walls were cold, radiating absence. I fumbled at my beads but my hands were numb, the fingers chilblained. Nights of no sleep and only the moonlight pouring through the window to fill the cell with its silver glowering. Then spring, which was the false spring. Easter passed and winter lingered, would not depart. One morning, a robin settled on the sill above where it remained throughout the day, its call drifting down to me where I lay upon the pallet, an impossible distance. With the song came summer, this summer. Lice in my hair and bedding. Rotten bread, fleabites. The floors gather heat with the sun shining on them, hot as hearthstones by the dusk. The air in damp rags lodges in my throat. The heat sits on my chest: a slow suffocation like that of men who die upon the cross. My wounds open, refuse to heal. They pus.

The scent transports me. Before me loom the hills of my childhood. Perfume wafts from the grass where the wind makes ripples on it. I can picture it all so clearly, the paths down which I ran with my brothers as children, the sights we saw. The priest who stripped himself naked and knelt beside the river to flog himself with a thorn-branch. The old mad shepherd who dressed in animal skins and sang hymns to his flock as he drove them cross the sward, howling like a wolf to speak the name of God. The cries of deer in their mating. We heard them over the next hill: the bellowing males, the yearning of the hart. By the time we reached them, they had gone. They left no trace of themselves but blood splashed in the grass. Writing these words, I lose myself to the memory as I once lost myself in prayer, in those days, long past, when I turned inward to the mansions of the soul. Sext, and the bells are tolling from the chapel. Their chanting washes over me. I answer. The words break from my lips, ragged as the hart's cry. Holy Mother, pray for us.

This cross becomes too heavy, the weight of my penance or sin. I am no longer sure of the difference or if it matters. The days are all the same, counted by this breviary. Evening falls. I watch for moonlight, then for the dawn by which I read the offices. I read without speaking, unable to give voice to the holy words. Once each week, the door is opened, and I am led past the other cells and storerooms to the staircase and the chapel where the Prior awaits me. He is a good man. He allows me to wield the rod for myself and takes it from me only when my strength fails me. Always the tabernacle is closed. It hides within itself the Host which is denied me. When the beating is over, the Prior dismisses me. He bids the limping friar, oldest among the brothers, to accompany me back to the cell. The old friar is kind to me. He gives me milk or broth and sneaks me quills and ink with which I write my verses, these words. Some mornings he sits with me and listens to the birds outside. He pleads with me to renounce my sin and to make full my confession that the Sacrament might be allowed me. He does not understand there is nothing to confess and no one who might listen.

Vespers. The day yields to its breaking but the heat does not relent. I thirst. I lick the damp from the wall and pant after memories, the frothing cool of mountain streams. Those days, too, have slipped away, emptying themselves like vessels inverted. I remember so little. I was so young. My father's face is as lost to me as his voice, though I can recall the tales he told us of the saints and of the priests and kings of Israel. After he died, my mother took the three of us to see his people, a journey of some days. On the road we passed a pond where a mule had laid itself down in the shade of the cedars. The animal appeared half-dead from hunger and its right foreleg was broken so it could not stand. Thinking of David, my eldest brother fashioned a sling from a tree-branch and hurled stones at the beast where it lay panting, our Goliath. The long ears split and separated from the skull. We joined my brother in throwing stones at the face till its eyes were battered shut. Blinded, the beast moaned softly, as though to itself, and stretched its bleeding head toward the water. My mother saw what we had done, but she was not angry. Without a word she wrestled the mule's head into the water and sat upon the neck until the thing was done. We were not punished. It isn't right, she said, to let a beast suffer. To prolong death when death already takes so much. She knew this too well. My father's people wanted nothing of us and gave us even less. Days later, returning home, we passed the pond in which the mule had been drowned. Around the corpse the waters had receded, exposing the wiry neck, the bleached skull. The buzzards had been at it and the flesh was stripped away. Only sinew and bone remained, wracked into the outline of the beast in its dying: all life fled from it, the lack made visible.

His absence haunts me. The memory of those inner mansions toward which I flew when first I was taken in chains. And found them empty: marble tiles gleaming, fires banked and roaring. The supper table was laid for the wedding with bread and meat and the finest of wines, but there were none to partake of them, and the musicians, too, had gone. They had left their instruments scattered about the room, but with the ghosts of songs upon them, melodies clinging like perfume to the strings. I floated past the supper table and crossed the threshold to the inner room, where the wedding bed was readied, piled with sheepskins and furs. Here the Bridegroom had come and from here again he had departed. His scent of myrrh lingered in the manner of songs just played, and the Bride, who remained faithful, lay herself down among the furs to wait. She looked up to the pine rafters as if to glimpse the sea of stars beyond. She grew anxious. At last she slept and did not dream, and when she woke, the fires were out. The house was cold, the wedding bed. His scent had faded from the air, faint as longing.

But the Bride was not content to wait. The inner mansions were deserted, but I went out from myself in the one way that was open to me. This was December, the killing time, and ice had formed in bands down the walls of the cell. I stood upon the bed. I strained my mouth toward the window and sent my voice soaring out into the night when everything round about was stillness. Where have you hidden yourself, Beloved? I asked, and the words ran together into a song. One of my jailers heard and came running. He was tall and thin and spidery, his flesh riven by old wounds. He was once a soldier, now a husk of scar tissue. He threw back the door and peered into the cell, haloed by the light he carried. I continued to sing, could not stop. He took up the filth bucket from its place in the corner and hurled it across the room. It struck the wall over my head and upended, dousing me with cold urine, clots of frozen excrement. The pail clattered to the ground. The noise shocked me into wakefulness and I realized that I was not singing but moaning, screeching like an animal in the agony of its abandonment. I fell quiet. The door slammed shut. The jailer departed and I was alone with the night, my mother, her weeping.

Mother, I am sickening. My dreams have become as one fever. Night after night, my body falls away from me and I rise untethered from the bed, breaching the ceiling to drift over the city with its black walls and spires, houses lit by candle flames. Last night the wind was up. Floating, I spread my arms like wings and allowed the breeze to carry me north from the city through hills and canyons lit by the moon. The landscape was familiar. I recognized the sweep of grass and wildflowers, the low mounds of sleeping sheep. There was the clearing where the mad shepherd camped. His broken voice drifted up with the smoke from his fire and spread itself in the same way till there was nothing left of it. Into this hush I fell, slowly, turning over like a leaf to see the stars behind me fade and slip into the dawn.

The Feast of Saint Lawrence. I was roused by the sound of the door, the bolt shooting back. The thin jailer entered, followed by the limping friar. The first man glared at me. Get up, he said, and I did, assisted by the friar who helped me into the hall. The door to an adjacent store room stood open, lit by a casement which overlooked the top of the monastery wall. The friar nodded slightly as we passed then walked beside me down the stair to the chapel with its windows lit up like jewels and the tabernacle locked against me. The Prior was there. He faced the altar with arms upraised and called for me to approach. I obeyed. I removed my scapular and stripped away my habit and shift. The fabric clung to my back, stripping away scabs and causing the warm fluid to wash down my spine. Blood mingled with corruption, the odor of living decay, and in this guise of death, I knelt before the altar. The Prior murmured a brief prayer and produced the rod that was my penance. Will you take it? he asked, softly, as is his way, but I was too weak to answer. I sprawled forward, sliding my belly over the stones. They were cool beneath my skin, blessedly cool, and I think I must have drifted off because I felt myself rising, as in my dreams, floating and weight-less. Then the first blow fell across my back and shocked my scars to life. I plunged toward my body, becoming one with my wounds as I vomited and convulsed upon the floor. The Prior struck me again and again. He wielded the rod not with hatred or with malice but with a suitable solemnity bordering on sadness. My wounds, opened, sprayed at each blow, and when the agony was over, the Prior said another prayer for my repentance. His features were sheened with blood and sweat and with white flecks of sickness like shattered bone.

Later. Evening? Again I floated from the room. I left behind my body and city and drifted north to the hills where I beached upon a mountainside. The valley spread before me, emptier for the dawn that rose behind it, gray and sapped of all warmth, and the sky itself was thinning, insubstantial as the smoke from a shepherd's fire. I listened for birdsong, but there was none, and the eye of the moon was on me in my nakedness. It sounded me to my soul's center: formless and boiling as the heavens above. The moon shone from those depths as from a black water and with a light like the chill that precedes life, the silence that follows a death. From the mountain, I watched the sun climb into the east, dragging the shadows behind it, waves after a fisherman's boat, and the moon did not retreat but recast dawn in its own image, rendering all devoid of color, as was the world before the world, before the Word was uttered. I waited, growing colder all the while. I listened for the Word of Light, but there was no god there to speak it, and all the sweep of time was revealed to me in this unfolding of the waves.

Canticle of Flesh. Song of songs, which is suffering. We enter into it as babes and endure it as we can and we do not leave it behind us until we are dead and the earth shoveled over us and none are left alive to mourn our passing. The fever is worse, I think. The days go by. The walls drip with heat and the sweat pours from me, dampening my robes. The weather will not break. My hands are shaking and greasy, useless. The window permits of too little illumination to read from this breviary and I cannot stand to reach the light. The limping friar brings me bread to eat but my throat is dry: I cannot swallow. The reed of my voice is broken. My tongue flaps against my gums but makes no sound. The lash-wounds fester and rot.

This night, the longest of nights, my mother came to me and dressed my wounds. I could not see her for the darkness but remembered her scent of bread dough and opened earth. She undressed me, habit and shift. The latter stuck to my back but she massaged the strands of fabric loose and washed the sores with water from a jug she had brought with her. She bathed me, scrubbing the grime from my skin with a damp cloth, the same as she had when I was an infant. I tried to speak, but she hushed me into silence and helped me to sit up as she changed the bed coverings beneath. She lifted my hands above my head and guided them into the sleeves of my habit. The scapular came next and I lay down against the bed feeling wonderfully cool and clean. Her voice came from the darkness, a whisper. She spoke to me the words of the master in Matthew's parable: Well done, my good and faithful servant. Her shoulder shook gently. She was weeping. The chapel bell sounded Compline. She limped to the doorway and went out.

☙

The cloister is quiet. The moon is down and still I write. I cannot see the page before me. Dawn is far off, but I am thinking of my mother and of the vision that was granted me. I have no doubt but that it was a vision, for she was a simple woman, and could not read. She could not have quoted scripture to me for all her faith was cut from stronger stone than mine, and even this availed her nothing when her husband died and his family rejected her. Mornings, she left the house while we slept and did not return till dusk with pieces of moldy bread or scraps of firewood, bones to boil into broth. Where did she go? I asked my eldest brother, who said that he would show me. The next morning, my brothers and I sneaked out of the house behind her. We followed her from church to convent, where she pleaded for alms they would not give. Afterward she sought for shade in the town square and sat down heavily with the begging bowl between her knees. I was young, barely three, but old enough to know shame as I watched her grasp at the cloaks of men who passed her by and paid no heed. One man lingered, a younger man, but it was only to look at her in a way I could not understand, and afterward, I heard them together in the street outside our house when we were meant to be asleep. He beat her. We woke to find our mother in the bed with us, cocooned in the rags of our blankets. Her right eye had swollen up, sealing itself closed, but she smiled to see me awake and offered thanks to God when we sat down to break our fast of many days. My eldest brother would not join us, being too proud, but she did not resent him his pride any more than she begrudged the Lord her suffering, even after her second son suc-cumbed to his weakness, and the cart came to fetch him away. My brother went after it. He ran with the tears down his face, but my mother merely lingered in the doorway and did not stir until sunset when the shadows lengthened and she murmured a prayer to the Virgin before going inside. We lay down together. She lay awake beside me while I pretended to sleep and did not cry out, or curse God, or scream for the pain inside her, but again tonight she was weeping, and I did not know why.

The night is passing. In the last hour of dreaming, I found myself adrift. Freed from my prison, I drifted south toward the coast and joined the birds in their migration. We flew across the sea, the seas of time, while the heavens seethed and divided to form the void that was the storm, its open eye. Tempest winds whipped at us, ripping the birds free of their wings and dragging their shrieks into the stillness overhead. The Holy Land was below me, the city of Jerusalem with its hill of Calvary, its three crosses. I hurtled toward them, dropping from the sky with the weight of a child spat, kicking, from its mother's womb. The Bridegroom was there, the one for whom I had searched. He had left his Bride on the night of their wedding, exchanging the promise of ecstasy for the cross to which they had nailed him and on which he had been abandoned in his turn. He dangled from the bar with the stink of death upon him, blood dripping from his wrists and feet. From above I noted the crown upon his head and the lash marks down his naked flesh like words in a foreign tongue. The hour was late: the crowds had dispersed. His followers, too, had deserted him, so only a few remained. The men among them were silent, while the women wept openly, without shame, all but for his mother who concealed her face behind her hands. She could not see me as I plunged to earth, falling toward the broken body where we were to be joined together, Bridegroom and the Bride, in this, our crucifixion.

Of course her face was hidden. She wept for her son on the cross as she has wept for me these nine months, as she weeps for all men in our suffering. Even now I hear her, though my fever is breaking. The long night past, I wait for night. Terce, and I am beginning to understand. Waking from the vision, I felt the bedclothes twisted up beneath me. From under my scapular I extracted a mass of stained and bloodied wool which I recognized as my old habit. It had been torn into strips and looped together with the remnants of the soiled bed coverings to form a crude rope, fifteen feet in length, which had been secreted under my scapular for me to find. I thought of my mother, who had limped when she left me last night at Compline and of the old friar, who had always been kind. I heard footsteps in the hall. His footsteps, I thought. But the door opened to reveal the thin jailer with eyes like dead coals. He squinted at me through the semi-darkness.

Please, Brother, I said. Where is the old friar?

He is no longer among us.

I do not understand.

He has gone to his reward.

Surely—it cannot be true.

He was old. The end came quickly.

It has just happened, then?

Yesterday at Sext he fell into a swoon. He did not awaken.

Thank you, Brother. For telling me.

I am not your brother, he said, and left.

Descendit ad infernos: he descended into hell. When the procession reached Golgotha, the soldiers drove nails through his wrists and feet and raised his cross high in the air so his flesh dragged on him and the blood drained from his wounds as from a butchered calf. The women gathered below him to weep while the emptiness loomed overhead, a silent storm. In his agony he cried out to his father, but the air swallowed his words, and gave no answer. He died, unable to breathe at the last, his lungs crushed by the weight of his own body, which was heavier than any cross. We are the same, Bridegroom and Bride. I am thirty-five and still the flesh defines me for all my yearning after heaven. This body breaks me with its aching, its awful weight, and even in dreams, God hides his face from me. Nine months have passed in this way, but everything is changing. The day is at hand, as the Apostle writes. In dying he smashed the gates of hell as I kneel now before the door to my own prison, my hands at the lock. My fingers grasp at the iron housing, taking hold. I pull myself up, hang my wasted carcass from it. The nails strain with the weight, then snap. The housing twists away into my hand and I fall, hard. The floor stones smash the breath from my lungs, but the lock is broken, the bolt exposed. A window in the next room gives onto the outer wall, and the rope is in my hand.

It has begun. Once begun, it must go quickly. This prison settles into itself, into a stillness like the void to which he cried, as I did, and with one word from his lips he turned the dark to light. I listen for it now, the voice of my Beloved. The quiet is complete. His Word, as yet unspoken, can be heard only in the silence of the night. Draw me: we will run. Through valleys and vineyards, where grapes grow fat upon the vine, to the hills with their fields of lilies and no steps visible among them, so light our feet upon the air.

> "I remained, lost in oblivion;
> My face I reclined on the Beloved.
> All ceased and I abandoned myself,
> Leaving my cares forgotten among the lilies."

The Account of David Stonehouse, Exile

PART ONE

The wind is up. It rattles the shutters, the roof-slates. The stovepipe moans, making music of its breathing to join the cries of wolves from outside. They are close, gathered beyond the orchard with snouts upturned and jaws slavering. With one voice they shriek to the half-hid moon and only me to hear them. Judah is asleep, his head on his paws. He does not stir with the howling or even with the singing which comes from upstairs. Every night it is the same. Her voice is high and thin and sad, the melody familiar. Mother Ann's Song. Here at the end of myself as it was at the beginning. The high notes shimmer and ache, little louder than the scratching of my pencil, the dripping eaves. Mud is everywhere, the earth wet to its bones in this dead season. The soil cracks and thaws to flood the streams and sap is running in the maples.

❦

The spring delays. Mornings, the ground is hard with snow or frost and the days are short, the woods gray-brown with dead leaves, naked bark. Game is scarce. The deer starve, weakening, and the wolves feast on them.

This morning was the same as any other. My sleep was poor, troubled by dreams of green shoots and black earth and trees hung with queer blue flowers unfound in any country. I woke with the singing or perhaps the memory of it. Judah was at the door, sitting with his back to me and tail thumping the boards. I rose from the chair and kindled the stove.

Breakfast was yellow cornmeal boiled into pottage. There is little else: the mountains are as yet impassable and the last of the meat long gone. No coffee, either, so I warmed myself with water heated on the stove and stepped outside with the rifle strapped cross my back and the cartridge box at my hip.

The house faces east, perched on a slight rise with the stillness of the wood at a hundred paces' distance. Judah joined me on the stoop. The sun was coming up over the trees, screened by low clouds shot through with colors as bright and unreal as those in my dreams. I waited as shadows appeared on the ground then on the house behind us, churned up like water by the swish of Judah's tail beside me. He waited too with snout upturned, eyes beseeching. I nodded and he bounded off round the corner of the house.

I stepped down. The earth had formed into frozen ridges dusted by the night's snow. Its surface gleamed as glass does and would not yield to the weight of my boots and body. Judah, too, left no prints, though I knew well enough where to find him.

He was behind the house seated upright under the cherry tree where last night I had set a snare. Now a half-starved squirrel hung by its leg in the noose I had fashioned. The thing was grotesque, all patchy fur and bulging eyes. It chittered when it saw me and bent double to scrabble at the thin rope, teeth and claws gnashing.

I struck with the rifle-butt. The squirrel, stunned, ceased to struggle. Its body swung from side to side like a pendulum and I hit it with the rifle til the life was gone from it.

Judah whined. He pawed at the ground with his foreleg, sending up snow. I slipped my gloves into my mouth and with fingers bare unhooked the squirrel from the noose. Its hands opened, closed, small as the hands of a child born early. I threw it away from me. Judah went after it, though I called him back, and he tore it to pieces as I looked on.

The other snares were empty. I wiped my hands and donned my gloves then walked eastward to the woods and lingered at the margin. Judah limped up beside me, muzzle smeared red with the squirrel's innards. His long tongue lapped at his nose.

Sunrise. The forest opened before us, shadows swimming down from the branches to hide a sky of fire. I looked back to the house where the lower windows showed as squares of red-gold. The upper windows threw back the sun and dazzled so I could not see beyond them. When I closed my eyes, the windows appeared there, black as pupils in the world under my lids.

We entered the woods. Our footprints from yesterday were visible, their outlines. We followed them north and east toward the river and the pine-grove and the pit-traps dug out this summer for deer. Judah went ahead, as he often does, leaving rusty streaks where his snout dripped and stained the snow-cover, the one thing of color in that gray world beneath the trees.

Quiet settled into our tracks, sifting down with the snow. The light struck through the branches overhead, painting the earth with its shine. The first of the pits, northernmost, was empty, as were the second and the third. Judah allowed these only the briefest of glances before continuing. His shadow, elongated, stretched behind him to reach me though I trailed at a distance of ten paces with the rifle at my shoulder: loaded, ready. I listened for turkey, woodcock, heard only snow beneath my feet.

We reached the river and turned with it toward the pine-grove to east, the dead-wood surrounding. We came within sight of it: three trees tall as ship's masts and acres of empty forest spread round, the soil barren with needles and undercut by pine-roots. It is a place for the dead, as is the whole of this valley, where no living crops grow. We skirted round to the south and were nearly clear of the pines when Judah paused.

His ears stood up, his tail too, and a wind rattled the trees, driving the powder in squalls between us. He ran. He took off toward the pine-grove, kicking up needles and powder though I shouted after him to stop.

He did not go far. Twenty paces, no more. He reached the edge of that expanse of dying wood. He slowed then stopped to bay at the white clots which dropped from the dead branches all round and shattered into whorls which glittered like sparks to hide him from sight til the wind fell and the snow with it, forming ripples on the ice-crust.

Two crows burst up from the ground. Judah barked again, retreating, and I brought the gun to my shoulder to sight the birds as they rose, though I did not fire.

A moose lay nearby. It had been felled by wolves which pro-ceeded to feast upon the flesh, rending the hide in strips, exposing the ribs. The organs were missing, tugged through gaps in the barrel-cage of its chest, while the haunches were likewise shredded down to bone, the fatty meat gnawed free. A mess of overlapping tracks showed where the pack had feasted then retreated north, the ground showing orange and white and spattered with black drips from the flesh they carried with them.

I turned my attention to the moose or what remained of it. The crows had eaten what the wolves had left and even the hide was beginning to fester. I slipped the knife from my belt and knelt down to saw through the ruined hindquarters. I cut away such tendons and ligaments as had proved too tough for wolf's teeth and traded the hunting knife for a hatchet with which I split the joints which held together the long bones of the thigh.

Judah came behind me, panting and eager. I swung the hatchet a second time, cleaving the bone through then braced one end with my boot to prize it free. Judah stamped, snorted, could not wait. He snatched the bone from my hand and bolted away with it to find some place where he might lie with it and break the bone and suck the juices from within.

He would be some time, I knew. Beside me the moose lay on its side with one eye open, looking up. Inside it my own reflection was visible, but darkly, shimmering in place with the light behind it. My face: bearded and haggard and without expression. The face of a man much older or of a young man from whom the soul has passed. I could not bear to see it. I kicked at the ground, spraying up dirt and needles til the skull was well-covered and Judah, at last, returned.

The thigh-bone was gone. Likely he had buried it, as is his habit, bedding it deep in soil like a seed to give no life, and the rest of the day proved similarly fruitless, passed without incident as we hunted in the wood. At dusk the tree-shadows lengthened to reach the shade cast by the mountains, closing off the valley. We turned back to the west with the daylight waning and allowed our steps to carry us away from the river, the pine-grove and its buried dead.

※

To this cold house, this darkened room. Three winters I have passed in the valley, a sojourner in a house which is not mine and never was.

The fall was past and winter settling when first I came to this place. I was exhausted, half-starved and near-killed of it, when the house appeared out of the dawn. It was square and small, two floors huddled beneath a single gable with a central chimney. The siding was stripped so the house showed gray as the morning, rearing up like Lazarus as I drew near, with whitewash for grave clothes and windows for eyes showing nothing: a house no longer but the mere ghost of one, a standing ruin of slate and timber, its spirit long departed.

But the mouth was open, yawning. The door, ajar, creaked with the wind behind it and the sound reached to the orchard with its un-fruited boughs, sounding down that field of beaten-down sedge that once had been a garden but wherein nothing grew. I called ahead of me as I approached but received no answer, and there were no lights inside, no hands at the curtains.

Weeds grew high about the doorway, brittle with frost and with summer's blossoms dried and clinging. Three slates, terraced, formed a crude stoop before the door, and this was scattered with mildewed leaves stained black with rot. I mounted the first of the slates, unsettling the leaf-cover and causing objects to surface: children's blocks, a girl's rag-doll.

The door fell open, an invitation. Again I shouted ahead of me but the house swallowed my voice and gave no echo. I went inside. The door screeched behind me but would not close. Its hinges were bent, the lock smashed, and I knew I was not the first to stumble on this abandoned farmhouse seeking for shelter.

By then, the Village was far behind me, a distance of weeks and miles. The autumn was spent like Cain in his wandering, feeding on roots or wild carrots while the flesh thinned and withered, the skin stretched. In logging towns, I begged for scraps at the doors of churches and even turned to thievery, stealing clothes from a blind couple and a hen from a poor farm.

I survived. The season in turning swept us north to a crest of bald mountains soaring up to halve the sky. I was ill-equipped to climb but followed along the rock-face til it opened into a channel where a river spilled to south from a gash between mountains. Here the ground was low and level, good for walking.

Late November: the air was cool and sharp with snow, the smell of it, the trees all bare and brown but for the pines in the grove. They beckoned, spreading arms to dim the sun and bring the night, longest night.

Then, in the morning, there was the house. The curtains were drawn, the windows shut, its interior as dark as that place under the pines. I drew back the curtains to reveal chairs and quilts, a long table with one place set. The wood-box was full, stacked with dry logs with a fur of dust upon them, and indeed, the dust was everywhere: it whirled up in clouds at every step as I climbed to the upper floor.

The smaller bedroom was bare of ornament while the larger was well-furnished with a bookshelf, a bedstead. A writing desk was placed against the wall near the window with two bottles of scotch on it, empty. The sash was fastened but the shutters swung back and forth, one then the other, causing the room to vanish then resurface with the changing light outside.

I opened the window. I pushed out the shutters, secured the latch. Behind me a washbasin took shape, dividing from its shadow. The bowl was full, choked with ash and scraps of burnt paper with the loops of a man's handwriting just visible—the same man, perhaps, who had broken the door and stacked the wood-box and slipped silently away.

He was a soldier. I found his coat in the nursery where it lined the inside of the crib as though for a bedsheet. The coat was dark blue in color with yellow sergeant's stripes while his cartridge box was laid within the crib where once a child had slept. His rifle was there too, leant up in the corner near the rocking horse. The barrel glinted, a flash of teeth.

In my twenty-four years, I had never before handled a gun, and for days after coming here, I allowed myself to starve because I could not stand to touch it. Each day I grew weaker til little choice was left me but to load the rifle and fell a rabbit in its running.

My aim was poor. The shot struck the beast through the hind-leg, dropping it to the ground. It shrieked for a time then quieted and it bled out as I watched, too weak to do what was needed though I had the knife in hand.

Winter changed me. The river froze, the mountain passes closed. Snowfall buried the orchard, the barren acre of the old garden, and I became someone else: I hunted game with the soldier's rifle and wore his coat. Afterward I warmed my hands at another man's stove and slept in the blankets his family left behind.

Even this book is his, not mine. I found it by chance three days ago when I attempted to make a fire and found the tinder too damp for lighting. Then I remembered the old almanacs and went upstairs to the larger bedroom. I knelt before the bookshelf, pulled as many of the yellowed volumes from the shelf as I could carry.

This journal slipped free from among them. It fell open on the floor. A name was scratched into the inside cover. *August Fitch*, it read, paired with a date nearly ten years before as well as a short inscription: *To war & arms I fly.* Pages were missing from inside, ripped from the binding so only blank sheets remained, and I recalled how the basin was full when first I came to this house, piled high with burnt paper.

August Fitch. A name and nothing more, a life erased by fire.

I crossed it out, wrote my own in its place.

David Stonehouse, Exile. Foundling.

☙

Judah, too, was a foundling. I was two nights in this valley when a wailing came from the woods, a high scream like a child's. It cut the gray morning and drove me outside half-clothed, half-dreaming. He was near the river-bend at the edge of the dead forest surrounding the pines. He was in the ground. I found him writhing where the soil, rain-soft, had given way beneath him. He howled and kicked against the mud so only his head showed: the long snout, the eyes wide with fright or madness. He showed me his teeth. He snarled at me but still I went to him.

I dropped to my knees and thrust my arms into the mire. He snapped and howled and did not quieten though I dug out the clay from the red roots which ensnared him then plunged in my hands again to grasp him about the middle, to haul him up.

He came out of the ground. I fell back with his weight upon me and attempted to shield my face as he slashed at me, his claws unsheathed. He kicked at my chest, tearing my shirt and carving channels down my breast. His neck snapped from side to side, biting at the hands which saved him, which held him still.

I let him go. He leapt up and away through dead trees and I did not try to follow. My fingernails were broken. The wounds throbbed down my chest, dampening my shirt. The blood clotted slowly and I slept and woke to find him standing over me, his legs spread and paws planted, head cocked to one side looking down. His mouth dropped open. The tongue unrolled and washed across my forehead, sweeping away dirt and dried blood.

He was pitifully thin, a hound of indeterminate breed. The hip-bones protruded. His coat was tawny in color and ragged, knotted into tangles about his throat so he resembled a lion, caked in mud and half-crazed with hunger. Perhaps he had strayed from his owner—or been abandoned—and for this reason if no other I forgave him my injuries and made him my own.

We walked back to the house. Our surroundings, it seemed, were of little interest: he trailed behind with his head lowered and made no protest though I scrubbed him down with water from the well and combed the mud-clumps from his fur.

He shook himself dry. The day was warming, a breath of spring in fall. He yawned and lay down and slept with the wind in his fur and the weak sun shining on him, a lion at ease.

~

I found a dead man in the river.

Yesterday was warm, almost unseasonable: the ice yielded in the night. The noise startled me from slumber and I lay awake a long time afterward. I could not sleep but waited for daylight then shouldered the fishing-rod and struck north to the river.

The channel was clear. The river had shattered itself to flat pieces like eggshell, which floated downstream with the surging current. The water frothed and spat, running high, and the sun made streaks upon the surface which folded back on themselves with the wind.

Judah chased the sun downriver and I was alone on the bank. Hemlock trees formed a wall at my back, green and fragrant and softly rustling. The pine-grove was visible beyond the hemlocks, their high branches like closed hands holding whispers. Inside the satchel I brought were hooks and a hatchet, a jar for bait. I threaded the hook with a maggot from the jar and cast my line toward the opposite bank.

The fish came up quickly, three in succession. Their silver bodies twitched as I drew them from the water but I clubbed them with the hatchet til they ceased to move. I whistled after Judah but he was gone, chasing scents or sounds invisible. I re-baited the hook and followed the bank eastward, drawing nearer the grove, where I cast again.

My line caught, tangled in the limbs of a drowned tree. I went after it. I sprawled on my belly with my hands in the water, and that was how I found him. The dead man was hooked in the crotch of a branch with the remnants of an undershirt and suspenders wound several times round him, fixing him in place as he bloated, decayed, and did not rise.

How long, I thought. At least since the autumn and likely earlier. Five years, perhaps. Long enough for the river to peel the fat from his hands and forearms so the bones showed through and the skull peeked out from a tangle of hair.

His head was submerged nearest the bank. I grasped at the hair, knotting the strings of it round my fingers. I pulled up, gently, meaning only to test the strength of my hold, but the scalp came away in my hand and I let go. The scalp did not sink but floated away downriver, turning on the current like a living thing. I gagged, tasting acid. My gut contracted, heaving, and I waited for the sickness to pass.

His bones cried out for burial: I went for the hatchet. The blade cleaved water and fabric together. The rags of his shirt parted round the hatchet and the body shifted, rolling onto its side.

With my other hand I caught hold of the exposed breastbone and tugged the man by his ribcage out of the water. I dropped the axe and adjusted my hold to drag him by his armpits onto the bank and then down the rise to the dead trees and the place where we had found the moose some days ago.

Pine-needles covered the ground, drifted inches deep in hollows where the ground lay low. The pines were visible on their mossy hummock with their three crowns like green lace spreading, doubled by the roots beneath my feet. How far they stretched. What horrors they compassed. The pines undercut the forest for hundreds of yards surrounding so the elms, uprooted, lay upon the ground. Sapling maples leant, gone bald where the bark had peeled from the trunk, and the hemlocks, too, were withered and sere.

I buried him between two maples. They were dead trees, standing snags, and the earth was hard with the winter just behind us and red roots webbing the soil. The hatchet served me for a spade. I chopped at the ground repeatedly, breaking through layered frost and hollowing a space in the ground as the morning passed and the sun reached its meridian.

The grave perforce was shallow, sufficient only to cover the pitted bones and ragged clothes, his fish-eaten boots. The shape of the boots was distinctive, as was the color, the toes tapered to steel points sheathed in dark leather where the rest of the boot was lightly tanned. The soles were rotted out, marked under the heel with Roman numerals or maybe the man's initials: what looked like an *I*, a *V*. His toes protruded from the ground, but I covered them with hemlock-boughs and marked the grave's head with a cross of sticks and fishing line.

I thought of nothing, or rather, would not think, would not let myself remember, and hours had elapsed when Judah appeared. He lingered at the margin where dead trees and living divided and would not come near the grave. His tail dragged on the ground. His limp was more pronounced than before and he was shaking, I noticed, body drawn taut like catgut struck to sound a single discordant note. His eyes were wide, jowls foamed with spittle.

I left the drowned man's graveside. I held out my hand with the palm open, up. Judah sniffed at it then recoiled as if I had struck him. His jaws snapped open, shut. He barked, whined. Our eyes met, and he was afraid.

A sound behind us: scarcely audible, a rustle of leaves.

Judah ran.

He leapt forward then stumbled over his bad leg. He fell, regained his footing, and continued to run, and would not stop. I gave chase but it was all for naught and I was breathless and dripping when I returned to the riverbank after an hour to retrieve my rod and bait and the fish I caught.

The sun was yellowing, shadows stretching to run together. I made haste to pack the satchel and turn toward home, crossing the orchard just as the wolf-pack awoke and filled the vale with screams and echoes. Judah was at the house, waiting. He sat upon the slate steps, gazing eastward toward the apple trees with ears and tail erect. In the wood, the wolf-pack howled at the kill, gorged with blood and near-frenzied, but Judah remained seated, a sentinel keeping watch. He would not abandon his post, not for anything, and would not come inside til I fastened the halter round his neck and dragged him cross the threshold. I closed the door, secured the bolt.

☙

Rain outside. The windows run with it, blurring the horizons, eliminating distance and perspective. I build up the fire and light a candle to see the page before me.

The storm is breaking. Thunderheads rupture with the gusting wind and hail spits down the roof-slates. A shutter has come loose upstairs. It bangs wildly, rips free, lands in the puddle where the gable empties.

On a day like this my mother left me at the gate to the Village and the stone house for which I am named. I was an infant, too young to remember, but Jerusha was a girl of nine when it happened and told me, later, how it was.

"The trees were shaking," she said. "The wind was in their leaves and shredding them. The noise was such I feared for the children's garden. I ran outside."

"But this was in October," I said. "The season was nearly past."

"So it was. But the squashes weren't yet picked and that is where I hid them, the dolls I'd made from cornstalks. I'd hollowed out a pumpkin which served them for a house. A mother, a father, and me their daughter. I couldn't leave them. I went outside, though the trees about were pitching and groaning. An oak came down and shattered like glass where it fell."

"You didn't run? Weren't you frightened?"

"I wasn't thinking of it. My thoughts were all of the family I'd fashioned and the hell that was coming for them. Rain slapped my cheeks and blurred my sight but I lowered my head and pelted cross the garden to the place where they were hidden. I opened the pumpkin and gathered them out. I hid the dolls under my skirts and was making to run for the house when I heard from the gate a sound like hollering."

"Me," I said.

"You," she said. "But I saw the woman first. She was at the gate in a crimson dress like none I'd seen, the color of it. The fabric shone like sparks from a flint in that evening dark with lightning cutting the sky. Her hair she wore pinned beneath a wide hat with a lacy brim like sometimes I saw in town. She didn't speak. She only beckoned. And I knew as I shouldn't but I went. She had a scent about her like crushed herbs or roses pressed in paper but nearer her I caught the tang of spoiled milk, which I thought peculiar, as her clothes were so fine. She carried at her breast a bundle of rags brown with dried blood or worse and this she held out to me. Plainly she meant for me to take it, but as I said, she wouldn't speak or even look at me but pulled down her hat so the brim hid all and I never saw it, her face. Only the hands which gave you up to me."

☙

The dreaming haunts me, the music. Her voice like soft bells striking.

I woke tonight with the singing. The stove was out, the house turned cold. I struck a drunkard's match and lit a candle. The flame stood up quickly, leaping to light the staircase as I climbed to the upper floor where the song doubled back on itself, echoing, circling round the candle's flame so the words could be made out.

In yonder valley there flows sweet union—

My breath was visible, forming vapors in the candlelight and veiling the flame as I walked down the corridor, passing rooms unused in the years of my exile.

Let us arise and drink our fill.

The high notes piercing: puncturing bone, ringing the brain like a bell, and all sound ceasing when I reached the door to the nursery. My candle, upraised, showed only an empty room, an empty crib, a child's horse faintly rocking. Overhead the ceiling appeared as lines of twilight where the slates had fallen away and the window was sealed with ice and frost in overlapping plates. The floor gleamed with old snowfall like the remnants of winter and no one to hear me when I spoke.

"Please," I said, only that, and went downstairs.

Past midnight, and the singing lingers. The song is done, but the house keeps the memory, held fast in its walls and windows. Judah is awake, restless, a lion roused. He paces the lower rooms with claws unsheathed and clattering. He pauses to scrabble at the wall or balance on the window-frame with his forepaws. He presses his muzzle to the glass, looks east toward the pine-grove. The window fogs with his breath and he resumes his pacing.

"Judah," I say, but he pays me no mind and will not listen though I urge him to lie down, to sleep. I have become as sounding brass: my voice jangles, fades, and is gone. The candle-flame flickers and dims, the dawn nearing, and I am alone in this house and only my own soul to haunt me. See its outline on the wall. See the thorns it wears.

☙

Always in its shadow.

With these words the Elder Job had sought to comfort me when I was twelve and could not sleep for the longing which racked me. For days I had lain awake, terrified, heart's blood beating down the dark. I hungered after the Gift, but the Gift eluded me, and I feared I might never feel the hand of God upon me or hear the angels singing. Their song: I craved the taste of it in my mouth as a man in the desert lusts after water. I would be purified, I thought. Cleansed of all that was rotten inside me. But the room was cold and silent and the blankets stank of my sin.

I sneaked downstairs to the library and lit a candle and applied myself to the study of the Word. Elder Job found me. Plainly, I was troubled, and the elder always was kind to me. He entered the room without admonishment and came to sit beside me. He did not speak but merely watched as I read, following my finger as it swept the shadowed page.

Behold the man, Christ said, and I closed the book.

The candle-flame wavered, went out. Job waited until I told him of what troubled me. When I was finished, he clasped my hand between his own and held it fiercely.

"You have come within the shadow," he said. "It is well, David. It means the cross is near. The tree on which the living God was hung and where He died. It is behind you now as it is behind all men who must live always in its shadow. I say to you again: it is well. You must first pass through the dark of the cross that you might learn to take it up and follow."

His voice was soft but urgent, pleading.

With the night between us, he told me, briefly, of his younger days. He was given to drink, he said, and gambling. A slave to the flesh and its impulses. He despised himself but was helpless to abstain from vice though it killed the living soul inside him.

"My life was all one shadow," he said. "As yours is now, I know. You long to be made one with God, to sing in tongues of angels. But first you must cast off the flesh as Mother did before us. Do you understand? The cross is here. It is behind you. Have you eyes to see?"

☙

Frost in the night but the day is warm. The mountains shrug off their burdens of snow. The pass to the south is open, though it comes nearly too late. The cornmeal is gone, the oats and tubers too, and only fish to see us through the coming days. The river teems with them but Judah will not go near the river and will not stray from the slate steps to join me at the hunt. He is frightened. Of the woods, perhaps, or of me. He broods, pacing, and will not be comforted.

Birds. This morning I heard them in the apple trees, singing to wake the earth to itself. Buds open with the sun's rising, shedding the night's chill and puncturing the prevailing gray. The soil is wet with snowmelt, good ground for tracking, and there were prints in the orchard this morning, moose-tracks, where the beast had paused to browse amongst the budding trees.

I followed them northward. The tracks continued into an old ravine, formerly a stream which fed the river. The channel is dry in summer but yesterday's meltwater flooded the gully, flowing down swiftly from ridges above. The trail reached the water's edge then vanished and did not reappear upon the opposite side of the gully where the streambed widened, draining to mud and shallow water. I listened for movement in the underbrush, steps in the dead leaves, but heard only birds, squirrels, the river plunging to the pass and the town six miles to the southeast.

I reached the river, wider here to the north of the pine grove, where the beavers had been at work. They had diverted a portion of the flow into a long, low shimmer fringed with reeds and tall grass and spruce trees forming rows beyond. Their lodge they built upon an island near the pond's center with the door facing outward, a black circle.

I had given up the moose. I thought I might collect a beaver pelt instead and so concealed myself amidst the tall grass with the rifle to my shoulder when the moose stepped from the trees, floating into view with a soundless grace. The beaver pond was still, as were the woods all around, despite the warmth of spring, and the moose inclined his head to nibble at the buds of a stippled sapling.

I sighted down the barrel, drew back the hammer. The moose startled at the scrape of metal and turned its head toward me, antlers wide as my own arms spread, and I fired. The rifle discharged, catching the moose through the broad of its chest. He turned and galloped into the spruce trees, snapping branches as he ran down the last of his strength.

I shouldered the rifle by its strap then stood and skirted round the beaver-pond. I reached the striped maple with its buds eaten away, the bark peeled down its trunk. Moose tracks were visible in the mud, dark blood splashed in the grass and spattered up and down the maple's length when he had wheeled then bolted away through the spruce trees, limbs all bent and broken to show where he had passed.

Into the spruces, their branches close. They whipped at my face and hands, abbreviating distance so I had no sight of the moose though the wound was surely mortal and his heart's blood darkened the ground. A hundred paces more and the spruce-wood opened onto deciduous trees, leafless to give a view of the river, glinting through the crush of limbs.

The moose could not be seen, though the blood trail continued for longer than I thought possible. It led me to the riverbank, the waters foaming white beyond so I dared not attempt a crossing. The beast was surely weak, near dead, but somehow he had walked across and so the trail was lost. I turned back toward the beaver pond, halting by the maple sapling at which the beast had fed. My fingernails settled into the grooves of the beast's teeth, elongated half-moons where the inner wood showed palely.

I looked behind me to the ranks of spruce where a second tree was missing its bark. A sheet of it had cracked and dropped away, revealing a deep wound ringed in red where the heartwood had splintered. The bullet. With a knife I dug at the bark, widening the gouge in the wood til I could insert the blade's tip and twist my wrist to wrench the bullet free. The bullet, flattened, rolled down the blade of my knife and landed on the ground.

I picked it up. The bullet was greased with red fluid, warm where it sat in the close of my palm. Strands of fibrous tissue were folded into the deformed metal, heart-muscle. My shot had passed through the moose's chest, tearing it open in two places before lodging in the trunk of a spruce tree. Unthinkable the beast should have survived such a shot yet it had done so and there was nothing for it but to rinse the bullet in the pond and slip it back into the pocket of my coat.

The day passed.

I reloaded the rifle and waited out the light with no sign of beaver. I walked home at noon with the gun unfired, my belly empty, thinking of the moose I had seen and of the shot which struck it. His terror like mine in that instant when he felt the end at hand and sought for shelter, a place of hiding where he might die alone and unremembered.

The bullet is in my pocket. It is strangely heavy, of a weight to sink a drowning man. The corpse I buried. Or the Elder Job in his youth when he thought to end his life.

"I wanted only to hide myself," he said. "The river was below me, flecked with light but with a blackness beneath. To vanish within it, I thought. I longed for it, to annihilate myself body and soul. I would drown and disappear and be like a child never born."

We were in the workshop adjacent the stone house. Job labored over the forge while I worked the bellows which fired the blast. I was there to help him, to learn his trade, but mostly, we talked. At seventeen, the Gift had not yet come into me, though children half my age had received visions of heaven or heard the spirits singing. I doubted. I told the Elder of my despair and he showed to me his own.

The story he told happened when he was a young man of twenty-eight and accustomed to the living death which is the life of sin. He borrowed money he could not repay then took himself off to a riverboat where there was gambling and drink and in such quantity he soon lost everything, even his pocket-watch, and afterward, made for the upper deck to be sick.

His creditors were close-by. He spied them from the deck-railing: two men on the jetty with pipes in their mouths, thumbs hooked in their belt-loops. A third man climbed down to a skiff which would row him out to the riverboat. This man wore a green plaid suit and sat at ease in the boat with his walking-stick between his legs and hands folded over the curved top, sharpened steel like a butcher's hook.

"He meant to rip me with it," Job said. "To cut me like a common swine."

The skiff drew near, cutting the water with each pull on the oars. The man in green looked up toward the boat and nodded to Job in recognition. He doffed his cap, half-smiling in the glow of the bobbing lanterns, and Job bolted to starboard, his head spinning.

The skiff drew up to port. He heard it: ropes thrown, caught, fastened. The waters roiled below him, the stars forming long shimmers between the waves. He larded his pockets with boat-hooks, one in each, then mounted the rail and stepped beyond.

The waters swallowed him. The current dragged him into that place of darkness, black as the shadow in which he lived with Christ dead on his tree behind him with arms spread wide to eclipse the sun—and like Christ he did not struggle but sank like a man already dead or indeed like one who had never lived.

"Such was my shame," he said. "If I had not lived, I could not have fallen, and if I had not fallen, Christ could not have died for me."

Sinking, he opened his mouth. He filled his lungs with the cold and plunged toward the river-bed with arms upraised and hands open, holding nothing. His chest was heavy with water, the boat-hooks dragging til he felt her hands upon him.

"A woman's hands," he said. "Or an angel's."

Woman or spirit she caught him by the shoulders and pulled him from the water, and when they reached the wooded shore, she leant her body over his to kiss him on the forehead. He slept and woke with a memory of her words to him.

"The cross is yours," she said, and so it was.

The end of the story I knew already. Job gave up drink and the pleasures of the flesh and took up the cross as he was bid. In time he learned to shoulder it with ease, with something like grace. He came to the Church of Christ and to the Village where other Gifts were given to him, and in abundance, for these were the days of Mother's Work when the visitations of the angels were a common-place. Job joined the brethren in their worship and danced with the spirit inside him, the holy words upon his lips. On the Sabbath he donned spiritual garments and ate of spectral food and drink which sustained him for days as the angels came and went among them and only their songs to show they had been there.

These songs we sang years later when Mother's Work was behind us and there were many among the brethren like myself who possessed only longing, for whom the duty of the cross meant weakness and failure, submission unto lust. Job's strength never wavered. At meeting he led the brothers in their ecstasy, whirling with them to cross the room with hands all joined while the strains of Eldress Rose's voice floated down from the rafters: it lit upon the dancing men who lifted their heads to catch the notes in falling. For hours it went on like this with the men dancing and then the women until all were exhausted and the Gift broke upon them while I watched, and ached, and prayed in words which went unanswered.

I was like Cain, my sacrifice found wanting. Though I walked with God like Adam, He was silent and would not speak to me as He did so many others. The cross was on my shoulders but the Gifts of the Spirit were denied me, just as the tree was denied to Adam, who likewise yearned after the thing forbidden, until in his yearning, he fell.

Job sensed this, pleaded with me to be patient. "You are young," he said. "The Gift will come to you as it did to me. The cross is yours, the angel said. And yours, David. Even now you sink beneath its weight, the waters rising all round you. But you mustn't despair. God is good: you will not be permitted to drown."

He advised patience. The Gift would come, he said, and so it did, when I was three-and-twenty. It was on Sabbath. I lingered at the edge of the gathered fold as the lamb does who fears the shepherd. Eldress Rose, eldest among the sisters, spoke of a Gift she had received in the Era of Manifestations when a spirit came into her and for hours spoke in words which none could understand for none among them had received the Gift of interpreting prophecy.

Afterward, when the Supper was taken, songs sung, I watched the thought of angels move through the assembled brethren, passed along hand to hand until it fixed itself upon a young boy of perhaps ten who let fall from his lips a stream of queer syllables. His voice wavered, a lilting music, but his words—if they were words—evaporated and would have gone unremembered save for the sleeplessness with which I was afflicted, later that night, which kept me awake despite my exhaustion and the snores of my bed-mate beside me.

The songs ran through my head, the same as they do now. The notes sounded clear as glass in my skull, forming themselves into melodies which circled round me, dragging me down toward sleep. In that place between waking and dream I found I could recall with exacting rigor the boy's song in every note and syllable.

> *Ash lach in*
> *bi mor na, o*
> *da rim a, e*
> *o*

I leapt from the bed and I think must have shouted, for my bed-mate started up with something like alarm about his face and said nothing though I dressed in the dark and ran down the corridor bare-footed. I rapped upon the door to the Elder's study, where he often slept. He opened the door to me. His hair was tangled, nightclothes damp with sweat as from a nightmare, and his eyes appeared black and sunken without the spectacles he was accustomed to wear.

But he welcomed me in all the same and bade me to sit and I sang for him the boy's song as I remembered it. With head lowered, eyes downcast, he listened to the boy's song and asked me to repeat the words, which I did, and afterward, I told him what I thought they meant. His hands were in his lap. His eyes glittered and he told me of the Gift.

"You carry within yourself a memory of language: the old tongue which was Adam's and which the angels speak. You are like those who waited on the Sibyl. The Gift is accorded you that you might listen to the brethren in their singing and transcribe the words to revisit them later, and pray over them, and with the eyes of your heart thus unravel their meaning."

All this I did, and for a time, it was enough. I was pleased to be of use, to be counted among the blessed, and if the eyes of my heart were open or closed, there was none to know it but myself and God—and He was only the silence which surrounded me such nights as I wrote by candlelight, pretending to faith, inventing meaning for words which had none. Always that silence was there, and even afterward, when I tried to sleep, it was a weight on my chest pressing down like that of the cross I carried but in secret: the taste of Jerusha's mouth, her lips on mine.

I fell with the weight of it. Christ did too. At the house of Ahasuerus He lay with His head against the wall, craving rest, but even this was denied Him. The man appeared from inside to send Him on his way and Christ up-rose in fury and splendor and cursed the poor man as He had cursed no other, not even Judas who betrayed Him.

The scene comes to me unbidden. The road to Calvary. The procession is halted before the rich man's house, the hot sun beating down. Light flashes from the assembled soldiers: steel armor in plates, spears they carry. Ahasuerus is there too with Christ before him, dressed in rags and kneeling for the burden on his back. He is a madman, a criminal. Ahasuerus kicks at the dust, blinding him, and wrestles Him bodily from the wall, casting Him down so the cross falls across Him, a crushing weight. The crowd applauds, jeering the prisoner until at last He stands with the cross upon his shoulders and turns His gaze upon me.

I think on it often. His fury in that moment when even falling was denied Him. His face is black with rage, eyes sharpened to points. His hand raised to curse me, to strike me, though I am as far beyond His reach as He is beyond mine and this my exile. I yielded to the cross and became dead to the spirit, a living beast with the murdered man inside me. The soul is gone but the flesh abides, its days made endless in this valley like those of Ahasuerus—or Cain— and I think sometimes I must bear the mark upon me, invisible to all eyes but my own, though I have killed no one: only the soul inside me.

God, but the flesh is heavy. This place is all one shadow, yes, but it is not the cross's shadow as Job once said but that of another tree, an older one. The planks and clapboards of this house are fashioned from its very heartwood while the circling mountains close off this vale as sure as the boulder which sealed His tomb.

He ascended into heaven, it is said, and in dreams, I return to the stone house. I walk the halls for hours with Job beside me. Some- times Jerusha is there as well. She takes me by the hand and leads me outside, and the garden is the Eden of her dreaming in the days before our banishment. All gone. I wake to this house, the ghosts which haunt it. The dream fades so quickly, no more substantial than the stain light leaves in its departure.

Rain again and lasting all day. I went out alone and returned with the stinging in my cheeks, numbness in my hands and feet, nothing more. We are all hungry, sickening with spring's advent. I can delay no longer. In the morning I will descend the pass and walk to town but for tonight there is only the last of the fish between us and the rain blowing hard outside, footsteps sounding from above: restless, pacing.

I build up the wood-fire and linger over the stove as it warms. My breath whirls before me, making webs of itself which spin, softly, into nothingness. The stove is hot. I scale and behead the fish and halve it lengthwise to draw out the bones. I call to Judah. He eats half the fish out of my hand and resumes his place at the window.

Trees loom out of the gray. The light gutters out of the sun.

The world retreats from us, but Judah will not forsake his vigil, lonely as my own and kept for no one. The glass dims to hold within it our reflections: his and mine and behind us the stove with flames banked high to brand our faces on the night.

The fish bloodies my hands, its butchered body. I scrub my fingers raw over the bucket then return to the stove. I melt lard into a pan and place the fish within to

[*The entry breaks off mid-sentence* .—*ed*]

Judah went mad. He was at the window, keeping watch while I prepared our supper. I stood with my back to him but turned when I heard him growl, a sound like thunder breaking in a place far distant. His claws were out, hooked in the sill. He balanced on his hind-legs with his snout at the window, breath misting the glass and his wet nose rubbing gaps in it. His teeth were bared. I leant down beside him to look east toward the orchard, the maples. All was stillness: no motion, nothing to see, not even moon.

I patted the fur about his ears.

"Easy," I said. "Easy."

He snarled through his teeth. He barked and would not stop and clawed at the window til the sill was nearly shredded and I feared the glass would give. I shouted but to no effect then grasped him about the middle to pull him from the sill.

He howled. His claws, flailing out, tore scratches in my chin and throat and we struck the floor together with my arms locked fast about his belly. He kicked against me, spitting, and I tried to hold him down, but failed, and leapt up myself at the smell of smoke.

The fish was scorched, starting to flame. I dashed to the stove and took up the pan and plunged it into the bucket while Judah bayed and would not quieten.

Supper was ruined, inedible. I was weary, worn thin. In my anger I grasped hold of Judah about the neck then threw him down, hard. His head struck the boards and I stood over him with the smoking pan still to hand, upraised as though to bring it down upon him.

He scrabbled at the ground. He was terrified, eyes wide as he tried desperately to escape from me—and I thought of his limp, caused by a beating, and of the master from whom he had run away. I froze. The hot pan struck the ground and Judah, righted, darted between my legs to the backroom, wherein he concealed himself and whimpered for fear and would not come at my call.

A voice from upstairs: Holy Mother's Protecting Chain.

The song had been there all the while but came now loud as strokes upon the forge in this new quiet with Judah whining for fright and night pressed to the windows, concealing all.

I shot upstairs, taking the steps two at a time. I reached the upper floor then sprinted down the corridor to the nursery, where the singing was loudest. The melody circled back upon itself, the air like black wings beating.

Vo o, vo nee
o har ka e
on a se

The song continued, louder as I crossed the threshold. The room was dark, the window covered, and the boards moaned underfoot: rotted through, warped by winter's frost.

The crib was before me, empty. I upended it. I dashed it against the ground then fell upon the cherry-wood frame with the fury of an animal. I broke the railing then the legs and kicked the remnants out to the room's center, scattering nails and sawdust.

It was done. Silence surrounded me, cold as frostbite. The song had ceased, but I sensed her, her nearness. Sweat froze to my spine and forehead, the backs of my hands.

"Forgive me," I said, speaking to shadows. "I am so tired."

I stepped forward, hands held out for pardon.

The floorboards gave way. Splinters pierced my ankle, wedging my boot into place so I fell forward. The breath went from me and I sprawled upon my belly with head upraised to watch the darkness detach from the window. The black became her shadow with its long dress and hair which trailed behind her, whispering, as she passed into the hallway and was gone.

I stood, staggered to the window. Clouds were thinning, shearing, opening holes in the sky through which a few stars glimmered. The moon was out, near to full. It scribed the weeds and sedges round the orchard, revealing the black shapes of wolves among the apple trees. Two beasts together, male and female. They were digging in the ground, eating autumn's drops in their hunger with the maple trees in unleafed lines behind them, stripped to shadows of themselves like rows of teeth.

A figure appeared among the maples, a silhouette. The height of a young child. It moved like a child as well, walking on all fours from out the forest's mouth and making for the orchard.

The wolves caught the scent. They stopped, listening, then turned to pounce, but already, I was in motion. I flew outside. The rifle was in my hand, kept loaded by the door. I fired into the stars and set the wolves to running then bolted down the stone steps.

The grass was sodden, shimmering. The beasts floated over it and made no sound, while the child, heedless, passed beneath the apple trees, and these were no longer bare, I saw, but silver with moonlight, laden with blossom.

The chill settled into my lungs, colder at each breath. I approached the orchard, a dozen trees with their branches joined to rain down flowers. Shed petals rose and fell upon the wind, batting like lacewings about my face. I smelled roses, musk, memory. The breeze in Jerusha's hair that morning when we met beyond the fields and she told to me the last of her dreams.

But there was no one in the orchard. No child there, no second fall awaiting me. The scent of apple-blossoms faded and I tasted the days of rain like wet stone in my throat. The soil boiled over with it, churning to mirror the shape of a storm so the worms struggled after air, stranded by rain to wait for dawn, birds. They writhed with one body save for places where the earth was trampled flat, patches of black stillness where the wolves had burrowed and feasted.

A light flashed from the ground. An apple, autumn-ripe. It was the size of a fist and so deep and red with juice as to absorb the moon's silver and cast it back black. I knelt amidst the twitching worms and steadied myself with the rifle-butt to reach with one hand, to gather the apple from the ground. I wiped away mud, grass, rubbing the red skin smooth till it gleamed in my palm, a perfect jewel. Then I returned to the house.

With the apple I coaxed Judah from his hiding-place in the workshop. He shied from me, still afraid, but sniffed at the fruit that was offered him and opened his jaws to take it between them. His teeth worked at it, mashing the fruit between them while the juices spilled out and puddled on the ground. Afterward, he licked the floorboards dry.

All is forgiven: Judah curls at my feet with his head on my knee. He sleeps despite the noise from upstairs, a din of breaking. A child's ball rolls slowly down the stair. It strikes one step then another, bouncing, before coming to rest in the shadows by the stove.

Judah whimpers, dreaming. Mist rises from the grass, promising fair weather for the journey ahead, and I am back in the Village, the stone house.

☙

My earliest memory.

I am a babe again and crawling. Like a snake I drag myself forward on my belly, crossing the boards of the meeting hall with the sun's gleam forming pools between them. The sisters' stair: I scramble up on hands-and-knees. I smell varnish, new that morning, the woodgrain rubbed smooth and slipping underfoot as I reach the upper floor, begin to walk.

The corridor stretches before me, endless with the shadows which fill its end, opening to nowhere. A woman is singing. Mother Ann's Song. The melody rises then swoops behind me, gathering me into it. I am compelled, captured, called to the hallway's end.

My child's shoes are wooden. They fit poorly so my steps clatter and scrape, but there is none to see me. The dwelling rooms are empty, scented with tallow soap or wildflowers picked from the garden, and the shadows retreat, forming two doorways placed opposite one another.

These rooms are smaller than the others, without windows and with room enough for a single bed. The first is empty. In the second a single chair is pulled out from the wall then turned toward it, faced away from the doorway. A girl sits in the chair, hands all knuckles where they knit within her apron and head uplifted with the strings of her bonnet falling down her back. She is perfectly still, motionless save for the rise-and-fall of her breath, moving with the song she sings as I watch, and listen, and she does not turn round.

❧

Judah stirs. The sun is up: light in the trees and a long day's journey before us—

PART TWO

[The following passages are written in a different hand.—ed]

The first dream was in June. I was a girl in the stone house but everything was different. The walls were veined with mold. The roof sagged. Flies circled me where I stood and there was a stench of rot from the floor.

This wasn't the stone dwelling but a dolls' house, the one I'd made from a pumpkin when I was ten. In the dream my parents were beside me though I was an orphan and had no knowing of them in life. My mother's face was that of Mother Ann while my father kept his hidden though I felt his hand at my shoulder, its weight.

The room had no door as I hadn't carved one but two windows opened into a fog which was thicker than any I'd known. It seeped into the room and whirled upon the floor neither white nor black but without color and with a taste like iron. It recalled me to myself, the flesh I wore in the dream, a girl's small hands and feet.

My father removed his hand, a burden lifted. I could walk. I stepped to the nearest window which was only a squared hole cut into the pumpkin's flesh. Through it I looked out upon a world of fog where there was no time or distance, no one and nothing to see.

Mother said, *You have not the right of it, Child.*

What must I do?

Have you not hands?

The fog swirled before me. I raised my arm and touched a hand to it. The fog yielded to my touch then curled about my fingers, bending to the shapes I made between them, though I knew naught of what I did.

Sights I saw, or made. A Billy goat, his eyes shaped from fog. Then a second goat beside him, a female. The beasts stood dumbly facing one another and didn't move or couldn't. A raven next and a dove. A milk-cow with fattened udders and a bull with horns. All these I made but all stood colorless, unmoving.

Mother said, *Look.*

I said, *There is nothing to see.*

Have my children taught you so little? All this Man has made, as is written, and named, as is his right. But a name is a dead thing as is the Word without the Spirit's fire to illumine. This world too is as nothing without color and to Woman is given the colors and their names.

Her gaze was on me, eyes cold and the color of ocean.

Blue, I said.

And her bonnet was pale as was the hair she wore bunched

beneath it and the bones which showed in her ancient hands.

White, I said.

Then *green* for grass and *brown* for trees and *red* for the apples which hung there, gleaming, so the whole of Creation took shape beyond the window—

In the morning, I told of this dream to the Eldress. She listened carefully and wouldn't speak til after I was finished. Then she crossed her hands in her lap and didn't look at me.

She said, *The days of Mother's Work are ended. The Gifts of late are few and granted only rarely. We must not be hasty or allow ourselves false hope. Tell none of what you have seen or of the words which Mother spoke to you. Rather you must work and pray as you have always done. If the Gift is real, it will come to you again and in time.*

I was dismissed. I saw to my labors. The days passed and I told no one of my dream though I thought on it often and wondered at its meaning. Mother's face appeared to me out of the brook when I washed the sisters' laundry and once I felt my father's presence behind me as I labored over the cookery with the grease brush in my hand.

In time, the Eldress said, but the time it passed too slowly. I was impatient. Nights I lay upon the pallet with my eyes open and arms upraised and fingers spread to brush the dark surrounding. *Come to me*, I said, whispering the words that none might hear. I did not want to be seen in my hunger, possessed by a longing like lust after that sorry dolls' house and all that it had meant or could mean for the life of toil which stretched before me.

Years before, when the storm had passed, Sister Candice found my dolls' house concealed among the gourds. She intended no harm but seeing the pumpkin was rotted through she shattered the walls with a rake and plowed the dolls into the soil where one of the boys found them. They were half-buried in the mud but he brought them inside and showed them to the Elder Job. Eldress Rose learned of it and later she looked upon us sternly when none would claim them. *These are not yours?* she asked, and I denied it, as did the other girls.

It was improper, Rose said, that we should harbor such notions, and she burned the dolls in the kitchen fire while we watched. I was afraid. I denied my family but afterward I repented of this betrayal with every year in passing through two decades or more til I thought I'd forgotten them and they returned to me in the night.

June was cool and rainy. It gave onto July, the dreadful heat. The waiting was too difficult. I slept poorly and sometimes not at all. I waited for the others to sleep before rousing myself to kneel before the bed.

Come to me, I begged. *Father. Mother. Daughter. Come.*

This Gift was granted me.

In August I dreamt myself back into the pumpkin's belly. Years had passed in the months of my dreamlessness and my body had aged. Now I was a young woman of thirteen as I was when first the curse had come upon me. Mother was there, as before, but my father was gone and the fog had lifted. From the window I looked upon a world of overwhelming color.

First the green of trees in summer leaf and then the black lines of their shadows. Wildflowers burst from the shade they cast, violet blossoms and gold which shone with the sun on them. Songbirds in the branches of the fruit trees. Their silver feathers flashed and winked.

Two goats appeared, male and female as they were made. They stepped from the tree-line and approached the window, trotting side-by-side. Cattle followed them, and sheep, proceeding two by two and the wolves coming last. They herded the other beasts as some dogs do, tails wagging as they ran alongside and nipped the sheep in their play. Their teeth were white and shining but their tongues were red, the color of raw meat.

The procession neared the window. The animals came within a few feet of my outstretched hand before turning with the wolves behind them and vanishing from sight.

Mother joined me at the window.

All this you have done, she said. *This world of color and light is yours as surely as it belongs to him.*

To him?

She took my hand in hers and pointed with it to the far corner of the garden. My father was there. He was faceless as before but walked with another beside him, a man, and this man's back was turned to me.

I don't understand, I said. *Who is the other man?*

Mother didn't answer. She spoke instead of the coming night.

The sun is in the west, she said. *Dusk is falling, and the heart of this house is rotten to its center. The walls are weak and must give way. None of this can last.*

Black mold down the window-frames. The ceiling dripped with it, spattering my face as I looked up. Liquid filled my mouth, throat, but the taste was sweet as honey, and beyond the windows, the beasts were coupling. Goats mated together and then with the cattle and even the wolves lay with the lambs before tearing them to pieces. The grass was red with it, the trees, and the wild corn turned crimson as it thrust from the ground.

A serpent moved among the other beasts, rippling and wet, muscled up and down its body as it circled the unknown man where he sat beneath the songbirds' trees. He was alone, I saw, and did not heed the snake though the pink length of it wound about his shoulders and throat.

I thought to warn him. I called from the window and he turned round. His face was familiar though I didn't know his name. The snake was gone but he stood naked, unashamed, and all the birds were quiet.

I awoke. The bed was wet. My breathing came fast and shallow and I smelled my body's juices in the sheets. I couldn't sleep. I sneaked to the basin and washed myself in the evening's water then lay down once more to await the morning's bell. It sounded. I rose with the others and sought the Eldress in the kitchen where I knew I would find her.

Again I told her of the dream but said nothing of the man or the serpent or of the way in which I awoke. She listened but was plainly troubled and wouldn't speak except to send me away. *Go and see to your work, Sister. I must think.*

Her pondering lasted a day and a night and it was morning again when she sent for me. The bell had struck but the sun wasn't yet risen and I went to the library as I was bid.

Eldress Rose was there and seated at the long table with her hands folded on her apron. Behind her the Elder Job stood with his face to the window, fingers at the glass. He heard me enter and turned away from his reflection. His expression was grave and he asked me to repeat it, all that I'd said to the Eldress. This I did while the Elder paced the room in his excitement, muttering to himself till a decision was made at last and he spun upon his heel.

The Dreamer's Gift, he declared, *is the Gift of prophecy. But prophecy is such that we must look to God to know the meaning thereof. Few possess the seer's eyes, the listener's ears, but there is one among us, perhaps, who might be trusted to interpret. The Gift was slow in its coming to him and now at last we know the reason.*

The Eldress said, *You speak of Brother David?*

Job didn't answer her. He addressed himself to me directly.

Write of what you have seen, he said. *Create for me a record of such dreams as you remember and give it to the Eldress.*

He looked at her. *See that it is done tonight.*

The Eldress nodded. She rose from her chair and shepherded me from the room.

We will speak of this later, she said and closed the door. But I heard their voices come winging down the hallway as I left and real-ized they were arguing. I thought

[*The passage ends abruptly. David Stonehouse's narration resumes on the reverse side of the page.—ed*]

PART THREE

The house receives me. The prodigal returns to find his father absent and no one to greet him, no feast prepared. The door creaks open on a frigid room, its windows dimmed, its threadbare curtains drawn to slits of dusk. My head throbs. The wound pulses in the makeshift dressings, fashioned from a child's blanket, and the pencil-tip scratches the page, going back and forth and no lines visible to guide me. The stove is cold and gives no light and Judah has been taken. He has gone to the deeper woods and I am too weak to follow, too weary in this moment even to rise and build the fire.

☙

Yesterday—

The skies were clear when I made ready to depart. I collected the winter's pelts for trading and bundled them into a length of folded oilcloth which I wrapped round twice and secured with a hemp cord. I cleaned the rifle, barrel and breech, and shouldered the cartridge box by its strap then buckled it into place over the sergeant's coat. Upstairs, I retrieved a cloth haversack from the first bedroom (this, too, had been the soldier's) and stuffed it with a sheepskin and blanket to serve for a bed. Into another sack I placed flint-and-steel and a skillet and such provisions as I would need for the walk down the mountain and back, a journey of two days.

Judah was restless. He panted to follow me about the house, claws clicking up then down the stair and round the room as I opened the stove-door and stacked inside the unfired logs. I added kindling and tinder and left the last of the matches too, for I carried the flint and would have no need of them. The stove readied I took up my pack and rifle and opened the door.

I called for Judah, but he would not come, and I could not let him remain behind to starve. He whined in protest as I fastened round the halter then shrieked for fear as I dragged him over the threshold and the door fell shut behind us.

The jamb stuck: I caught the handle and pulled it in, the noise echoing like a shot from the lawn and woods surrounding. Judah moaned and stayed close. With the halter round his neck he allowed himself to be led down the slate steps then cross the orchard.

The woods were quiet. They held within themselves a silence like that before the Word was spoken. The wolves had retreated to their den and such deer as remained were bedded down in the thorns and briar-bushes. The pits we passed were empty, their coverings undisturbed, and we were near the dry creek-bed when Judah scented a hare. His hunger mastered his fear and he nipped at my hand which held the rope. I released him, and he leapt, thrashing, into the undergrowth.

The brush rattled and heaved with the struggle and the hare was surely starved or injured for Judah caught it with ease, emerging from the underbrush with the long body clamped and twitching in his jaws. I finished the hare with a blow from the hatchet then skinned and dressed the carcass. Its haunches I cut into long slivers and held these out for Judah to take. He sucked the flesh from my hand then licked my fingers clean of blood. I discarded the skin then swaddled the butchered meat in cambric to be cooked and eaten that evening when I stopped to pass the night, as was my habit, on the bald lookout over the river.

An hour's walk, and we reached the end of the valley. The river surging in ages past had hacked a channel through the ridgelines surrounding and this we followed for hours till we were clear of the vale: I un-looped the halter but Judah stayed close, and would not stray, and together we descended. The forest thinned as we neared town. Fir and spruce gave onto aspen and birch with green leaves curled to give more light. Late in the afternoon we left the spring woods and passed between unseeded fields black with upturned earth. The town took shape before us, forming out of the dusk as from a mist: the church-spire first then the mill and the red bricks of the general store which showed the evening's glow.

The journey had taken longer than I anticipated. I feared I reached the town too late, but the doors to the general store were open and a band of four farm laborers off work lingered outside. For the most part they paid me no mind, all but one man who was older than the others and who looked upon me queerly.

I returned his stare. He did not look away but neither did he speak and soon returned to chewing his pipe stem with eyes half-shut as in thought.

Barstow appeared in the doorway. The shop-keep is a glutton, a drunkard: red-faced and fat, his apron smeared with sawdust and flour and streaked with dark molasses.

He said: "Been expecting you these last two weeks."

"That so."

"Come in," he said. "Leave the animal."

I slipped the halter from my coat and with it secured Judah to the hitching post. He gave no protest, no reproach, but slumped against the post with his head laid down between his forepaws and ears standing up.

I entered the store. Inside I exchanged the furs for credit as was our arrangement then purchased oats and rice and coffee as well as bacon and butter. Other items too: hooks and line, matches, gunpowder, jerky. I laid these provisions out in the oilcloth then bound it shut with ropes before taking the bundle onto my back. I strained with the weight of it, more tired than I realized. Barstow made no comment but merely watched me go.

The sun was low and sinking, nearing the tree-line. The hired men had gone, all but the oldest among them, who lingered with the pipe-stem clamped between his teeth. He was leant up against the wall of the saloon wherein the others had vanished with his gaze fixed on me as I unhooked the halter from the post and took the lead into my hand.

I withdrew a length of jerky from my coat-pocket and held it out for Judah. He sniffed at it but showed no interest and allowed himself to be led without protest, staying close behind me all the while, sheltering in the shade I cast.

We passed the saloon-doors and the old hired-man. I was lost to my thoughts and did not hear his voice and only halted when I felt his hand upon my arm. I spun round. My eyes met his, and he must have seen something there for he removed his hand, as though scorched, and retreated from me with hands raised for fear that I might strike him.

"No need of that," he said. "Wanted a word with you is all."

"Then have it," I said.

He hesitated. "Just something you should know." He struck a match then cupped his hands round the flame to re-light his pipe. "There was someone behind you," he continued, coughing, the smoke on his lips. "As you came into town just now. Someone following. A man."

I shook my head. "I would have heard him. The dog would have scented him."

"He kept his distance. Walked some paces behind you and hid hisself behind that hedgerow as you came off the hill. Been watching for him ever since."

"You haven't seen him?"

"No, but he could've sneaked off, I suppose. If he made for the woods, I mightn't have seen him."

"Or he is still up there," I said. "Waiting for me."

He nodded. "It's why I stopped you. In case he's planning to jump you. The others, mind, they wanted no truck with you. They say you're a strange one, and so you are, but it isn't right, is it, a man should turn toward his home without knowing what's there waiting for him."

"No."

The old man made his goodbyes and disappeared into the saloon. From inside I heard the young men shouting as he joined them and this was followed in turn by the first strains of a song in voices rough and wild as the wolves'.

The moon was shining brightly upon the battle-plain…

I did not stay to listen. I un-slung my rifle to check the breech then placed my thumb upon the hammer, readied. I willed my hands to be still and my breath to slow and climbed to the high fields. The halter slipped from my wrist to my elbow, but I did not adjust my grip upon the rifle, did not dare. I pulled Judah along by the throat so he lost his footing again and again.

We gained the hillside, the juniper hedge where the man was said to be hiding. I approached with the rifle at my shoulder, the barrel outthrust.

There proved no need of it: no one behind the hedgerow, no one waiting for me in ambush. But Judah's fright was catching, I suppose, because I started to run. The breath pumped through me as from a bellows and I made for that line of hills at such a pace as I could manage.

The sun was down when I reached the overlook with its view of the river and the vale below. I made camp upon the promontory, as I often do, building a fire from windfall strewn about the hillside where winter blasted the summit and splintered the last of the shade-trees.

I took a bird for our supper. A woodcock ventured too near the fire and I downed it with a shot from the rifle. Wild turkeys were nearby and there were chipmunks and squirrels and such game as I had not seen in months. The bird I prepared by the light of the fire then drove in the rod by which to roast its carcass over the logs.

The flames licked up: the flesh charred, bubbled, dripped. A hunger came over me at the scent, heavenly after weeks of rice and fish, but Judah only stalked the edges of the firelight, as though compelled, his eyes showing white about the sockets where they turned to the dark surrounding. He whined, softly.

The valley was below us, the river unheard at this height. Wind whistled in the broken trees and made the flames to leap and dance, shedding sparks in clouds like fireflies for all the summer was far off. Supper, then. I filled my belly while Judah paced and finally halted opposite me with the fire between us, hiding him from view.

Exhaustion overcame me: I slept.

I awoke to a ring of smoldering embers and Judah keeping watch with the darkness cinched round us and tightening. The fire in dying was like a storm's eye with a chill wind rustling all about and no other sound but footsteps close-by and circling the fire. I heard them in the undergrowth, mulching leaves and twigs together.

Judah heard them too.

He spun round, mad with fright, and snarled through his teeth. His jaws snapped at the air clotted with smoke and embers whirling up as I leapt half-dazed from dreaming and planted my boot amidst the coals of the fire-pit. I cursed and stumbled back, smoke-blind and coughing on sparks as I dropped to my knees and rooted in the grass for the rifle: dead grass in blades, the thorns of a creeping briar. The gun was gone, stolen away. I hugged the cartridge box close with one hand while with the other I pulled a coal-red stick from out the fire and waved it before me.

Judah yelped and howled and tore round the fire-pit. The thief, it seemed, was near, his footsteps close, but he evaded us. I could not see him though I thrust out the torch before me and waited for my eyes to adjust: naked trees at clearing's end, the forest massing far below.

The footsteps were louder now, faster. They revolved about the fire-pit with Judah keeping pace, snapping at shadows as they winged through the firelight. I was shouting, hoarse, the words tearing in my throat though I recall nothing of what I said. It hardly matters: I wanted only to drown out Judah's frenzied yelping, the sound of footsteps circling.

His tread was that of a heavy man but he moved with the speed of a bat so that even Judah flagged and fell behind, panting. The hound's breath failed him. He snarled with the air that was left in him. I swung with the torch, so wildly the glow extinguished in my hand. I slipped the hatchet from my coat and hacked at the air, cutting the man's shadow to pieces though he did not cease or slow and Judah collapsed by the fireside. His barking yielded to a long, low moan, and the man was gone.

His footsteps retreated. They faded from the grass, the underbrush. The moon slid down the sky to reveal an empty expanse of hilltop, a clearing starred with frost and the loops of a man's bootprints breaking through. The gun was missing. Plainly the man had taken it with him, carrying it off with the shadow he dragged behind.

I kicked at the coals and rekindled the fire, striking sparks with my flint from off the hatchet's blade. "Eat," I said to Judah, and he was too weary to refuse. He slurped the flesh of the woodcock from my hand and swallowed down the burnt fat. My hands were wet with saliva, blood: I wiped them dry on my coat then lay down awake to watch the stars go out of the sky.

They did. The sky flared violet then dimmed into gray. In the fog of the morning, I shouldered my pack and smothered the fire and with Judah beside me walked down the hill to the river and the valley beyond. We were silent just as the land was silent: no birds, no wind. Only the river as we drew near. The flow was up. The waters gurgled through the mist like the phlegm trapped in a sick man's chest and driftwood formed a kind of dam where the rains washed down the slopes of the hills surrounding.

We neared the pine-grove, that low hill with its three pines like Calvary and the small grave at its center. I could not think of it, not now, and did not look to see the markers I had given them, twin crosses fashioned two years apart. We went on, striking southwest from the river toward the pit-traps and the house. I walked half-asleep, shambling forward with the cartridge box at my chest and the oilcloth-wrapped bundle strapped to my back, heavy with powder and shot and no gun now to fire them.

Traps alone would not suffice. Without the rifle we would starve and starving must go south out of the mountains to the Village and the stone house. Its gates are shut against me, sealed fast in my exile, which was Adam's, impassable though no flaming sword appears to cut me down. It is hardly necessary. Those doors will not open to me though I lose my voice in calling to them—my brothers, my sisters—and beat my fists bloody on the oak.

Morning unraveled toward noon. We neared the house. In my reverie I did not notice Judah as he stole away. I did not even realize he had gone til I heard that awful howling at my back and realized I was alone. The screaming was to the east, the outermost ring of pit-traps. Such pain in it, such fear: he must have fallen. From the depths of the pit he howled out for rescue like a child starved for mother's milk. The pack unbalanced me: I secreted it away in a hollow log and took off toward the pit-trap, leaping clear of fallen limbs where I spied them and somehow keeping my feet for all I stumbled, arms flung wide. I reached the pit, running, and nearly tumbled over but drew up short, and skidded to the edge, and found it empty.

The howling had ceased. The earth opened into a deep shaft with slick sides like a burial pit and meltwater pooling at bottom to reflect my features, pinched and pale, and the shape of the man behind me. His arm snapped across my throat. The blow burst on my Adam's Apple, bruising the windpipe and causing my vision to flicker. He kicked at the backs of my knees, and I crumpled. He caught me by the armpits and with one white hand took hold of the cartridge box. His strength was incredible: he snapped the leather strap in two across my chest then ripped the box free. His voice was in my ear, low and spitting.

"Take my coat too, will you."

He relaxed his grip. I dropped to my knees, coughing after air. I could not remain upright: he cuffed me about the ears, drawing blood from the scalp, and hammered at my ribs with his fists til I slumped forward with my face in the muck. His boot was on my neck, a crushing weight. I was drowning, pinned as was the serpent, unable to breathe for the weight which held me fixed. He cursed me with a voice like broken glass and wrestled with the coat I wore, twisting my arms round in their sockets til the garment slid free of the shoulders, a skin shed.

He called me a thief and worse. He said I meant to steal from him his very life, which I could not understand, and then the weight was gone from my neck. Air exploded into my mouth and lungs. I gagged and sputtered and turned my head to see my assailant stalking away.

He was tall, at least six feet in height, broad-shouldered and strong. In age he appeared around thirty, though I could not see his face, and for clothing he wore boots and gaiters paired with blue trousers, suspenders, a linen undershirt with sleeves rolled back. He carried my coat and cartridge box together in a bundle under his arm with the rifle resting across his shoulders.

Judah was beside him, limping. I could not call to him, had not the breath for it, and there were open wounds down his side, thin gashes made by a blade or willow-whip. His gait was slow and shuffling like that of a man to the gallows and the two of them were nearly out of sight when Judah looked back. His eyes met mine but he did not see me, somehow, and his face appeared human in its hopelessness with an emptiness like mine on the morning two years ago when the worst of the nightmare was past and I woke within the pine-grove.

༄

Such things I felt in that moment:

I was like the Elder Job, perhaps, when he had gambled all, and lost, and the black waters opened before him, but no angel's voice to call me back. Christ was dead and crucified, his bloodied face written on my bones like scrimshaw.

I closed my eyes, though just awake, and the image of His broken body appeared from out the darkness, nailed to the cross of my transgressions and Mother weeping at His feet, grieving what was gone and gone forever. For I had given my soul, and given it gladly, though months had to pass before I understood what I had lost.

All this was two years ago. I was more a boy than a man, and I stood up, shaking, and stumbled to the river. The surface had frozen in the night and the earth was hard with frost and slippery as I scuttled down the bank. With the hatchet I smashed a circle into the ice and plunged in my hands, scrubbing them raw, sopping off blood and grave-dust.

A moaning came from behind me, a low sound, and empty, like the wind in November. I looked down toward the water and glimpsed within it a face like death, which was my face: a skull with all flesh and feeling stripped away and eyes left open to look on everything, nothing, a world of winter.

The same face I saw today in the pit-trap, a ghost's image in mud. The gaze vacant, unblinking to watch me cough and choke and regain my feet. I touched my fingers to my scalp. They came away warm, wet, and my ribs throbbed with every step to carry me back toward the house, this house, and the chair at which I write—and sleep.

Another morning. The day is mild with the sun in squares upon the floor and soft wind in the trees, shaking leaves out of the buds.

Rising, I brewed coffee for the first time in months and fried bacon and potatoes together in a pan for breakfast. I spent the day by the window, watching the woods as Judah did in the days after we found the drowned body.

That was where it began, with the wet slip of his hair between my fingers. With the stench of mud from his ribcage, sealing the gaps between, and the organs inside rotting. But if that was the beginning I find I cannot imagine an ending or guess at the fate which awaits us all: the living, the dead, or those halfway between.

Even spring is a place halfway, as was that summer of three years ago, when the fierce heat lingered into September and the wind set whorls in the yellowed grass. Mornings, the sun beat down from the south, warding off rain for weeks, so the fall, we thought, would never come.

How little I understood. I was naïve, a child in soul if not in body. With Eden blooming all round I became like Man in the days before Woman was made and all of the wonders of the earth were brought to him, each in turn, and all for him to name. Or the first disciples when Christ made wine from water or cured the blind or herded demons into the driven swine. Of course they believed. With such evidence before them they could scarce have done otherwise and my faith, too, came easily, if only for a time.

One morning in July the Elder Job sought me before the break-fast bell. The meaning of my Gift was revealed to him, he said, and ushered me toward the library where we could be alone. He closed the doors and paced the room and finally halted to withdraw from his jacket a folded sheet of brown paper.

"The dreams of our sister Jerusha," he said.

He unfolded the page and smoothed it over his chest before handing it to me. The paper was plain butcher's paper covered front-to-back with angular script unlike any I had encountered. Plainly it was written in haste for the paper was often torn in chevrons where her quill had moved over the page and through it, cutting.

"The Gift of interpretation is yours," said Job. "And your hand is accounted a fine one. Therefore, Brother David, you will take the day to study Sister Jerusha's words and transcribe them as you have done the songs of the spirits. When this is done, you must give yourself to pray upon their meaning and shape your thoughts to the form of the Gift within you. Then you will tell me all you have learned. Beyond this I will say nothing more lest I cloud them, the eyes which have been given you."

He departed. The page was before me, the lines of her cramped handwriting which I strained to read as the mist boiled off and breakfast ended and my brothers and sisters went about their labors. The sun breached the tree-line to south and east and I turned my attention to my work, transcribing her words in my own hand and on white vellum as the dreamer's words demanded.

She dreamt of the days of Creation and saw the beasts of the earth emerge from a fog, formless and void. Goats and birds and cattle all appeared in the same order as in Genesis but they were white and flat, unmoving til she named the colors as she was bid and the whole of the Garden burst into flower. This was but the first of her dreams.

The weeks passed. When next she dreamt she bore witness to the Fall. August: the rot which is in life surfaced and with Mother beside her she watched the animals breeding, one with another, moving in rhythm to birth a broken world. Trees sagged with the weight of fruit on their branches, the hedgerows forming snarls of thorn and berry which went unpicked though the animals were more numerous than before. Of fruit they had no need for they feasted now on the flesh of one another even as they coupled, male with female and wolf with ewe.

Time's glass was fractured, the grains of it poured out so the wild corn sprouted and shot from the ground to attain a man's height: red in stalk and leaf and overtopped with crimson blooms the color of heart's blood. The color lingered in her mind, she wrote, even after she woke with summer's heat sitting on her chest and her nightgown soaked in sweat. She tasted the word like salt on her tongue. *Red.*

I dwelt too long upon the image. I closed my eyes and saw her waking with the blankets sliding from her, the nightgown clinging: the shape of her breasts, the dark thatch of hair between her thighs. She struck a match to light a tallow then sat by the window with the candle casting halos about her eyes and hair-ends and skin like pale syrup in its glow. She wrote as one does in the grip of mania, inclining herself over the slate and brown paper and the quill racing cross it, scratching through to stone. So quickly the dreams faded and were lost.

Once in September I rose and dressed myself at the window and watched the fog descending on the stone house. It rolled from the surrounding hills, forming waves to hide the farm-fields and the mill. A door opened downstairs: Jerusha. She had woken with the bell and donned her apron to fetch the morning's water. A footpath led from the house to the stream, a distance of fifty yards. She walked with the buckets slung from a beam across her shoulders, bent forward beneath it so she did not lift her head to see her way but entered the fog and was lost in it.

The soul contains a memory of Eden, Job once told me, while the body holds within it the memory of its Fall. By this he meant we must be vigilant, faithful to the cross we bear, but in the quiet of the stone house with fog at the window and the others at their prayers or just awaking I watched Jerusha reappear from the mist, the water weighing heavy, and thought not of Eden but of the first sin and panted after it myself, though I could not know what it would mean. Even in my sin I was an innocent.

Night has fallen. The windows are dark. I do not light the fire.

I was asleep: I had no warning.

The door shuddered with a blow which roused me and sent me stumbling cross the room, scrambling for the rifle which wasn't there. The hammering came again, splintering the paneling. The bolt, drawn fast, rattled but would not yield though the cracks widened and joined to form an elongated oval like an eye turned on its side and faced outward to catch the flash of moon from the man's eyes and rifle as he smashed in the damaged panel.

I fumbled behind me. In the dark I swept the cold stove with my hands til the matches tumbled into them. I struck one. The flame-tip leapt up shimmering to reveal the bed and the stove and the long table toward which I lunged while the assault went on and on.

The match went out in my hand and I struck the table hard. My lungs emptied. The table bucked with the impact of my body against it and skidded cross the room toward the door just as the cracked panel shattered and fell.

A hand appeared, a man's broad hand with tendons like steel wire. It snaked through the opening with fingers spread to grasp at the bolt, to pull it back.

The moonlight swam, ribbed with shadows, but I kept my feet, somehow, and drove the table-end to the door, jamming it fast under the handle.

The bolt shot back. His hand disappeared and he kicked at the door. The handle jumped but struck the table and would not turn though he redoubled his fury and ruptured the lower panel with his boot, heavy boots, like those worn by soldiers.

He was panting, grunting like a beast in heat. My lungs, bruised, expanded painfully with the breath which filled them as I dropped to hands-and-knees. The hatchet I found in its place by the door, knew its weight in my hand. I crouched beside the table.

The kicking subsided. I swallowed my breath and willed even my blood to silence as I watched for the hand to reappear, the fingers first, and then the whole of a milk-white forearm which was thickly muscled up and down its length.

I swung. The hatchet struck him below the elbow, severing tendons, glancing off bone. He bellowed. I brought the hatchet back but the hand vanished and the body with it and the shattered door gave onto a slate stoop bathed in moonlight, shining and silver but for the shadow he cast behind him as he retreated out of sight.

I listened for footsteps, heard splashing in the muck beyond the slate stair. Then a faint metallic scraping which was a hammer drawn back. I threw myself forward and was on the ground when the rifle discharged, punching a hole in the door. The ball struck the tabletop and lodged there, sawdust whirling up to catch the light through the door.

He reloaded, and again he was in motion, boots striking like flints. He thrust the gun's barrel through the broken door and drew back upon the hammer. I tasted sulfur, smoke. Silence, then, with him listening for me as I was for him and still the shot did not come.

He withdrew the rifle. A scraping of boots, a rustle of fabric, and no other sound audible as the moon slipped out of the sky. Only the blood at my temple as it circled my skull, constricting to drum about my ears, an awful pressure. The air whistled in my nostrils.

A crash from the backroom then a noise like rain on the boards as glass poured from a broken window frame. I was in motion, scuttling on hands and knees out from under the table then hurtling into the other room.

Momentum alone sufficed. I barreled into the man as he clambered through the low window, off-balancing him so that he tumbled backward out of the frame. His legs went up, showing bare feet white as bones where he had removed his boots to steal away from the steps. He hit the grass and rolled into a crouch, swinging the rifle round to fire from the shoulder.

My legs were numb, useless, but I scrabbled at the window-frame and contrived to pull myself forward, behind the wall, so the shot went wide through the window, passing close enough to rattle teeth, steal away hearing.

I could not find the hatchet. I had lost it somehow and stood up near-blind in the dark and with ears only for the bells which deafened me with the retreat of lightning which was the rifle's discharge and the thunder of its voice. He was reloading, I knew, and did not think, but plunged through the window head-first, striking him in the chest. He flew back with my body against him but threw me clear and straddled me about the center so we rolled together down the rise.

We struck the ditch, the mud which pooled round the steps and the first weeds pushing through. We wrestled with our hands about the rifle, but he would not let go or loosen his grip for all I perched upon his chest and trapped the barrel with my weight. We were quiet, had breath only for the struggle. His legs flailed behind me, useless, but he pulled down on the rifle, dragging me with it til our faces were close, separated by no more than half-a-foot. His eyes were open, I saw, and very wide. I shifted position. I drove my knee up between his legs and leant into the blow to mash the soft tissue. He did not react but met my gaze with eyes showing black for the faint sheen of light on a raft of passing cloud above us.

His head snapped up, pulping my nose. I stumbled back and struck the hillside, swallowing the iron taste of blood as my nose split and emptied itself down my face. The man rolled over onto his hands and knees and stood up, shaky, then staggered toward the wood with the rifle slung cross his back, favoring his right leg as he ran.

Clouds were passing, flowing with the Milky Way across the sky. The moon re-emerged to light upon the man as he stumbled through the orchard to the forest's margin where the trees like nets parted and closed round him.

His boots he left beside the door. Pointed toes. Dark leather and light. They were the same as those I had buried with the dead man but appeared new. The insides stank of mold as though left for weeks with water standing in them. The soles. I turned over the boots to scrutinize their undersides, his initials carved upside-down in the bottom of the heel. *A.F.* rather than *I.V.* I brought them into the house and placed them near the stove to dry then turned the table upright to cover the door, nailing two boards across to secure it into place.

I saw to the backroom. The window had shattered inward, showering down glass which winked and sparkled on the floor. One hound's tooth bit deep, savaging the man's ankle and spraying down the wall. I swept up the glass-shards from the ground and retrieved the blankets from my pack, untouched since my return.

My nose was leaking. Warm blood filmed on my lips, painting them scarlet, like the color of the corn in Jerusha's dream. I tore strips from a blanket and used these to wipe my mouth and staunch the flow and sop the blood from the wall. The other blanket I nailed to the frame to ward off the draft then blocked the window with a low shelf.

Inside I lit the stove and breathed upon the coals. The spirit came into them. Sensation returned, and pain. The bells of my ears ceased from striking and I heard soft footfalls overhead. Her voice from the nursery: no longer singing but weeping, wailing over the shattered crib where no baby slept.

I stopped my ears with wadded cloth and stoked the fire high, making light enough to see the blood-flecks on my hands and spattered down the page, showing crimson where firelight fell across it. The color, like her grief, held within itself the whole of hell's terror and desolation, as did the screaming which came from the woods in answer.

Judah whimpering, beaten, howling in his pain. *Red.*

❦

Midday and the wind blows warm, the flue thrown wide to catch it so the fire wells up bright and hot. The man's boots steam, releasing an odor of old rain. I wake with the stink, breathing in blood through my ruined nose. I ache. I lie upon the floor with the journal resting open on my breast and the pencil moving over the page, keeping pace with my mind, as the past weeks return in fragments. The memories twist in my hands, bending to one side and another in the manner of a blacksmith's puzzle.

Job made one for me. I was a child of seven or eight and the puzzle occupied my attention for hours upon a rainy Sabbath when I should have been at my prayers. The puzzle was fashioned from three black twists of metal which Job had forged himself and contrived to braid together with a delicacy which seemed impossible given the broadness of his hands. It was a thing of beauty, and of grace, inasmuch as it was made to be broken and the pieces separated with ease if one but knew the trick of it.

For the whole of that Sabbathday I tested the iron twists between my hands till the workings of my mind came to mirror the shape of the puzzle and I saw at once how it was done. The pieces separated and fell from my hands. They struck the ground, skittering, but I did not move to collect them. I did not move at all, being like John at Patmos when the Revelation was visited upon him, wonder mingling with awe in that moment and Heaven's weight pressing down.

Years later, and it was the same when Jerusha told me of her final dreams, the two of them together, which came to her on a night in September and which she kept secret from all but me. She would not confide even in the Eldress but contrived a meeting between us in a place beyond the cornfields where the rubble wall was highest. By then the peak of summer was past and the year had slumped into autumn. The wall was over our heads, and we were hidden, but the brothers were at their work amidst the corn so Jerusha was obliged to whisper as she spoke.

In the first of the dreams, she said, she woke to find the Garden crumbled into chalk. The earth was barren and gave no life and the beasts had gone from it, breeding til their numbers stripped the land bare of sustenance whereupon they resorted to cannibalism so there remained but a single wolf, a male, who fell upon himself in his hunger, consuming his own flesh. The pain was such he screeched and moaned but appeared unable to stop till his bones, licked clean, settled into the ash which was the soil and always the wind blowing dust like snow.

For if they do these things when the tree is green what will they do in the dry? There was soot in her mouth, its bitter taste on her tongue, and her doll's house had caved in upon itself. No roof, the sky's open maw overhead, and even Mother had deserted her.

"I was alone," she told me. "And then I saw him."

The man roamed naked through the wild, solitary now where once God had walked beside him. He covered his face and wept for grief and saw his way through the gaps in his fingers. He was tall, muscled and sleek with fine hairs bristling down the length of his body.

She went to him, though she did not see his face, and afterward she slept in his arms and woke to a damp bed, a freezing room. The rain which had delayed so long now tapped upon the window to call her from the Garden. She thrashed beneath the blankets. She shivered and prayed til sleep returned to her and with it the dreaming.

The Garden was transformed. The soil was dark and rich, the color of spent coffee, raked and plowed and planted by unseen hands which had sowed the earth with new growth. Blue blossoms shaped like stars surfaced from the black and bloomed themselves inside-out, forming the trees which groaned for the weight of fruit upon them: white lemons, green plums. All was fruiting, all fecund.

There were pumpkins and squash the size of a man's head and the corn-stalks all round soaring to a height of twenty feet and laden up and down with corn like knobs of polished silver.

She hungered: she ate her fill. The plums were crisp but with a flavor like new-churned butter and the corn was sweet as berries picked at summer's height. She filled her belly then took to wandering in the Garden and was not surprised to find the man beside her. They walked together, hand-in-hand, though she could not discern his face or that of the girl-child who danced toward them out of the rows of sweet corn.

"My daughter," Jerusha said, though she could scarce believe it. Her body was a fallen thing, made of flesh and sin, while the child before her was a being of radiance knit from threads of light, or joy, or the laughter which trailed behind her as she whirled and spun and came to a halt before Jerusha.

The child giggled, nervous. She joined her hands and lifted them together with an apple cupped between them, an offering. The skin was smooth, without blemish.

"What did you do?" I asked.

"I had no choice," she said. "What could I do but take it?"

All this she told to me. She leant forward, expecting no answer, but whispering with her face concealed for the hair which hung before it.

Her words were as a blacksmith's puzzle: it twisted in my hands with the meaning of her dreams. In June her first dream showed the creation with the naming of the colors like the naming of the beasts and all the world made blessed and new. In August her second dream portrayed the serpent, which was lust, and the sin which was our Fall. Her doll's house buckled beneath its weight and so too did Man when he yielded to temptation.

Then came autumn and she dreamt of the Garden in ashes, seared down to bedrock and lost beyond reclaiming when Man fell and Christ Himself was dead. He had gone up on the tree as was prophesied with the two thieves beside him and even Mother was in the ground.

But Jerusha had dreamt again. In her early dreams she beheld the Creation and the Fall but this her final dream was a Day of Resurrection, the spirit and the body together and the Garden made new from the rubble of itself. Sweet corn thrusting from the earth and blossoms unfolding in a riot of color, rippling as they spun, like the robes of the world's dead emerging clean from the earth, arrayed in robes of the spirit like the invisible garments worn at meeting.

All this I told to her, but Jerusha smiled and shook her head. Her body, she said, was made for more than dreaming, and she took my hand in hers. I was shaking—she was too—and the future opened before us to give onto a world of endless flowering. Tree of Knowledge. Tree of Life. Her hand in mine as the child, our child, danced out of the corn, and the puzzle slipped and separated in my hands, a revelation.

That sensation.

I am thinking of it now to recall the graves in the pine-grove, the river with the dead man in its grasp. His body in its tattered clothes. The boots which sit beside the wood stove.

"Take my coat too, will you."

My thoughts turn to the soldier, the man who had lived in this house with his family and who had left it to the forest when it was full to the rafters with his belongings: furniture, farm-tools, the journal in which I write these words. He had torn the pages from the front and burnt them in the basin, leaving only a name by which to remember him.

August Fitch. He had flown to war and arms and returned with his sergeant's stripes to find his house deserted, his wife and child gone. He must have stalked the woods like a wild thing only to return to the vale after all these years wearing boots with his initials and a dead man's stench upon them. Perhaps it happened in this way. Fitch came over the snowy pass in the latter days of winter. He lingered at the forest's margin, watching. Without question he was an able woodsman and left no tracks nor sign of his presence, but Judah sensed him, his nearness, and was afraid. He feared the man as he feared nothing else, and hated him, and followed him, and went to the man as though to his master, his first master, the man who had abandoned him to that shallow pit with the red roots closing round.

A final image. Blackened leather, white bone. Rotten soles carved with a man's initials: not *IV* as I had thought but *AF*, the letters inverted, the finer lines erased by rot. A.F. August Fitch. He had seen me with the drowned corpse and returned at night to dig the body out of the ground. He had wrenched off the boots to have them cleaned, and stretched, and later he donned them himself for all they still carried the reek of decay. The drowned man, then, was not Fitch. He could not have been though he wore his boots, and Fitch had reburied the bones after the theft, tamping down earth to give no sign.

All nonsense, of course, but I see no other explanation, and Fitch is real enough. He stole from the dead as he stole from the living, and last night, he meant to take from me this house and all it holds within it. And I did not let it go. I fought him for it and with a fury I had not thought possible so that I believe I would have died for it and for nothing where there is nothing left to save. Only this season's emptiness, ghosts of winter's ending.

The hour is near. Dusk is upon me, smell of spring upon the air. Some few birds in the orchard, wind in the shattered frame. I will go back to the grove. I will take the hatchet with me, a spade to open the ground wherein the drowned man lies.

In my hands, the puzzle-pieces twist and bend, will not be parted.

⁊

Things I have witnessed—

Evening, and the sun was gone, the moon as yet unrisen, when I stole from the house. I dropped from the broken window and scuttled away on all fours to the shelter of the apple-trees. I expected a shot from the woods, which did not come, and regained my feet within the shadow of the trees. Orchard's edge: I paused with that stretch of open grass before me, the blood pulsing in my ears and throat. Then sprinted for the tree-line.

I reached it. I covered my face to breach the wall of branches with buds like thorns which whipped at my hands then yielded to the dark and silent spaces of the night. I slowed. I strained my eyes for gaps in the leaf-cover where I might walk and go unheard. For the man had my rifle whereas I carried no weapon save the hatchet at my belt and the spade which I held with both hands, the steel head gleaming with the bands of moon through which I passed.

The distance to the pines is scarcely a mile but I had to be quiet, careful, and did not reach the grove for hours. The moon was up and wreathed with stars like the brow about an open eye, round at the full to scatter its glow about the pine trees' canopy. The light shone back flashes from the ground, glinting off damp needles and the rain-washed cross which marked the dead man's grave between two dead trees.

I was quick. I crouched in the moonlight, exposed on all sides, and chopped at the ground with the spade's sharp edge. The grave was shallow, the frost melted away, but the work proved harder than anticipated, for the ground was tangled in wiry roots that ran in knots beneath the leaf-mold so my spade was near-blunted by the time the first bones surfaced, looking like old ivory or fish-bones hauled up in nets of red root: they severed down the spade's head, releasing gouts of dark fluid to stain the spine, the ribcage compassed about with suspenders and hung with cloth fragments turned brown with their days in the earth.

The skull appeared. The jaw was broken, hanging, cracked by roots which massed like red wires in the hollow of the cranium. They pushed out from the mouth, writhing with the moon behind my head and my shadow stretching before me. The stench—

I coughed up strings of bile but did not cease from my labors. The spade was useless and so I chopped at the root-mass with the hatchet til all was soaked through in the same dark fluid and the pelvis lay exposed: half-fleshed, the blue-gray trousers clinging. The boots were on his feet. They were warped with rot, toes tapered to points and *I.V.—A.F.*—cut into the sole. They were identical in all respects to those Fitch had left behind him and indeed the corpse was clothed as Fitch had been in gray pants and suspenders and a linen undershirt.

The air whistled over my head, the clap of a rifle following. The shot struck the trees beyond and I threw myself forward, striking my elbow and jarring loose the hatchet. I reached for it but could not get hold and besides there was no time: I heard from behind me the scrape of the rod in the breech, the hammer drawn back with a click. I slithered forward on my belly, tumbling into the grave even as Fitch's second shot set the earth in clots to spitting.

I was cornered, a fox at bay. I burrowed with my nails in the roots which walled the edges of the grave. From above I heard the rifle primed and cocked then the crunch of old needles as Fitch drew near my place of hiding.

He walked with an unhurried ease and paused to whistle cross the dead wood. Three shrill notes: a huntsman's call. I raked my fingers through the earth, searching for aught which might serve for a weapon. My hand closed round the skull, and I clutched at the eye-holes, tearing it free of the spinal column and the roots which held it fast.

The skull was in my hands. The moonlight wavered, dimming, and I waited for his shadow to cover me. The air soured in my lungs. I tasted bile but still there came no shadow, though I listened hard for his breathing and did not dare to raise my head until I heard the din of movement from the living trees at the pine grove's edge.

Judah. His muzzle black with dried blood, his coat streaked and matted as he staggered toward the grave, favoring his good leg. Fitch had vanished. Even in the dark the man's bare footprints were visible, approaching the grave then ceasing abruptly, as if in mid-stride, and the rifle and cartridge box lay nearby, abandoned.

My grip relaxed. The skull slipped from my hand.

"Judah," I said. He whined but turned from the hand I offered. I retrieved the cartridge box and shouldered the rifle. "Come," I said, and he fell into step beside me, the moon riding high to light the way. Soon we were out of the dead-wood with the river-sounds fading behind us, but the stench of mud clung to my hands and nails and lingers there still, hours later, as I write these words, though the whole of another day has passed and the dusk is settling in.

I returned to the pines at dawn. Judah accompanied me. He was scarred and limping, seemingly half-starved, but his fear had left him and he trotted beside me with ears erect and nose to the ground and even chased a squirrel to the mouth of its hiding place, pulling it up shrieking. I winced at the snap of its neck, the silence which followed. I sat down, aching, and trembled for sleeplessness, cold and wearied at the core. I closed my eyes to hear him gut the beast in his teeth and sup the heart out of its ribs. When it was done he deposited the ragged thing before me. He pawed at the mud, whining, imploring me to eat, but I shook my head. I could not touch that ropey mass of fur and could not meet Judah's gaze.

His dark eyes were half-obscured, cupped in a face which was puckered and swollen where Fitch had cut deep and the lash-wounds down his side were beaded with clear fluid, dry blood. I covered my face with my hands and would have wept, I think, but felt the warm tongue lapping at my fingers and knew we must go on.

We gained the dead wood, the drowned man's grave with the earth heaped up round it and the skull mired in muck at some yards' distance. The eyeholes were packed tight with soil while scraps of flesh clung to the forehead and red shards of root and vegetal matter protruded from the teeth. I knelt to collect it from the ground then straightened up with its weight between my hands.

Judah growled, barked. He hovered over the open hole with his snout in the dirt and his tail whipping about, yelping till I saw them, the tracks which surrounded us, wolf-tracks. The pack had passed through in the night but lingered on finding the open grave and fell upon the corpse with unusual savagery. I inspected the grave. The wolves had gnawed through the roots and sucked the last of the flesh from the bones, lapping out the marrow then leaving the cracked remnants in white chips scattered like pebbles surfacing from the soil.

The ground, I observed, was curiously warm, damp with a greasy substance like half-congealed blood. The dead man's under-shirt was similarly red and sopping where it lay half-shredded in the mud and his boots were stiff with it, as were my own, when last night I crouched within that open grave with the severed roots belching warm fluid in rhythmic spurts, as with the beating of a great god's heart.

The skull I placed upon the ground behind me then inclined myself over the grave with one arm extended. My fingertips brushed the broken roots where they breached the earthen wall. They were soft and yielding, fibrous. Red liquid dripped from them, staining the earth and filming on my skin. I raised my hand to my mouth but the substance, whatever its nature, was without taste or odor. I stood. I wiped my hands upon my trousers then picked up the skull and carried it before me as I descended the bank to the river's edge.

I did not hesitate. I heaved in the skull and watched it sink and did not look away till the water's surface again was smooth. Then I struck away to the west, moving upriver, following the course of it for some hundred yards along the boundary of the dead and dying wood.

I found the place without difficulty. The soil was stripped, washed out where heavy rains had flooded down the bank and left the earth a mess of exposed roots: ruddy and dull and sheathed in bark. Some were grown thick as a man's neck though the ground all about was barren, flooded clear of vegetation but for withered sedge, sagging elms, and below them, the roots of a great pine tree which was always spreading, finding its anchor by doubling its shape in the ground.

Here I had digged Judah out of the earth. Two years and more have passed since then and the pit has vanished into the root mass. I looked eastward to the pines, which were plainly visible, even at this distance. They burst out of the spring wood, unfolding on a slate sky and somehow taller than I remembered, as though they had never ceased from growing.

My mind was full of dreaming. I made my way back toward the tall pines and did not notice Judah as he appeared and walked alongside me. We reached the pines, that forest of snags and rubble with the black grove at its center, pine-boughs like rafters high above.

The sun was out. It tilted through gaps in the greenery to fall in bars on the barren ground where wolf's tracks joined and tailed like the script upon a page. I counted the tracks of at least half-a-dozen beasts weaving in and out of one another and circling the blooded pit where the man's bones had lain. Some tracks were broad as a mule's while others appeared far smaller. Among them I discerned the naked footprints of a human child, a baby's feet, and her palm-print too where she traveled on all fours, nails like claws making furrows in the earth.

The light shifted: I was on the ground.

My face was in the mud, one arm outthrust to touch my palm to hers and cover it completely. The shadows moved round me, curving toward the grove at dead-wood's center, and the sun had passed from view when I stood with the pines behind me, looming up taller than the Stone House and older than its granite, soft wind shaking down dust and the fallen needles glinting. Judah whined, anxious to be away. The palm-print had vanished, obscured by my own, and her footprints had faded from the earth.

PART FOUR

X X X X X

Five days of nothing, no words, and only these marks to show the time.

Judah is sick. His wounds have turned bad, his coat thinned into patches. His joints swell so the pain keeps him from sleeping. He lies awake moaning through the night and will not eat but lifts his head only to drink from his bowl and sop the bottom dry. Otherwise he is listless, unmoving, and does not move from his place beside the stove where he pants and shivers though the weather is changing and I build the fire high.

He is unrecognizable or near to it, eyes sunken and muzzle swollen. The lash-wounds scab and suppurate. Pus runs from his chin, mingling with a crimson fluid redder than any blood. I wipe it away. For the second time in my life I am become as a nursemaid, gentle as the mother I never knew. With such tenderness I wash away the blood and filth and afterward wring out the soiled dressings. Then I walk outside and vomit into the bushes.

Spring is come. The white blossoms wither and drop from the trees. Buds explode into green sheaves like waving hands which turn with the wind passing by them. The air outside is balmy, perfumed, but the stench indoors is unbearable, fetid and sweet like fresh decay.

I am conscious of a quickening, unfelt these many years since those September days when Jerusha and I contrived our meetings beyond the fields when the others were at their work. The corn grew high enough to overtop the fieldstones, and we were well concealed, hidden from human eyes though the whole of the world opened to us like a flower.

The flesh had ceased to drag on us. We felt instead a sensation of lightening. The realms of the spirit were at hand, descending from heaven like the New Jerusalem to enfold the flesh within itself and join us together, body and spirit, even as we were joined in that moment with the stone wall at her back and her single shuddering cry of ecstasy or pain.

We were made new. Our bodies were as resurrection bodies, not crosses to carry but vessels to fill. The heat of the spirit overbrimmed us, pouring forth like an anointing oil heady with the smells of wet soil, churned earth: the dead garden of her dreaming which we seeded with new growth til we were exhausted and panting and summer's glory spent.

September into October. The corn was cut and carried in. The first frost settled into the ground and the dreams they came no longer. In truth, we had no need of them for our waking life was become one dreaming, but the Elder Job grew anxious. The weeks passed and he sought out Rose of a morning and begged her for news she could not give. By October he believed himself abandoned. His sleep became restless, broken, and he took to pacing the brethren's halls by night, meditating on such Gifts as are given and taken away.

The Eldress Rose, by contrast, was pragmatic. The dreams, she said, were plainly false visions, sent to tempt the fellowship of believers into the sin of spiritual pride. The two quarreled fiercely over this point. One evening, after supper, I heard them in the library. The door they shut behind them, but I listened at the keyhole.

"You yourself feared the devil's snare," she said. "You forbade us speaking of the visions lest the whole of the fellowship come to share in your affliction."

"My affliction," he repeated. "You liken it to a sickness."

"A sickness, yes. And in the same way, Job, it will pass."

He laughed, hollowly. "I am all bitterness. All hell."

"You disgrace yourself," Rose replied, furious. "Your despair is ill-suited to your place within the Church. Your self-pity! It is that of a drunkard when the spell of intoxication has passed and he finds the bottle is dry. Or have you forgotten what you used to be?"

She left him. Her great bulk passed over the keyhole and I flattened myself to the wall as the door opened and closed and she hurried away up the sisters' stair, long skirts swishing.

I lingered at the door. I listened for the rise and fall of his breath behind the door then thrust my eye to the keyhole.

The Elder stood at the window with spine erect and a world of falling night before him. He did not move though the minutes passed but stood and stared into the glass which showed only his reflection. I watched and did not go to him, though I yearned to give comfort as he had once comforted me, to tell him what I had learned.

If only he might understand, I thought. The Gift had not been stolen away as he believed. Rather we had taken it into ourselves where it had bound us spirit and flesh, joining us together in the heart we made between us.

"Listen," Jerusha said and lowered my ear to her belly.

࿇

Hear it now. Judah's blood beats fast for the sickness which has him in its vise, which will not let him go. Sweat pours from his paws like drool from his ruined mouth and the end it must come soon lest I be forced to make of things an ending.

Already I have lingered too long. He is nearly blind, eyes vanished into the swelling about his skull and snout. The purple scabbing rips open with every movement of his head, releasing gouts of fluid which splash between his paws, forming clots where they pool in the cracks between the boards. He cannot sleep or eat or partake of water though I force it on him.

This afternoon I knelt before him and took his muzzle into my hands, easing his jaws apart and wedging them open with a pencil. He made no protest, and did not stir, though I brought the canteen to his lips and tipped the water down his throat, and all to no purpose, for he could not swallow. The liquid dribbled from his teeth, mingled with bile and spattering the floor.

An hour or more was spent in this way till the canteen was empty and Judah, moaning, dropped off to sleep in a puddle of water flecked red with blood and white with his sputum. He woke up screaming. That was an hour ago and still he has not ceased from it, though his cry is hoarse and ragged as a wildcat's.

The wolves, emboldened, draw near at the sounds of his agony. They pace beyond the orchard with the maple trees behind them, moonlight on the apple-blossoms as they fall. Their voices they lift with the rising crescent to attain an unearthly pitch, high as that of the sisters in the ecstasy of their dancing but with such sorrow in it, such pain, a lamentation.

Judah moans. The voice fails in his throat, his tongue near-to-shredded. Outside the wolves continue their baying while upstairs she stomps and screams and bangs through the ceiling with her fists upon the floor. I stop my ears with wadding and shout myself hoarse then slip through the window with the rifle in my hand. I fire toward the orchard, the wolves. I mean only to frighten them, but they do not move and the howling does not cease.

They are as watchers at a deathbed. They sense his end as Judah does, watching me through slits in the scabbing as I return inside and reload the rifle.

I sit at this stove with the gun barrel laid cross my legs and my eyes on the window, the room's reflection swimming there. I close my eyes, unstop my ears. The wolves depart and the house lapses

into silence: his wheezing breath and no sounds from upstairs, the
eastern sky still silver with the moon in its descending—

ॐ

I carried him outside. He weighed little more than a child where the
muscle and fat had sloughed off the bones and he was half-bald
besides, the fur coming away clumps, his face made tumorous with
swelling. I cradled him in my arms. I pressed him to my body,
hoping to still the shivers which racked him despite the warmth of
the morning and the sun shining from a sky of lapis lazuli. His
breath was shallow and rapid: blood-warm, reeking of fever. He
whined.

We entered the orchard, where I laid him down amidst the crush
of fallen blossoms. Sunlight flashed from the rifle's barrel then
green where it streamed through branches surrounding, the layer-
ing of leaf on shadow. Judah heaved onto his side, collapsing, a
house tumbled into its foundations. The swelling blinded him so he
could not see me but listened as I saw to my labors with the rifle on
the ground and the dull spade in hand.

Birds flitted between the orchard-branches. Their songs formed
rings about us, moving outward in concentric circles toward the
woods to echo in the trees with a sound of distant church-bells, fast-
running water. His ears twitched, listening, and the flowers drifted
about him.

My footsteps thudded, spade cutting sod. Two years of exile,
three graves dug. I have become a tiller of soil as Adam was, and
Cain, and only crosses to show for it. The hole I dug narrow but
deep, its sides shored with pine planks, deeper by far than the pit in
which I had found him two years ago.

I could delay no longer. I knelt before him and gathered him into
my arms. Then walked with him to the grave and placed him within
it as tenderly as I could manage. He settled to the bottom, all sinew
and bone and his chest heaving with the effort of breathing. I
brought the rifle to my shoulders and pulled back the hammer.

His head twitched, raised. He gazed up, blindly, eyes like slits in that gash of earth. The muzzle dropped, exposing the bald crown of his head, an invitation. I depressed the trigger.

A thunderclap and all the birds were quiet. The wind dragged itself through the orchard and across the grave's opening, raining down blossoms. White petals filled the hole I had dug, the wound I had made. They clung to the gray flesh of his brain, which was visible for a moment where it sat within the ruptured skull before the blood boiled out of the wound, hiding all save the floating blossoms which turned upon the flow til they were red and sodden, sinking.

He did not fall. His shattered head lifted to show the sightless eyes, red fluid pouring from behind them. His mouth dropped open, the tongue dry and twitching. The voice rattled in his throat as with a dying breath but the noise went on and his head did not drop. From the grave he watched me through eyes which showed nothing. He pleaded for death, a second shot from the rifle which did not come. The gun was discharged and I had brought no cartridges.

I panicked. I took hold of the gun by the barrel, jabbing downward at the open bullet-wound. The skull splintered at the impact, collapsing inward. The brain, exposed, pulsed in its casing, woven throughout with red wires which seemed to resist the blows somehow though I swung at the head with the rifle til all else was reduced to shapeless tissue, chipped bone: red and gray and the apple-blossoms falling, covering all.

But still his suffering went on and knew no end even as the awful rattling continued and would not cease though my hands and arms grew numb with exhaustion and I dropped the rifle. It cratered the mud and glistened where it lay, greasy with brain-matter.

I was sick with horror, guilt. I could do nothing though Judah watched without eyes, the tongue clicking in his throat.

He exhaled. A strangely human sound, heavy with defeat.

I ran.

🍎

Hours later—

The dusk is here, and I am still running. I light candles down-stairs and fire the stove and sing to myself in the words of the angels as I pace the upper hall shutting the windows which were left open this morning to vent the smells of illness.

The night-sounds vanish—peepers, songbirds—but the hell of his anguish roils in my brain: the clicking of his tongue, the thin strains of his moaning. Silence breaks over me like the waves of shaking which seized the Eldress Rose when the angel was upon her.

The shadows lengthened, spreading to blacken the walls and I turned my face from the shapes which swam within them, glimpsed in a mirror dimly. Judah's snout all ruins and the shattered teeth thrusting through. The brain pulsing inside its red net. Pine-roots over-spilling a drowned man's grave. I cannot bear it, cannot sleep.

The puzzle is unraveled, its pattern revealed, but there is nothing for it now and nothing to do until daybreak. I sit beside the cold stove and keep this vigil though the candles sputter and go out till only one is left burning. The wick gutters and spits to give the lambent glow by which I write, conjuring the past and its ghosts.

Autumn's end. The end of her dreaming and the days which fol-lowed. Jerusha was often sick of a morning and given to oversleeping so her work was affected though she took pains to conceal her illness. But she could not hide her pallor or diminishing appetite any more than she could extinguish the light which glowed within her.

One or two among the sisters were heard to remark on Jerusha's sickness and what they termed "her changeable temperament," but they were as naïve as I was. They were raised within the Village and knew of no other life. Only the Eldress Rose suspected. Though she did not speak of it, she had come late to the faith and left behind her a brute of a husband who had killed her infant son. Late in October the Eldress took to watching Jerusha when the younger woman was at her work or at worship and noticed the way her hand strayed toward her stomach to speak the name of the Lord. Like a spider, then, the Eldress lay in wait while frost formed up and down the windows, turning the stone house cold and dim.

Then pounced. The Eldress cornered Jerusha in her retiring room after breakfast when the others were long ago risen and about their work. Jerusha denied nothing. She did not speak at all but only bared her belly to the Eldress to show the rounded flesh and God's heart beating behind it, ripples spreading on the skin.

Mid-morning: the Elder Job was at the forge. Rose shouted for him from the house and her tone was such that he came at a run while still in his apron. He feared a kitchen-fire, perhaps, or some other disaster but little guessed at the nature. He found Rose in the meeting hall and Jerusha beside her with her breasts plainly showing through her nightgown and both hands cupped over her belly.

The Eldress said: "We must send for Brother David."

Job called to the orphan boy Aaron who was raking the garden. Aaron found me at work in the mill fitting bolts to the lathes. The boy was nervous and given to stuttering but said I must come with him. I entered the meeting hall and found Jerusha seated on the floor with back straight and eyes forward and the Elders to either side of her, their faces somber, stripped.

Job dismissed the boy. He paced with his back to me. He said nothing, waiting, while Rose stared ahead unblinking with fingers like claws where they hooked in her skirts. Jerusha's eyes found mine and she smiled through the hair which fell about her face and with a glow like August sun about her so I knew we were found out.

"Tell them," she said, softly, and I did.

I was passionate, eloquent. I was a man on trial with the Judge in robes and glory crowned and seated silent before me as I pled my case. I told of my abandonment at the Village gate and of the girl who found me and brought me in though the storm raged all about. We were joined together even then, I said, though we knew it naught, and I endured years of anguish and doubt til the Gift of Interpretation was granted me that I might understand the Gifts which were sent to Jerusha, the dreams which carried in themselves the weight of prophecy, its awful import.

"Inventions," Rose said. "False visions. They ceased as suddenly as they came."

"They did not," I said and addressed myself to Job. I told him of the Final Dream and of the promise of the New Jerusalem, speaking to his back while Rose gazed on in fury.

"You often spoke of the cross," I said, "the long shadow it casts. You said I must recognize it for itself so I might take comfort in its burden. This I have done. Only this. The cross is our sin, as you said. In our ignorance we murdered the living God and nailed His body to it. But through death was our redemption and the cross we made became the instrument of our salvation. It stands on Calvary as it has always done but its roots are in Eden, the same as those that feed the Tree of Life. The Garden, then, is immanent in the cross and we carry it with us all our lives just as Jerusha carries inside herself the seed of a new spring, a flourishing without end. She is to be mother to a world as Mary was and Ann. But have you eyes to see?"

With these same words Job had sought to console me when I was young and afflicted with doubt. But he found no comfort in them himself and merely shook his head slowly, without understanding, his broad hands hanging at his sides. His voice failed. The words cracked and dropped from his mouth like pebbles. "No more," he said.

"Please," I said. "Look at me."

He turned. Our eyes met and I beheld in him the black gulfs of his despair, the depths toward which he had plunged himself all those years ago. He survived his fall, but the river's blackness remained and appeared wider now for the reflection which swam within it, my reflection, and I did not look away till the dark in him eclipsed the lights of his eyes and he turned from me to hide his weeping.

The Eldress took him by the arm and spoke some soothing words into his ear, though I could not make them out. Then she turned her gaze on me and it was venomous and black as a serpent's with undisguised hatred. I was shamed by it, and looked away, but Jerusha was unaffected. She smiled at Rose or perhaps at no one and did not cease from smiling with her hands folded over her belly as though to catch between them the sound of a heart beating.

We were punished. We were orphans alike with nowhere to go and exiled to nowhere in our un-repentance. Others before us had been found out in their sin and separated man from woman and sent to east and west, never again to meet. This was the custom within the Church but Jerusha and I would not be divided. We refused all inducements to atone and pledged ourselves to leave together with the babe she carried though it meant our condemnation. When the appointed day came we were allowed nothing save the clothes we wore and a little money, enough to see us to the next town.

The money was Job's doing. Of this I feel certain though he would not speak to me or to anyone and withdrew deeper into himself—his true self, as he saw it—which was the flesh he had left behind. From a peddler he acquired a bottle of gin or whiskey, something foul, and drank it down himself on the eve of our leaving. Later that night with the lamps all extinguished I heard him from the sickroom, his heavy tread up and down the brethren's stair. He sang bawdy songs then hymns and all with such desperation, such longing.

Ash lach in
bi mor na, o
da rim a, e
o

His shattered voice like the tongues of angels, singing the first of the songs I had transcribed. I heard Jerusha too. Her voice drifted down to me from the sisters' sickroom where she was prisoned. The same room where I had seen her so many years ago when I was a child and my mind held only music: the song she sang, which was Mother's.

We did not sleep. The dawn came and we walked out together. None were there to bid us farewell. Man and woman, the believers carried on with their work, tending to the animals or building up fires in the kitchen. The Eldress Rose watched us go, if only to make sure of our leaving, but turning back toward the house, I glimpsed a face at the library window.

Job. His drowned features, black stones of his eyes.

The cattle-track struck north toward the woods and ridges beyond, and Jerusha and I walked hand in hand along it, skirting wood-lots and rubble-walls, the fields by which we lay together in the cradle of our summer. All was transformed in the wake of autumn's passing, the corn reduced to rows of stubble and a fine rain falling as we passed beyond the outermost wall and the Village disappeared, lost to sight behind the veils of blowing mist.

Forest-sounds enfolded us: music of drifting leaves, dripping boughs. The songbirds were gone, though crows remained, and ravens. They called to one another as we climbed for the whole of that first day, the track rising sharply beneath us to meet that distant rim of hills, white with frost like winter's breath upon us. We were not afraid. In our exile we were even then in Eden, knowing nothing of this valley or the pine grove. That low hill with its three pines like crosses at Golgotha where Adam's skull was buried and the living God succumbed.

Abba abba lema sabachthani? Saying this the breath passed from Him and so too the soul we shared like the flesh of our flesh, dead in the womb with the cord wrapped round.

Daybreak. Judah's cries cut deeper and I must go.

It is done. I brought matches with me and rags, a length of cord which I looped into a coil and tucked into a pocket of Fitch's haversack. The haversack I slung from one shoulder where a wood-axe also rested, the blade newly sharpened. At my side I carried a small ironbound cask, which fit snugly in the crook of my arm but was heavy, and it pained me to carry it. I resorted to use of a strap. This I cinched round the body of the cask and secured it to the cord that I might drag it behind me as I walked.

Progress was slow, tending to east while the sun swung round behind me to shine out of the south. The day was warm and fragrant. Leaves twitched with birds in their singing while the undergrowth rustled, red squirrels surfacing, darting out of sight.

The pines appeared, adrift like ghosts in the crush of greenery. I was close. I reached the edge of the dying wood and turned again toward the river, striking north to the bend where I had found Judah, two years ago, writhing in the grave his master dug.

Fitch. He was a beast of a man, well-suited to war and arms, his sergeant's stripes. His family deserted him so the house was empty on his return and he had no one, no companion but the dog who feared his master too much to flee from him as did his family.

He raged. He tore the pages from this journal and drank down the bottles of scotch which I had found years later then left the house without his gun, his coat. He followed the river to the east past the beaver pond, his dog beside him. They came to the bend, where the river turns to south and narrows, running downhill.

He meant to leave the valley. Perhaps he intended to ford the river and Judah defied him: I do not know. But in his frenzy he savaged the dog with his boots then buried the beast in a shallow grave before splashing into the water, drunk and half-mad. He lost his footing and was swept downriver. He drowned, hooked like a fish in a forked willow-branch, and there he lay for years while the pines grew taller, deeper, and the roots crept farther afield for purchase as their crowns unfolded and spread.

In time the roots reached the hole wherein he had buried the dog. They breached the earthen walls. They shattered the bones and compassed the skull within their grasp, puncturing the spine first then the brain til from the broken flesh there rose the resurrected body.

Judah. He was not of the flesh but of the spirit and could not die so long as the tree held his bones within its grasp. I was blind. I had mistaken spirit for the flesh and lived with his ghost for years while the tree's roots churned and collapsed the bank and his grave was all a snarl, filled with roots as pale and tough as horn. For this reason I had brought the wood-axe. The first blow shuddered off the bark as did the second and third til I repositioned myself and stood with both feet braced to bring the axe down over my head.

I swung. This time the blade bit, cutting a narrow channel the width of a fingernail's mark. The cut burbled and overflowed to spill out crimson sap the color of new blood. The liquid trickled from the wound then flew in droplets from the axe-blade as I struck home again and again. The root shattered. Warm sap gushed out of the wound, pouring down over my feet to fill my boots, and the air itself was greasy, reeking of offal.

The flow slowed and ceased. Morning passed to a heat like summer. I removed my shirt and mopped the sweat out of my hair then hacked at the cut to widen it. The axe breached a second layer of root-matter and again the red water spurted out, wetting my pants and soaking them through so I appeared as though I had crossed an abattoir on hands-and-knees, blood pooled shin-deep on the killing floor.

I dulled the axe. I sharpened it then dulled it again while sunlight licked cross my back like a fire's twitching tongue. My vision blurred. My hands went numb for the twist of the ash within them and I clambered down the bank to the water to wash my hands and face and drink down the sweat I had lost with the sunlight still on me, blinding, beating down.

I returned to the task of destruction. With the axe in both hands I broke through the masses of braided root til the muscles failed me at last and I could scarcely heft the axe though my strength it must suffice for the final task before me.

The sap drained out of the cut. With my shirt I blotted the edges of the wound to dry them then knotted the rags and cord together to feed the length of it into the hole. The tail-end protruded, trailing a distance of five yards over the piled-up roots toward the river.

I opened the cask and held it fast with both hands to upend its contents into the cut. The black grains of gunpowder rolled out to fill the axe-wound and trap the rags into place that they might serve for a fuse. The cask empty, I retreated down the bank.

My hands trembled. The first three matches went out in my hands. Then the flame took, and I ignited the fuse. The cord burned slow, spitting, but the fire quickened upon reaching the knotted rags and I scurried away down the bank. I submerged myself in the freezing water and grasped at the trailing weeds, anchoring myself in place below the level of the explosion which I knew must come—and did—and shook the planet on its axis, stealing the sound out of my ears so all creation was made to ring: a death knell.

But I was not dead. I recovered my wits and scrambled up the bank. The roots were gone. The great mass of them had burst out of the ground like a wine-cork, leaving the soil stained and sodden and stinking of sulfur, shattered bodies, exposed innards. The stench of Jerusha's body where she lay on her back with legs spread and face upturned to the pine boughs overhead. The dead thing which dropped out of her.

Bones. White shards of them everywhere, scattered like eggshell among the broken roots and jutting from crimson puddles. The day dwindled in the stench of hellfire. I searched amidst the bones with dusk thickening on the air and the clangor of bells in my head, though the woods were quiet, all birds and animals fled.

The skull I found some distance from the hole. I knew it by its elongated snout, the yellowed teeth fixed in the top of the jaw and the red root-matter clinging. I carried it down the bank with both hands and lifting it over my head I cast it into the river.

The splash came. The waters closed and were still. All was silence, full on night, and I waited for moonrise that I might see my way back.

An hour passed on the river-bank with the falling dark and the trees in leaf around me, hiding me from view. The waters rippled, the wind from the south and building. Thorn-bushes swayed down the curve of the opposite shore with the void of the night-forest beyond, a space permitting of no observer, no human eye.

Wolves appeared on the opposite bank. They emerged from the wood as from a thick fog and paused upon the waters' edge, the wind in their fur. Clouds were moving, quickly now to catch the moon and shred across it so a light flashed through like storming. It stole into the eyes of the assembled pack, set them glowing.

They stood flank to flank watching me, a hundred paces away and still their shadows covered me. The great pines sighed with the wind in their branches, heavy crowns dragging. His lowered head hanging with the wreath of thorns upon it.

Into your hands I commend my spirit.

These same words I spoke two years ago when the hole was dug and the stillborn body placed within. I sealed the grave with earth. I spoke these words and the very soul went out of me—and of Jerusha too—exiling us to the world of flesh, hell of bone and sinew.

We haunt ourselves. We are dead but unburied and with nothing left to us save the haunting. In the delirium of that summer we were as the first man and woman and joined our spirits together even as we twined our bodies to forge from ourselves an Eden which flourished and died and now lies buried in the ground.

The moon emerged. The pack moved with one body, lifting their heads to loose a blast of sound like the angel's trumpet, howling even as the trees howled, as all of the world screamed for the weight of the flesh upon it. The sound moved through me, vibrating my hair-ends, my fingertips. The river, frothing, cast up the moon from its depths to illumine the far-bank.

And I saw her. A young girl, perhaps two years old. She crouched amidst the screeching pack on hands and knees and naked save for the long hair which covered her like a pelt. She did not look at the moon as did the others but at me and did not howl but sang, sweetly, in the language of the spirits all infants know.

Vo o, vo nee
o har ka e
on a se

☙

The moon passed through a ribbon of cloud, climbing up the sky. The wolves turned and vanished, the girl following, and the trees fell silent as the wind withdrew into the south.

I stumbled home. Moonlight shone in the tracks I made, silvering the orchard wherein I had placed Judah, his resurrected corpse. All about was quiet. My body twitched, a drawn string, but there came no sound of moaning and the grave stood black and empty.

His suffering, then, is at an end even as I sense my own is just beginning, for such is the task before me.

I am thinking again of Ahasuerus, who denied Christ a moment's rest and received in exchange the curse of eternal life. How well the old storytellers understood the truth of the scriptures. It is an awful thing to fall into the hands of the living God, where living is a fire never quenched. Job born new out of the river but with the same hole inside him. Fitch in the teeth of his madness, rage undiminished in death. Judah blinded and broken, unable to sleep, panting after water he could not drink. A child with long hair, a girl: two years old, nearly three. She ran on all fours like an animal, the wolves pressed round.

I climbed the slates to the house. I passed the broken door and fell upon the stores of food with a hunger like none I have before experienced. Rashers of bacon I ate raw, chewing fat to jelly in my gums and washing it down with frigid water hauled from the well and splashed over my hands and face. Then I sat down by the window to write this account.

I am nearly finished. The world outside is a sea of fog and the bells in my ears are striking, calling me to work: the pines, the grave I dug and must unbury. The spade is blunted but will serve. Let me wait only til the morning, for the first hints of color in the orchard.

[David Stonehouse's narration ends here. The concluding passages are written in a different hand.—ed]

PART FIVE

This book was my mother's before it was mine. She carried it with her always. When I was a girl, she taught me to read that I might know my father by the account it contains and later entrusted the journal to my keeping. But my father died with his story unfinished and so it is for me his daughter to provide it with an end, though for me, as for Mother, there are no endings.

The last part of the story alone I remember and this is only pieces. The river's chill, colder than the air. Sensation of fur between my fingers. Holding fast as we swam across, the others close. Smell of pine-sap, needles. A figure in the grove, thin and quaking. Crouched at the foot of the hole with its hands in the earth, busy about the work of burying.

The rest I know because Mother has told me.

Autumn days they wandered the wood without means of forage, their hunger after one another become craving after food of which there was not enough. My father's faith waned. His fear grew like a shadow to cover all he saw so he would not touch her, my mother, though her labor came early and the awful pain was on her.

She told me of this too. How she lay within the grove with needles for a bed and strained against the pressure in her gut, her chest. Her body closed in upon itself, crushing organs and babe alike til the slick pieces of it shot into my father's waiting hands.

Silence then, my father unspeaking.

Is it a boy? she asked.

A girl, he said, nothing else, and still there came no birthing cry.

The after-birth slipped free. It splashed upon the ground. She smelled a scent like raw meat, new killing, and hot blood belched from the rip in her body.

David, she said, but he did not reply. She wanted to say more but couldn't. Words she lost but music came to her, the notes of a song. They passed from her lips as she passed from consciousness and all around was darkness and cold and worse when she awoke.

The child was gone, the after-birth too. My father had torn his clothes into strips and with these bandaged the wound between her legs and staunched the flow of life from it. Pine needles spread between her legs, webbed with blood and shreds of tissue.

David was nearby. She heard him over the bank, his steps like hammered nails. They punched through her gut and thighs. She ached with it but was too weak to call to him, to ask after the child. Her voice escaped her, a moaning, and soon his steps approached. The eyes rolled in her skull. They would not fix on him as he crested the bank. His outlines shimmered, faintly, and his hands were clean. They gleamed like new snow, fields of it at dusk and every bit as empty.

The child, she said.

He shook his head, looked at his feet.

She asked, *Where have you taken her?*

Her neck, he said. *She was caught up in the cord.*

Bring her to me. I am her mother.

She wasn't breathing—

What have you done?

What was necessary. Only that.

He gave no other answer. He could not speak the words to tell what he had done but only nodded toward the pines and the needle-strewn earth about them, a black patch of soil which was newly disturbed and overtopped with a cross.

Her horror in that moment, her rage—

I was too weak, she told me, years later. *I couldn't move for the hands he held on me. He grasped me about the shoulders and forced me down to keep me still though I shouted and thrashed til the wounds reopened, spilling, and the rest of the day is lost.*

It was snowing when she awoke. The ground was white, the sky. The trees shed plumes of white dust which hung in the air and did not fall. Hours had passed or days. Her dressings had been changed, the filth wiped away, and a fire was burning before her, the blankets piled high. She was too ill to rise but rolled onto her side to face the cross my father had fashioned.

The snow was piled on it, she said, *and it gleamed with the ice which formed there. The light shone out of it, so bright I was blinded, just as Paul was. I couldn't see but there was wind in my hair like a baby's breath and David was beside me, kneeling. He said he'd found a place for us, a house. He carried me on his back across miles of snow and wilderness then up the crooked stair to this nursery, the empty crib which waited for me.*

I am there now.

Much of my childhood was spent in this room and I linger now to write these words while Mother busies about the lower rooms, making ready for our departure. The crib is before me, empty again, its purpose served. My fingers find the cracks in the legs, just visible to show where Father dashed it upon the ground.

Mother repaired the legs herself. She used wood-nails and

plaster then painted over the joints to hide the staining. The work was done quickly and the paint flaked away in spirals, revealing patched cracks white with paste. I noticed them and asked my mother how it happened.

I thought she had not heard me. She was so quiet. Finally she spoke.

I have told you that faith is a gift of God. You were born with it, my darling, touched with grace as I was and as your father longed to be. He was a good man, a clever one, but for his cleverness he was blind and couldn't see the Gift when it was offered him. All was made plain to him but he couldn't understand it, and because he had no understanding he gave you up for lost and would've given you up forever.

She continued, *Do you remember the sower, how some seeds fall on good ground? Others fall among the weeds and are choked by them. Something of the kind happened to your father. He saw the crib and thought only of absence, of loss. But an empty cradle speaks of expectation as well as loss and I had carried in my womb the very seed of Eden.*

He knew this the same as I did. But he couldn't believe it. He had no faith and faithless himself mistook mine for madness and all because I never doubted, never ceased to hope. Everything else followed from that. It's why he broke the crib—and it is why I mended it.

I have read my father's account. He was a clever man, Mother said, but I think he trusted too much to cleverness. He sought understanding, always, but the eternal lay beyond his understanding and became for him a thing of the acutest terror. It resisted his attempts at reason, a puzzle without solution, so all Creation came to seem a madness, a place of exile. The world of the spirit surrounded him but he had not eyes to see. In his blindness he perceived only the flesh and shrank from my mother's belief to make of her a ghost while she was still alive.

Consider his account, how she haunts it about the edges. A voice in the night. A presence upstairs. She was invisible to him, or nearly so. He mistook spirit for flesh and flesh for the spirit and this was his final error. After two years in the vale, he forgot himself and scribbled in this book as though he really were alone in the house for all my mother read it while he slept and once she wrote in its pages when he was away. Strange that my father makes no mention of this. Probably he never read the things she wrote or realized they were there but continued to confide himself to this journal until the night he died.

Let me wait only til the morning, he wrote. *For the first hints of color in the orchard.*

He lowered his pencil, his head. He slept in the chair, exhausted, and did not stir when Mother descended the staircase. She had heard the explosion in the wood, and wondered, and spied the journal clutched between his hands. She eased it from his grip. She had no light but stood by the window to read of what he had seen and all that he intended.

The grave I dug and must unbury.

She closed the book, let it slip from her hands. It struck the ground but he did not wake. She turned and climbed the steps. Her tread was soft to make no sound and she reached the nursery where she had taken to sleeping through the daylight, singing songs to the crib by night. Back then it was still broken, heaved upon its side where my father had cast it down. One of the legs lay splintered on the floor, a length of cherry-wood crowned with jutting nails. She retrieved it from the floor, held it in both hands. She went downstairs.

The sun was up, birds singing to meet it. She crossed the room to the chair in which he slept. She stood over him with the light at her back. Her shadow fell across him and he awoke.

Afterward, when it was done, she dragged him by his armpits to the orchard. The grave was open, dug deep but short where it was meant for a dog rather than a man. She folded his knees into his gut and bundled him into it.

His hands she arranged over his breast, the fingers laced together. The face she covered with soil, kicking at the ground to rain down earth and apples til the grave's walls collapsed and he vanished into the ground. Only the white hands visible. They sat upon his chest, folded together, as though he were praying.

An apple tree grows there now, its branches naked as are those of the trees surrounding and there is snow in the air, spring snow.

The lights are drawing near. At dusk they creep out of the valleys to dance upon the ridgelines, cutting paths in the snowfall. The south glowers with them. They float in a sky where there should be only birds.

Mother and I are the last left in these hills. Game is scarce, the farms have failed, and the wolves departed years ago. When I was younger, I would hear them in the woods at night or find their tracks of a morning. Sometimes they left rabbits for us in the garden, scraps of savaged meat which Mother collected from the ground to cook for our supper.

Once I woke from a nightmare to find the pack of them gathered before the house. They were seven in number, seated in a row with heads uplifted. Motionless, silent. They were keeping watch, it seemed, with the moon behind them turning all to silver, even the sparks of their eyes.

But that was decades ago and the land itself is altered. The forests were cut for timber, harvested like wheat, and a dam was built down the river. The town is under the water and so too the great pines, submerged about their middle but still growing, still spreading, just like the river which is now a lake and rises with each rainfall.

Soon the waters will reach the orchard, the house. We will be gone. We depart in the morning, making for the north where there are wolves yet, and winter, and no lights to hide the stars from view. I do not yet know what will become of this book. It is my decision, says Mother, and I think perhaps I will bury it with Father. Or perhaps I will take it with us when we go and carry it at my breast, keeping it hidden as my mother did, and for so many years, til the winter's night she sat with me and told of its existence.

I was thirteen—old enough, she judged. We sat together after supper, the stove between us roaring. Inside the fire danced, turning blue-white at the tips and buffered by the chimney-wind. Mother vanished into the shadows then reappeared beside me, the journal in her hands.

This book belonged to your father, she said. *It's written in his hand, which was counted a fine one. He was known for it when he was young, but it suffered, I think, for the cold of this place and there are passages inside which I cannot make out. Others I know well enough to speak from memory though the words they weren't meant for me.*

She placed the book in my hands. It smelled of mold, of Mother, and black damp had seeped into the binding. The inside pages were rippled with it, rank upon rank, forming waves barbed with the lines of his script: *David Stonehouse, Exile.*

It is yours now, she said. *This book was all he left us when he died and I've carried it with me for years so you might know him by it. The journal bears his name but there are pages inside on which he never wrote. He died before his story's close and so the end is ours to tell as we would and in our way.*

Mother's voice, the things she told that night.

How she buried my father in the orchard. How she wandered from the house and was lost to the wood. She crashed through underbrush, trampling down thicket in a haze of mist and birdsong and the journal under her arm.

The day was getting on, the sun swinging slowly to south. She came to the river and followed its course to the pine-grove and the rings of sparse growth surrounding, undercut by pine-roots, those two graves within sight of one another, two crosses listing, about to fall.

Sunset, the sky aflame. Fitch's grave was sited between two snags. The gash was shallow, not two feet down, and lined with chips of bone which once had been a man. Still it sufficed. She lay down within it and rested her head against the earthen wall with its webs of shattered root and the cross above her, its shadow thrown down.

The weather turned. She did not move though she shook for hunger, for cold, her eyes closed fast and the rain running over them. She lay with the journal on her breast, covered with both hands, waiting down daylight and dark alike until all remembering failed her and she passed beyond herself into the moon of another night.

The stars dazzled. Mother knelt over the open grave. The clothes she wore were new like robes of the spirit donned at meeting while the body which lay before her was half-decayed, blotchy with rot and clad in scraps of cloth recalling the sack in which a babe takes form.

Pine-roots fastened about the exposed skull. They beat through the wires of its hair, their rhythm slow and even, sounding in the earth below her knees and in the milk which filled her breasts, dribbling through the dress she wore.

She buried herself. She collected the journal from the corpse's grasp and filled the grave with her hands, raking her fingers through soil til the nails were cracked and bloodied and she heard a splashing from the river.

Wolves. The pack surfaced out of the water. They swept silently up the bank, moving seven abreast and the great male at the center. He was gray-black and grizzled and the unsheathed organ swung between his hind-legs, red as the roots beneath her feet. The pack slowed, stopped, all eyes turned to Mother where she stood, trembling.

The male advanced. He bore down on her as upon his prey and on his back he carried the child. She rode him bareback, straddling the ridge of his spine. Her knees fitted to his ribs. Her small hands knotted in the fur at his neck. She was naked but wore the loops of her hair about her to conceal her face so the two were nearly indistinguishable, child from beast.

The wolf halted before her. His breath blew into her face, damp and stinking of slaughter. Mother opened her arms to him, her hands. He snarled. The red tongue snapped, teeth shining, but the child remained motionless upon his back, watching through the curtains of her hair.

Please, Mother said, and offered it up, the heart from her chest, and because it was given he would not take it but lowered his head, and looked away, and so the child came to her.

Mother held the baby close. Her body was frigid but the child's was warm and her breasts dripped for the heat of it. Milk sopped through her shirtfront, making clouds where it splashed in the mud and moonlight shimmering in streaks on the ground.

Drink, she said, and this I remember. River's song, the wolves withdrawing. Softness of skin together and the smell of earth about her. My fingers opened, closed: they grasped at nothing. The moon went out of the sky and we slept.

Publication History

"Below the Falls" first appeared in *Nightscript I* (ed. C.M. Muller), 2015 and was subsequently reprinted in *The Year's Best Dark Fantasy & Horror 2016* (ed. Paula Guran), Prime Books, 2016.

"The Woman in the Wood" first appeared in *The Children of Old Leech* (eds. Ross E. Lockhart & Justin Steele), Word Horde, 2014.

"Lucilla Barton (1857-1880)" is original to this collection.

"Lilies" was first published under the title "Unhallowed Ground" (electronic format only) DarkFuse, 2012. It has been extensively rewritten for this collection.

"The Lake" first appeared in *Aickman's Heirs* (ed. Simon Strantzas), Undertow Publications, 2015 and was subsequently reprinted in *The Mammoth Book of Best New Horror 27* (ed. Stephen Jones), PS Publishing, 2016.

"A Shadow Passing" first appeared in *Autumn Cthulhu* (ed. Mike Davis), Lovecraft eZine, 2016.

"Dream Children" is original to this collection.

"Lincoln Hill" was first published in verse form in *The Silent Garden* (eds. The Silent Garden Collective), Undertow Publications, 2018.

"A Sleeping Life" first appeared in *The Madness of Doctor Caligari* (ed. Joseph S. Pulver, Sr), Fedogan & Bremer, 2016.

"Arena" first appeared in *Nightscript II* (ed. C.M. Muller), 2016.

"Canticle" first appeared in *Marked to Die* (ed. Justin Isis), Snuggly Books, 2016.

"The Account of David Stonehouse, Exile" was first published as a limited-edition chapbook by Dim Shores Press, 2016.

Acknowledgements

My deepest thanks to Michael Kelly and Undertow Publications and to C.M. Muller, Ross Lockhart, Justin Steele, Simon Strantzas, Mike Davis, The Silent Garden Collective, Justin Isis, and Sam Cowan. I am likewise indebted to the encouragement and vision of the late Joseph S. Pulver, Sr. Without him many of these stories simply would not exist.

Passages from St. John of the Cross's "The Song of the Soul and the Bridegroom" and "Stanzas of the Soul," quoted in "Canticle," are taken from public domain translations by David Lewis (1909) and E. Allison Peers (1959), respectively.

About the Author

Daniel Mills is the author of *Revenants* and *Moriah* and the creator of historical crime podcast *These Dark Mountains*. His nonfiction has appeared in *The Los Angeles Review of Books*. He lives in Vermont.